Copyright

Table of Contents

First Heat

Allie is a young omega, and her first heat is coming up fast.

The problem is that she's never been kissed, let alone had sex, and the prospect of getting busy with a stranger to satisfy that primal need doesn't interest her at all.

When Allie reluctantly chooses Sidney, an alpha who works as a heat helper at the local clinic, her expectations start to shift.

Between the heat hormones and his charming smile, Allie stands no chance and she's about to discover a whole world of sexual possibilities under Sidney's guiding hand.

Content notes: This omegaverse story is m/f and contains a heat, knotting, nesting, purring, growling, biting, and bonding. Birth control is readily accessible in my omegaverse for all genders, sexes, and dynamics.

There's an emphasis on exploration so there will be sex toys, light bondage, butt play, and mild sensory deprivation.

It's pretty fluffy so don't worry about any dark content. Just spicyness, sweetness, and a cinnamon roll alpha.

Chapter One

Allie stood frozen on the clinic steps, staring at the doors, apprehension bubbling inside her. It wasn't fair. She didn't *want* to be an omega. She was *supposed* to be a beta and not have to deal with this nonsense.

A woman at the front desk noticed her loitering and pulled open the door. She bobbed her head, the gray-streaked auburn strands swaying as she offered Allie a brilliant smile. "Can I help you, dear?"

Allie stared at her feet. "I'm supposed to have my first heat soon."

"How wonderful! I assume you're here because you'd like to procure our services?"

"Yes ma'am," Allie mumbled, thoroughly examining the scuffs on her shoes. It took every ounce of fortitude she possessed to not turn and run full speed back the way she'd come.

"Would you like to come inside? Or do you need a minute?"

Better get this over with.

Allie squared her shoulders. "I'm ready."

"My name is Muriel." The woman smiled again. "I'm an omega as well. You have absolutely nothing to worry about. The staff here are all very knowledgeable and excellent at their work."

"Yeah, that's what the website says." Allie dragged her feet as she entered the clinic. She thought about asking if Muriel had used the clinic's Heat Helpers before to back up her claim but didn't particularly want the mental images that would accompany a yes.

Panic fizzed in Allie's gut.

She'd been chickening out of coming here for two weeks already, and when her doctor had phoned to check in she'd had to confess that she still hadn't arranged anything for her heat. The doctor had lost their shit on her (in the most professional way possible) but it was enough to motivate her.

So here she was...

Great.

Muriel led her to the front desk and handed over a clipboard full of paperwork to fill out. Grateful for the opportunity to delay any further conversation, Allie sat and scribbled out the information. Most of it was medical information, with an uncomfortably in-depth section on sexual history and preferences which Allie had left blank. Muriel looked over it all when Allie passed it back.

"You missed a spot, dear."

"Nope. Nothing to fill out. I'm as pure as the driven snow." Allie made a face, half-hating herself for saying anything.

"That explains the additional nervousness." Muriel glowed warmly. "Please come with me."

Allie trotted along behind, and Muriel took her to a room where one wall was full of tiny containers.

"What the heck are those?"

"Scent packs. It'll help you find an alpha for your heat."

"How's this supposed to help? Shouldn't there be a visual catalog or something?" Her mind flipped through high school biology lessons. It was common knowledge that scenting was a big thing between alphas and omegas, but she didn't want to choose her first sexual partner based on that. It was *weird*. What about personality? Looks? Life goals?

Okay.

Deep breaths.

She inhaled sharply, held it a moment, and let it flow out.

Panicking helps no one.

"You'll see whoever you choose based on this," Muriel assured. "We used to start with visual but often the matches weren't optimally compatible so now we start with scent and go from there. You'll know when you find one you like."

Allie scrunched up her face. "If you say so."

"I do." Muriel handed her another canister. "Coffee beans. It'll help cleanse your nose if you need a break. I'll be down the hall but if you need anything before I return you can push the yellow button by the door."

Then Allie was alone, clutching the coffee canister like a lifeline.

"This is so dumb," she moaned.

She picked up the first container on the wall and pushed the button on top. It released a puff of air that smelled like roses and wine. She shrugged and put it back, moving to the next, and then the next. Her head swam from the plethora of scents. She made it through the entire first two shelves and hadn't found anything special. They'd all smelled nice, but she didn't feel like meeting any of the alphas each container represented and none seemed any better than the others.

Maybe I'm broken...

Allie reached for the next and pressed the button, sinking straight to her knees as a rush of sweet citrus and cloves flooded her senses. "Jesus Christ on a cracker."

She shoved the coffee canister up to her nose and inhaled several deep breaths to clear her head. Goosebumps covered her head to toe.

Her nipples poked against her T-shirt. "Excuse you." She slapped her hands over them.

Allie stared at the offending container and dared to pick it up again. She was already sitting on the floor so at least she didn't have to worry about her legs betraying her. She pushed the button and it puffed out another rush of sweet citrus and clove. Lust rippled down her spine and pooled between her thighs.

"*God*. What the fuck?" She pushed the button again and let out a low moan, warmth prickling over her skin.

The door opened and Allie flung the container away like she'd been caught huffing glue.

Muriel chuckled. "I see you've made a selection. Did you want to see if there are others you're compatible with?"

Humiliation draped Allie's shoulders like a lead cape. One embarrassment was plenty. "This one is fine."

"Excellent." Muriel retrieved the container and turned it to see the information on the bottom. "Come, dear. Let's put this code into the system and see who you chose."

Allie followed at a sedate pace, both dreading and needing to see the face that matched the scent.

Muriel tapped away at her computer and turned the screen toward Allie. "You picked Sidney. He's a delightful person and I think you'll like him."

Allie gaped at the image. Rippling muscles, dark brown eyes, chiseled jaw, wavy black hair, and a smirk that made him look like the devil himself.

He's so hot.

Panic careened into her brain and exploded on impact as she reminded herself that she was looking at someone she was going to fuck.

A stranger.

A *really hot* stranger but a stranger nonetheless.

She stumbled back and sank onto one of the empty chairs. This was too much to handle.

"Are you alright?"

"Nope."

"Should I call your emergency contact?"

"*God* no." The last thing she needed right now was her mom showing up. She'd already fought to come by herself and she was *not* going to chicken out...again.

"Would you like me to contact Sidney then? We could arrange a meeting in quite short order."

Allie opened her mouth but nothing came out. How was she supposed to be in the same room as him? What if she fainted because of the scent? But she'd have to meet him or someone else eventually. Every doctor cautioned against going solo for a first heat and she'd become morbidly obsessed with reading about the horror stories of unplanned ones. She had every privilege available to her to be able to plan hers with a professional. That didn't make it any less awkward though.

Not trusting her mouth, she nodded.

Muriel beamed, picked up the phone, and dialed. "Hello, Sidney! I have a beautiful young omega here about to present. Would you happen to be free for a quick meeting? Excellent. We'll see you shortly."

Allie wanted to curl up and let the ground swallow her whole, but it remained steadfastly solid.

"Come with me. I'll get you comfortable in one of the meeting rooms." Muriel got Allie a glass of water and a cup of some calming tea that smelled like a grandma. Allie sipped it anyway and scarfed down a packet of chocolate chip cookies while she waited.

When the door finally opened and Sidney stepped inside, she was a ball of nerves and almost ready to pass out. She tried to greet him but only a whine left her lips. She pressed her hand to her mouth.

What the fuck was that?

"Nice to meet you, Allison." His smile was sweet and he moved slowly, as if worried she'd get spooked.

"Allie," she corrected.

"Allie."

The way he said her name was so smooth it had her toes curling.

"Can I sit down?" he asked.

She nodded and he perched on the chair across from her. Her lungs burned like she'd been doing sprints and it quickly became impossible to breathe normally.

"Easy does it," Sidney murmured in his smooth as silk voice. "Do you want to come closer?"

Allie was already out of her chair before her rational brain could stop her. He didn't protest one bit when she climbed straight into his lap and pressed her nose to the scent gland on his throat. "Fuuucking hell, you smell so good. Why do I feel like this?"

"You're very close to your heat," Sidney murmured, running a soothing hand down her back, but it did the opposite of soothe. It made her ache in places no one but her had touched. "You're going to have to take a suppressant to sign a contract."

"Contract?" Her brain was so hazy. She'd read about it on the website but the info eluded her now.

"I can't help you without a contract, and you need to be clear-headed to sign it."

His words melted away. All that remained was the feeling of being pressed against him and that maddening, intoxicating scent that she wanted to drown in.

She was half-aware that they were moving and then he put a pill in her hand, telling her to swallow it, and then to drink the glass of water he held out. He tipped the glass in her hands and she chugged it, pulling away with a gasp.

"Good girl. Take a minute." He let her rest against him again while her fingers curled into his shirt.

The haze slipped back in small increments until she realized she was plastered all over the hot stranger and she shoved herself away, backing right up to the wall. "What the fuck just happened?"

"You came here too close to your heat," he answered. "You're not in a good headspace right now, but the medicine will help. It'll delay things for a few hours. It's tricky to know for certain with presentation heats. They're never quite as reliable as later ones."

Sidney stepped towards her and her hackles went up. He paused at the sound that tore from her throat.

Did I growl?

God. I hate this.

"Easy." There was a swell of the citrus and clove scent that followed the word and she bit back a whine.

"One of the physicians is going to have a look at you and make sure you're okay to proceed. If you want to spend your heat with me, then you can sign the contract while the medicine is strong enough to manage your symptoms. If not, you can head to the hospital."

She cursed herself for not already having a sexual partner so she could avoid all of this and spend her heat with them. But nooo. She'd had to focus on *school* instead of dating.

A fat lot of good that did her now.

Sidney crooked his finger and she followed like a hooked fish.

Stupid sexy alpha.

He led her to the next floor of the building and into an exam room where the doctor was already waiting.

"Hi, Allison. I'm Dr. James." The physician was a middle-aged woman with brown hair and a warm smile. "Cutting it a bit close, I see?"

"If I could have avoided it forever, I would have," Allie snapped.

Dr. James exchanged a look with Sidney. "You're not being coerced into coming here, are you?"

"Not technically, but what else am I supposed to do?"

"If you're that uncomfortable with having a heat partner, we could always take you to the hospital and sedate you for the duration of your heat. It's not ideal, but we could manage the symptoms for you well enough."

"Because that's *so* much better." Allie shoved her hands into her hair where they tangled in the dark curls. "I want to be a different dynamic. Why hasn't science figured that out yet?"

Dr. James pursed her lips. "Sidney, could you please excuse us for a moment?"

"Of course." He stepped outside and shut the door behind him.

"Talk to me, Allison. How can we help you through this?"

"I don't know." The tears snuck up on her and she wiped them away. "I'm so scared."

"Of what, in particular?"

"I've never even been kissed and now I'm supposed to think

about getting naked with a stranger for days, letting them…"

"Ah. Yes, I can see how that would be daunting." Dr. James flipped through Allie's documents. "Well, you're nineteen, so you can make whatever choice you think is best for you. Presentation heats don't agree well with long-term suppression or we could have delayed for you, but that's something we can look into afterward. What do you think about the hospital option?"

"That's equally terrifying."

Dr. James nodded. "I'm sorry there aren't better alternatives."

"I don't want to sleep with a stranger." Allie wrapped her arms around herself.

"Do you think it would help if you spent some time with him first? All the alphas who work here will do their very best to make your heat comfortable however they can. If you want to talk until the wee hours of the morning or go out for dinner with them that's perfectly allowable."

"Really? It's not just a wham, bam, thank you ma'am and everyone is on their way?"

Dr. James snickered. "Only if that's the preference of the client. Typically with presentation clients, the omega will be in the home of the alpha they choose, or the alpha will come to them if the omega lives alone. It allows time to get comfortable, lets the omega engage in nesting behaviors, and move gradually into the heat as opposed to someone being contacted to come to them when the heat begins."

"That sounds not too bad."

"There's also the option to request the alpha use only toys if that makes you more comfortable. It takes a little while longer for the heat haze to lift with that method, but it can be managed."

That particular mental image, of Sidney wielding some wild sex toy with that smirk of his, bringing her to climax without their bodies even touching, sent a ripple of need over her skin. She smothered down the whine that crawled up her throat. "I guess that would be okay."

Dr. James's smile brightened. "Perfect. Let me do a quick exam, and then we can talk about your alpha choices."

Allie sat patiently while her vitals were checked.

"Now, how many alphas are you going to be meeting with today?"

"One."

"You only liked one from the whole batch?" Dr. James seemed surprised and paused her ministrations.

"I stopped when I found one I liked."

"Why?" Dr. James quirked her head.

"Because it's embarrassing!"

Rein it in, Allie.

"Sorry." Her cheeks flared with heat. "I'm having some emotional difficulties with everything. I was really hoping I'd be beta so I could continue on like normal."

"Sometimes normal can be overrated. There's plenty of things about being an omega that betas will never get to enjoy. I know you're uncomfortable, but there's no shame at all around any of this. We're all here to help."

"It's not that I don't want to do stuff. I just don't *want* to, you know?"

"You'll have to clarify a little for me."

"It's like, I know what my body wants, but my brain is taking longer to catch up."

"Completely fair. Would you be interested in someone like Sidney if you weren't in heat?"

"Well, I mean, yeah. He looks like a model. But I was hoping for a little more than that for my first time."

"One moment." Dr. James rolled over to her computer and tapped away on the keys. She snatched a page off the printer and handed it to Allie. "Here's his full profile."

Allie scanned over it. Middle child. Twenty-four years old. Leo...

"He rescues puppies! Are you *kidding* me right now? There's no way that's real."

"Quite real. Sometimes he'll bring fosters into the office." Dr. James smiled over her laced fingers. "We're very selective about who can be a heat helper. They have to demonstrate compassion, in addition to being knowledgeable about omega care and being physically fit enough to handle the demands of the job."

Allie's resolve wavered.

Stupid sexy puppy-saving alpha.

"Okay, so, say I agreed to have him as my heat partner. Then what?"

"Your form says you live with your parents, so in this case, you'd pack yourself whatever supplies you need, and he would take you to his home. All the alpha homes are professionally cleaned after every heat, so you don't have to worry about a thing. Once your heat is over you'll have up to three days of recovery time with him though you're free to leave before that. You can either come here or go to your regular doctor for a post-heat check-up and that's it. You're free as a bird until your next heat."

Allie groaned and dropped her face in her hands. Logically she knew it was the best choice. She just had to convince her brain that it was fine.

"Can I hang out with him for a little bit before I decide?"

"Of course. Why don't you head back to the meeting room? I'll be here to sign off on the contract if you need me."

Allie was taut as a bowstring as Sidney rejoined her and they went back downstairs.

She plopped down on the couch and he diverted to the mini-fridge, glancing over to her. "Juice?"

"Uh, sure."

He tossed her a juice box and sat down on the leather couch. "So...puppies?"

Sidney's face lit up and he pulled out his phone. "Yes! This was one of my last fosters."

He turned the screen revealing a little blue-eyed puffball that made Allie's heart explode.

"His name is Brutus. He was part of the Roman senator litter of Australian shepherd mixes."

Sweet merciful God. I am so doomed.

"Senators?" She squeaked out.

He grinned and flipped to another photo of five equally precious pups. "Brutus on the left, then Cicero, Tiberius, Augustus, and Julia."

Allie let out a whine. "How many of them live with you?"

"None now. Brutus was the last to get adopted, and he went home three days ago."

"Unfair. I'd have gone home with you just to pet them."

Sidney laughed. "I'll take in another litter when I can but certainly not immediately if I'm taking care of you for the next while."

"How many puppies have you fostered?"

"Seventy-six."

"Holy shit." She imagined his beautiful face, laughing, the rest of him covered in puppies that yipped happily.

"I've been doing it for a little while now, plus a few came in big litters."

"How many heats have you shared?"

"Seventeen."

Allie swallowed hard. "What's it like?"

"Exquisite." He propped his elbow on the couch and let his temple rest against his hand. "Omegas in heat are perfect in a way I can't quite describe."

She nodded breathlessly, squirming. "Do you actually want to share my heat? Like, is the idea of it palatable besides the fact that you're getting paid?"

Allie held her breath as he looked her up and down with a focus that made her tingle.

"Of course. You're a gorgeous woman. If you'd approached me outside of all this I probably wouldn't say no, though I might take more than a couple of hours to get to know you before taking you home."

Focus.

Deep breaths.

The very hot man said he'd have been open to sleeping with you outside of this situation. What do I do with this information?

"Have you slept with anyone outside of a heat?" Sidney asked.

Allie's cheeks erupted in heat and she shook her head. "I've never...I mean...I don't think anyone even wanted to."

Sidney snorted. "I find that incredibly hard to believe."

"Well if they did they certainly never made me aware of that desire." Allie squeezed her hands together. "Not that I would've paid much attention if they had."

"Oh?"

"I took a lot of advanced classes in high school, and I may have overscheduled myself a little with university. There hasn't exactly been a ton of time to dedicate to dating. Plus, I still live with my parents, and that would put a damper on bringing anyone home."

"Fair enough. I've had a few students before. Are you having to push any exams?"

"Nope. I wrote them early to get them out of the way."

His eyebrow quirked. "Impressive. I graduated last year, but I took everything online and spread out classes so it freed up a bit of time without the commute and I could do things as quickly as I wanted."

"I like the classroom experience. I love studying, but I also really like the guidance."

Something in his eyes flashed and it sent a bolt of lust swirling in her gut.

"If we share this heat, is there anything in particular you're interested in being *guided* on?"

"Um..."

"Heats don't have to only be about satisfying that primal need. They're great for exploration. Your body is as ready as it's ever going to be, so if you want to play, I'd be more than willing."

Her brain short-circuited.

Play.

He smirked. "Are you purring?"

She snapped back into reality and smothered down the sound. "No!"

"There's not a thing shameful about being excited to explore. Heats should be a positive experience, not something to dread."

"Tell that to my brain."

"I can do that."

First Heat

Sweet citrus and clove wafted over her like a cloud, and she
gasped as heat pooled between her thighs. He crooked his finger, and
she slid across the couch towards him. Then he patted his lap and she
moved before she could think better of it. His teeth grazed over her
throat, over the scent gland, and she thought she might pass out from
the spike of pleasure that shot straight in opposite directions, making
her head swim and her clit tingle.

She made an awful, desperate sound when his tongue dragged
over the same spot. His cock twitched beneath her.

Okay, maybe the sound wasn't awful if it made that happen.

"This is you on suppressants," he murmured into her ear.
"Imagine what it would feel like in a heat."

"Kiss me." She squawked at her own audacity, but he only smiled
against her skin. "I'm sorry."

"Don't be sorry. You're asking for what you want and that's good."

"I... I can't think about having sex with someone when I've never
even kissed them. My brain wants a particular order to thing—"

He leaned in, cutting off her words, his mouth on hers, and his
hard fingers digging into the base of her skull.

Every thought melted straight out her ears. His lips moved,
soft and demanding in their quest to make her a helpless mess. She
whimpered when he pulled away.

"You're absolutely perfect." His brown eyes had turned molten. "I
want to share this heat with you. Choose me."

"Okay." She sounded hoarse to her own ears—or at least what
little she could hear over the thundering of her heart.

"If you hop off, I'll let Dr. James know we're ready for the contract."

She didn't *want* to hop off, but she did as he suggested. He
looped an arm around her waist to keep her steady as her legs
wobbled like a newborn foal. She zoned out while he was on the
phone and returned to reality when the doctor came into the room.

Dr. James laid out a small stack of forms. "Before we get started I
need to take a quick check to make sure your heat hormone levels are
low enough you can legally sign a contract. Hold out your hand please."

Allie did so and jumped when the doctor pricked her finger, squeezing out a tiny droplet of blood and sticking a strip up to it that turned a pale green.

"You're a little high, but still in the safe range." Dr. James slid the papers towards Allie. "We'll get through this as quickly as we can. Have a read over the basics and then we'll customize a bit."

It was awkward reading with both of them watching her. She read over the timelines, care practices, risks, and liabilities. It all seemed pretty standard.

"Looks fine to me."

"Condom allowances?" Dr. James asked.

"What?"

"For your heat. All of our staff are regularly tested, you haven't had a sexual partner before, and I'll be administering your birth control after you sign so they wouldn't be strictly enforced. The additional skin contact can help with the heat. Both parties have to agree to whatever is chosen."

"Without is fine." She shoved that particular image out of her head and tried to focus on it from the clinical side to avoid embarrassing herself.

Sidney nodded. "Agreed."

The list of various sexual acts they went through both piqued her nerves and left her breathless. She was hesitant to strike too much in case her heat brain wanted something. Who knew what she might agree to when she was stewing in that hormone soup? She only scrapped anything that made her internal self want to hurl, which all in all still left a lot of things open.

They worked through the contract until she was red as a beet, then she laid down her initials and signatures next to Sidney's and watched as Dr. James's signature sealed the deal.

"Now you're all mine." Sidney grinned.

All his.

God help her.

Chapter Two

"Here's my address." Sidney handed her a business card. "You can leave the information with your parents, and I have their info in the emergency contact form if we need it for some reason."

Allie tucked the card into her pocket.

"Where's your vehicle?" he asked. "I'll walk you there."

"I walked here." She shrugged. "I'll probably walk to your place, too. I'm saving money to travel, and I've never needed a car, so I don't have one."

Sidney's brow furrowed. "I don't want you walking alone when you're this close. It's dangerous."

Allie shivered.

He crooked his finger. "Come. I'll drive you home."

"Okay."

Sidney led her to his SUV, and she slid into the front seat, turning to him when his door opened.

"Could you stay in here while I pack? I don't think I can handle my mom meeting you."

His smirk appeared. "I can wait for you."

The trip to her house went by in a blink and she dashed from the vehicle to the front door, slamming it shut behind her. She slapped her envelope with the contract onto the kitchen counter and set down the business card next to it.

"You're back?" Her mom looked up from the stove. "How'd it go?"

"I found someone. I'm going over now."

"Already?"

"They had to give me a suppressant so I could sign the contract."

Her mother clucked her tongue. "I told you to go last week."

"I know. But I went today and now I need to pack. Here's the contract. Please, keep it safe and, for the love of God, don't look at it."

"I'll put it in with the taxes." Her mother tucked it into an accordion folder. "Do you want something to eat before you go?"

"No thanks." Allie was already running towards the stairs.

What do I pack for a week of mostly sex?

She hauled a suitcase out and laid it out on the bed. Her phone buzzed in her pocket and she yanked it out.

Sidney:
Bring at least four days of clothes
We can do laundry as needed
Pack any sex toys you have

Her face burst into flames reading the last text.
"Fucking hell." She danced in place.

Allie:
I don't have any sex toys

Sidney:
None at all?

Allie:
I'm not leaving anything
around for my mom to find
She's a snoop

Sidney:
Fair enough
Bring anything that'll make
you comfortable

She grabbed things mostly at random, filling the suitcase
with pajamas, toiletries and various other comfortable clothing.
Lamenting that she didn't have anything that passed for lingerie or
even time to shave her legs before going over, she shoved the suitcase
closed and zipped it up, dragging it down the stairs after her.

"Bye, Mom! Love you! See you next week!" She flew out the front
door before her mother could even respond, knowing that if she
stopped she'd probably lose her nerve.

Sidney was standing outside the vehicle when she got there and
took the suitcase from her to load it into the back.

Allie hopped into the front seat and swung the door shut, nearly
catching her toes in her haste.

"Is she watching me out the window?" she asked when Sidney
slid into the driver's seat.

He glanced past her towards the house. "Yep." He smiled and
waved at her mom before turning on the vehicle.

Then her mother was marching across the lawn with a teddy bear
in her hands.

Oh God, no.

"Drive!"

"I'm not blazing out of your driveway when your mom is walking
over here. I could get in trouble with the company for being a dick."

Allie whimpered as he pushed the button to roll down the
passenger side window and her mother thrust the teddy bear
through it.

"You forgot Mr. Bear."

"Mom! For the love of God."

Allie tried to sink into the chair, covering her face with her
hands. The teddy bear plunked onto her lap and she resisted the urge

to fling her beloved plush onto the lawn.

Sidney chuckled. "You should bring it. The comforting scents will help you adjust."

"Fine. I'll bring it. Can we go now?"

Her mother kissed her head and Allie groaned.

"Mom. I'm not five. Please don't kiss my head in front of people."

"You don't mind, do you? Mr…"

"Sidney Marino." He passed her one of his business cards. "Here's my information if you need it."

"Lovely to meet you. I hope my sweet girl hasn't been a bother to you. I'm going to miss her so much."

"Mooom. *Stop.* I'm a grown woman, and I need you to not be in my head for what I'm going to go through in the next week."

"Oh hush now."

"We really should be going," Sidney interjected. "I promise I'll take the best care of her while she's with me and return her to you safe and sound."

Allie wanted to throw herself under his SUV.

Her mother opened her mouth to speak again but Sidney was already rolling up the window as he smiled brightly, waving to her as he pulled away.

He turned to her as they pulled onto the street. "Okay, I see why you wanted me to drive."

"I love her, but holy shit."

He looked at her lap with a smirk on his lips. "Cute bear."

"Shut up."

"Your place is weirdly clean." She glanced around from where she was rooted in the entryway. "Why do you have so many blankets everywhere?"

"Nesting material." He wheeled her suitcase down the hall and turned back, waiting for her to follow.

She kicked off her shoes and scampered after him.

"Bathroom is here," he pointed as they walked, "and the bedroom is at the end of the hall. If you don't want to sleep in the same bed until your heat starts, that's fine. I can sleep on the couch, but it's generally better to have me close by. If it starts during the night you won't be able to come find me. You might be safe tonight with the medication you took but definitely not beyond that."

"Good to know." She glanced around. His bedroom had a king-sized bed so there was plenty of space for everything her imagination might bring up. "I don't mind sharing."

"I'll let you unpack while I get started on the grocery order. The plastic drawers are for guests."

Guests.

I guess that's one way to put it.

She unloaded her suitcase into the sterile drawer set, trying not to think about the seventeen others before her who had also used it. It would be hypocritical of her to be weird about it, but that didn't stop her for a second. She didn't care much about what other people did, but she wasn't at all prepared for what *she* was about to do.

His bedroom smelled like heaven, at least to her omega senses, and she followed the compulsion to drape herself face first over the bed. Relaxation seeped into her bones.

He laughed softly when he returned and found her in that state. "Enjoying yourself?"

"I really wish I wasn't." She'd have groaned if she wasn't so comfortable.

"You don't have to be embarrassed about anything. I'm very used to omega behaviors, and I think it's cute." He sat next to her with his phone out. "What do you want me to order? Pick anything you want, the more calorie-dense the better."

"Lasagna and garlic bread?"

"Sure. What else?"

"Chocolate cake, please."

He held out the screen for her to look over the pre-prepared meals from an omega-friendly food provider that took the specific needs of a heat into consideration.

"All of this looks so good. I'd happily eat everything on the menu."

He nodded, added a few things, and placed the order. "How're you feeling?"

"Super weird."

"You can do anything that'll make you more comfortable. Want to put on pajamas and watch a movie?"

"I'm down with that."

He left her alone as she exchanged her clothes for flannel pants and a tank top, leaving her bra in the laundry pile in a fit of boldness. He was in the kitchen when she emerged. The gaze he swept over was like an electric bolt up her spine, and she bit her lip to hold back a squeak.

"Snuggle up and pick something to watch while I finish dinner."

"You got it."

By the time she settled on a cute comedy, he passed her a bowl of fried rice and sat next to her, draping a blanket over their laps. It was hardly cold enough to warrant the blanket, but she rolled with it. She inhaled the fried rice and tried to focus on the movie, but every time he shifted or had any reaction, her attention was drawn to him all over again.

She'd gotten somewhat acclimated to the concept of her upcoming heat but was still displeased that her first time was going to be something she probably wouldn't even remember. She watched his profile discreetly from the corner of her eye. Maybe it didn't have to be...

"Question."

"Hmm?" He turned to her.

"What happens if someone wants to do stuff before the heat starts?"

"Then we'd do *stuff* before the heat starts. Is something specific prompting this question or are you horny?"

She hated how warm her cheeks were and knew she was probably glowing from the strength of the blush. "I'm not super comfortable not having a choice for my first time. I'd rather go into that knowing it's because I want to and not just because the hormones are pushing me."

"If you want to, we can have sex beforehand."

"Wait. Really?"

"My job is to make sure you're as safe and comfortable as possible through this process. If having sex on your terms beforehand would make you feel better, then we can do that."

"Part of me wishes you hadn't said that because now I have to actually choose."

His brows knitted. "Isn't that what you wanted?"

"Yes. But I'm also chicken-shit and I'm only good at making academic choices, not life ones."

"I'd say take your time, but you're on a bit of a deadline."

"Ugh. Don't remind me." She inched away to give herself space to breathe. "I want to do things on my terms and I'm trying very hard to not panic, so I need you to cooperate with me. I need to go slow, and I need you to keep me from freaking out."

He nodded, gaze focused on her with an intensity that made her burn. "Understood. Why don't you lead each step? I'll respond from there, and you choose when we move ahead."

"Okay." She sucked in a breath. "Okay. I can do that."

"I'm here when you're ready. No rush."

Her heart was beating so fast it made her whole chest vibrate with the punching staccato.

You can do this.

It's just sex.

You're gonna do it again tomorrow and pretty much all day every day for the next bit. You gotta push through and do this.

She held her breath, pushed the blanket away, and slid to sit on his lap, knees on either side of his legs so she could face him but also leap away if her panic got the better of her.

"Remember to breathe."

She gasped in a lungful of air, her head instantly swimming with sweet citrus and cloves. She braced her hands on his shoulders and closed her eyes to focus on calming down. Her senses were tuned entirely to him, to the warmth of every point they touched, to the firm muscle beneath her hands, and to the sweet scent that continued to emanate from him.

"Can I touch you at all? Or would you prefer I stay totally still?"

"Touch something non-sexy."

She caught his soft laugh a moment before he set his palms on her calves. The warmth went straight through her pajama pants and her eyes snapped open. He was *so* close. Every fleck of gold in his eyes was visible, each perfectly styled hair, each tiny whisker crafting his five-o'clock-shadow.

"Kiss?"

He abandoned her calves and sank his fingers into her hair, curling them to get a firm hold at the base of her skull, pressing her forward until their mouths met. She melted into it and dug her nails into him, trying to keep up with him even at the slow pace he'd set. Adapting to him took her some time, but he was patient, letting her get to know the rhythm and feel of the kiss. Her teeth scraped over his bottom lip and she jolted back, surprised at herself.

He smiled beneath her. "Doing okay?"

"Mhmm." She took a deep breath. "Again."

She sank closer, plastering herself against his chest. The taste of him burned through her and she wanted to devour him. A low growl built in her throat. She shifted again and dipped her head to tongue the scent gland in his throat.

"Bite if you want to. You can't bond me until you're in full heat." He shivered.

She scraped her teeth against his throat, the growl coming free as she indulged some ancient part of herself. He groaned beneath her, his grip on her tightening with every nip she made against his skin. Her fingers locked to his hair and tugged his throat to the side for better access, nibbling along the length of it as she inhaled deeply, citrus and clove so strong it coated her palette.

The deep answering growl from him snapped her into reality, and she shoved away so hard she tipped backward. He grabbed her before she hit the ground and hoisted her back into his lap, his arms locked around her.

She pushed away again, gentler this time, and stared him down. "What the *fuck* was that?"

"That was you getting out of your head." He traced soft fingertips over her cheek, and she relaxed under the attention. "You don't need a heat to feel that. It's part of who you are."

"That sounds like a pile of lies, but I'm going to trust you." She shook herself, flinging away the nervous energy bubbling under the surface. "I can do this. Focus."

Allie snatched both of his hands and set them on her chest so they were cupping her breasts. She stared at them for a long moment. He moved his thumbs. She bit back the sound that rose up, but the shudder slipped through.

He did it again. "Can I go under the shirt?"

She hesitated and then nodded, decisive.

He took his sweet time with the request, inching under the hem of her tank top, his long fingers fanning over her back and sliding up. She squirmed restlessly in his lap. The smirk on his lips appeared and she wiggled, trying to spur him on.

"Hurry up," she whined.

"Nope. You put me at this stage and I'll go as fast or slow as I like." His grin was sly and extremely self-satisfied. Then he brushed thumbs against her nipples with nothing in the way. She almost leapt straight off his lap, but he anticipated it and braced for it. "I'm going to touch you again. Try not to fly away this time."

Allie whimpered softly.

Sidney moved with agonizing slowness over her skin. His mouth found her throat, and she let out a low moan. Her breath turned ragged as his lips explored the expanse of skin and then his hands were back where she wanted them. He rolled her nipples between thumb and forefinger and she gasped into his ear.

"Hng." She shifted her hips, grinding against him. "Jesus fuck."

He paused and she bucked in his lap, pressing closer.

"Why are you stopping?" She fussed, her hips demanding more again.

"I was trying to give you a moment."

"Don't. Stop," she growled.

She almost regretted her words when his eyes darkened. It sent a spiral of lust through her, but then his hands were on her hips, pulling her closer. He hoisted up her shirt and closed his mouth over the pointed peak. The sound she made didn't even sound real to her ears. She clung to his head, panting and squirming. Each lap of his tongue had her reeling. Her blood sizzled, and her pulse pounded like a kettledrum in her ears.

"Please. *Fuck*." The next words dissolved into incoherency under the attention of his mouth. There was only a brief second of relief before he turned to the other breast and set upon it with a relentless focus that had her quivering.

He cupped her breast, lifting it a little higher for his mouth and she grabbed his wrist, pushing it towards her lap with frenetic energy she didn't quite understand. He let her guide him, but the layers of fabric were *in. The. Way*.

Her pants needed to be off.

Torn between having to get off him to remove the pants and staying where she was so he could continue with those delicious circles he was doing with his tongue, he made the decision for her.

A protest formed in the back of her throat, but then he was lifting her, carrying her towards the bedroom.

Oh.

He laid her out on the bed and stepped back. A whine left her throat before she could clap a hand over her mouth to stop it. All it took to get him to join her was for her to reach out. Her brain blinked out of commission when he hovered over her.

"How're you doing, little one?" He murmured in her ear, spurring an electric sensation that sparked over her skin.

When the fuck did 'little one' become hot?

"Good!" she squeaked out.

"Put me where you want me." He held one hand aloft for her and she grabbed his wrist, maneuvering his hand to rest on her hip. She needed to work back up to that mental state that kept her from thinking.

"Please don't make me say it. I'm awkward."

"Mmm, nope." He nipped her earlobe. "Your terms remember. You tell me *exactly* what you want me to do or you put my hand there yourself."

She held her breath and squeezed her eyes shut, pushing his hand over so it rested between her thighs. She let out a sound she didn't recognize when he curled his fingers.

"There's a good girl. See, you know what you want."

He stroked her through the layers, but it wasn't nearly what she needed.

"Please."

"Please what?"

"I hate you so much right now." She barked out a laugh and shuddered when he pressed a little harder.

"No, you don't." The smirk was back on his lips as he moved his hand in maddening circles.

Allie let out a frustrated sound and wriggled her hips. "I don't want to say it."

"Then I'm not moving from this spot, and I think you might be a little tired of having these pants in the way."

She whimpered and gathered up her courage, grabbing onto the waistband of her pajama pants and shimmying them down her hips. They made it as far as her knees before he reached to assist, pulling the fabric with that same deliberate slowness that had her aching.

"Panties, too?" he asked. Smugness infused his expression. Instead of slapping the pompous upturn at the corner of his lips like she wanted to, she dragged him down for a kiss, letting herself drown in the taste of him.

"Them, too," she said when she resurfaced.

The look he gave her might as well have melted the panties straight off her, but since it didn't, he removed them for her. He paused again and her patience was gone. Her thighs fell open as she snatched up his hand, settling it exactly where she craved his touch.

Her back arched until she was almost sitting upright when his fingers glided through the slick folds, swirling over her clit.

She dragged the pillow over her face to muffle her sounds, but he snatched it away.

"No hiding. I want to hear every little noise you can make." He moved bit by bit over her core, teasing and stroking. Then he lifted his shining fingers up for her to see. "You're so wet for me."

She shuddered and rolled her hips to encourage those fingers back into place.

Finally cooperative, he stretched out next to her and settled his hand between her thighs. One vexatious finger slid inside her, and she clapped both hands down over his. He froze and raised a questioning eyebrow.

She pressed against him, demanding the movement continue. "Don't stop. It's just a lot."

"A lot how? Because you're going to have plenty more in there than a single finger soon."

"No one's been in there except for me." She drew in a shaking breath. "I'm adjusting."

He resumed, pumping the digit in a fluid motion until a groan leapt from her mouth. He teased her relentlessly before adding a second finger, moving to the exact pace she set until she was light-headed from breathing so hard. She lost track of how long they lay like that, each thrust of his fingers sending tremors through her.

"More."

He paused, rolling another finger in the slick. Her eyes lost focus as he added it, her mouth falling open to pull in more air.

"*More.*" She'd been teetering on the edge for too long.

"Be specific," he chided.

She shook her head.

He sighed and withdrew his fingers, his lips turned down.

"Nooo," she whined.

"You know the rule."

"I just want to come."

"Good girl." He shifted over to lay between her legs and slid those wicked fingers back where they belonged, adding his mouth, tongue flicking over her clit.

"Mother *fucking* hell." She gasped and buried her hands in his hair, pressing her hips up against him.

The intensity of the combined sensations was like fireworks and her volume pitched, incoherent syllables dancing past her lips to the pulse of his tongue. Impossibly wound up, he undid her in mere seconds. She came with a cry, shaking and desperate, but he stayed unrelenting, driving her straight through one orgasm into the next. He had mercy on her after a few and finally pulled away, settling to watch her as little twitches and shivers skittered through her body.

"Take off your tank top when you're ready."

Her brain vaguely understood the instruction, but she was languid and satisfied and in no great hurry to move. Until he slid off the bed and pulled off his T-shirt.

"Jesus Christ. You're a puppy rescuer, sex god, *and* a fucking model."

He laughed. "You're so good for my ego. No modeling though. I have to be in good shape to keep up with the omegas. Likely by this time tomorrow you'll be putting these muscles to *very* good use."

She whimpered again.

"Tank top," he reminded her as he unzipped his jeans and let them drop.

Lust rippled through her at the sight and she yanked off the shirt bunched above her breasts. She tossed it to the side with an eagerness that had that smirk rising again. But then he slid off his underwear and her eyes widened.

"Are you *kidding* me? There's no way that's going to fit."

He laughed and stepped closer. "Oh, it'll fit. If you were in heat already you could fit two of me if you wanted to."

She gaped at him, a small sound escaping as her brain supplied her with the image of Sidney clones sandwiching her at front and back.

Instead of crossing the bed to her, he walked around the side and settled against the headboard. He crooked his finger and she followed the wordless instruction, climbing into his lap. Goosebumps decorated her skin.

"I have to do everything?"

He chuckled softly. "Not everything. You get yourself on this cock, and I can handle the rest."

"God. You can't *say* things like that."

He snared her around the waist. "I can say anything I like, and, if you want to pretend you don't enjoy my audacity, that's up to you, but I don't believe it." He dipped his head, tongue curling around her nipple, hands pressing against her back. Arcs of electricity zipped through her and she wrapped around his head.

You can do this. It's just a dick...

She brushed tentative touches over it and hot breath puffed out his nose against her skin. She rose up and inched closer, dropping a hand between them. Her fingertips didn't quite meet when she closed her hand around him. Guiding him, she rubbed him experimentally through her folds, groaning at both the sensation and the way his breathing shifted.

Relax.

Lining him up, she shifted her hips and worked in fractional increments to take the head of his cock inside her. He dragged her closer and devoured her mouth while she moved in a slow undulation, letting herself adjust slowly, sinking down on him inch by inch until she was seated in his lap.

She blinked and stared down. "I did it."

He laughed and squeezed her into a hug. "You did. Want to explore a bit before I fuck you into the mattress?"

"What did I *say* about the saying of things?" She pressed a hand over his mouth. "You're going to give me a goddamn aneurysm."

He flexed his hips and she lost her train of thought, letting her hand fall away. She rose up a little and sank back down, biting her lip and squeezing her eyes shut as she concentrated. He nuzzled her throat, nipping at the scent gland until she was melting under the attention.

"Thank you," he murmured in her ear.

"For what?"

"For wanting to share your first time with me. I've shared a few first heats, but none of them were virgins. I like it more than I expected."

"Is it because of my sparkling personality? Or maybe the crippling awkwardness? I bet that's super charming."

"You've got a smart mouth," he nibbled her bottom lip, "and I want to devour it."

She trembled, her muscles squeezing around him. "Jesus Christ on a cracker. I'm not going to have a single brain cell left when this is all over."

"Maybe not," he shrugged, "but at least you'll be extremely satisfied."

She held his face in both hands. "I think someone should put their money where their mouth is and get to work on making that happen right now."

"Hop off."

"That's the opposite of satisfying me."

"Well, we can stay in this position, but then it's all you. Maybe you want to fuck *me* into the mattress?"

"I...could give it a go?"

"I'll help." His hands fastened onto her hips and guided her upwards.

The sensation of gliding on him left her half-delirious, but it was even better when he pressed her back down, and better still when he guided her to roll her hips and took her nipple back into his mouth. She keened sharply, head thrown back as she followed the rhythm her body craved. He took advantage of the new exposure and suckled the scent gland, sending her down a new spiral.

The crest of pleasure broke over her and she leaned forward, sinking her teeth into his shoulder to muffle the sound as she was overwhelmed. He jerked sharply pressing upwards into her, hands digging into her hips with a ferocity she could already tell was going to bruise. When the tremors finally subsided he wrapped his arms around her and she flopped like a limp noodle against him.

Her throat hurt from breathing so hard and every time she shifted to get more comfortable it sent fresh ripples through her. She darted out her tongue and lapped at his scent gland.

"You smell nice." She buried her face against him and sighed.

He trailed firm hands up and down her back. "Do you think you might be a little blissed?"

"I feel drunk...maybe high. Or both. Drigh? Hunk? Does a word exist for both?" She nestled closer. "I wish I could feel this good all the time."

"But then you'd stop noticing." He tipped them to the side and slid out of her even as she made tiny sounds of protest. "Come on. You had a big night and you should have some water before we continue."

"Carry me. My legs don't work anymore."

He scooped her up, cradling her against him. "Did you know you're incredibly fucking cute right now?"

"Mmm, no, but you should tell me again. No one ever thinks I'm cute."

He carted her to the bathroom and set her on the counter. "Well, everyone else is stupid then because you are completely perfect. Cute as hell, absolutely sexy, and you felt like heaven when you came on my cock like that."

"Oh my Goood. You're doing the saying again. Stop that."

"Nope." He turned on the shower and ushered her under the hot water, turning the detachable showerhead between her thighs until she came again on the pulsing stream. "I'm never going to get tired of the sound of you."

She hummed happily and pressed her nose to his scent gland.

"They should make a perfume of you."

"You're fun like this." He laughed, the sound loud in her ear.

"I didn't know orgasms made me fun."

"To be fair, they make most people fun." Sidney pressed her against the tiles and she was entirely too relaxed to feel awkward about it.

She'd always thought she looked a bit like a drowned rat when she stepped out of the shower, but he didn't seem phased by how round her head looked with soaked hair. In fact, he was rather focused on entirely different round things. He squeezed both of her ass cheeks and took possession of her mouth with his.

He tasted so *good*. It was wildly unfair, and he had her tingling all over again. His scent was muted with the shower running, but the steaming spray didn't remotely affect the way his tongue dipped into her mouth.

His lips tugged into that devilish smirk as he pulled away. "Having fun?"

"I refuse to answer that and feed your ego."

"You don't really have to answer. You've already made it perfectly clear." He laughed and tugged her closer. "We should get you fed a little more. First heats are already unpredictable enough, but I don't want to trigger you early with all of this."

"But then it would be over faster, wouldn't it?"

Sidney shrugged. "Hard to say. First heats aren't as reliable as later ones while your body is getting used to things."

"That sounds vaguely ominous."

"I'm sure it'll all be fine. It's just a new, extremely intense experience, and I'm not sure how you'll react." He turned off the water and dried her off, wrapping her in an obscenely soft robe before carrying her out to the kitchen.

Their grocery order arrived while she was cocooned in blankets. He pulled out the cake they'd ordered and served her a slice.

"Dessert first?"

"Of course. The lasagna will take a little while, and I don't want you hungry."

She shoveled a bite into her mouth. "How am I supposed to go back to normal life after all this?"

"If ever there was a time you should be spoiled with every indulgence, it's during a heat."

He leaned against the counter looking like an absolute snack. She covered up the thought with another bite of cake, but he was already smirking anyway.

"Thinking about me?"

She took another bite. "Nope."

"Your scent changes when filthy thoughts slip through."

"That's not fair." Allie pouted.

He shrugged and put the lasagna in the oven. "You don't want me to know?"

"No. You get too smug about it."

"That's all part of my charm. Don't pretend you don't love it."

"Whether I love it or not is irrelevant."

"Mmm, I don't think so." He stepped away from the counter with a hot, predatory gleam in his eye.

"You stay over there. Cake is sacred and I need to be able to eat it again after this without thinking of you getting up in my business."

He laughed. "But would that really be so bad?"

"Yes, it would! Because I will blush red as a goddamn beet and my parents will *inquire* what's prompting the blush and that will make it a million times worse."

"I think the solution is to let me get up in your *business* so much that you're no longer at the mercy of your blush."

The glint in his eye shot a bolt of lust straight to her clit, and he beamed.

"Quit taking advantage of the fact that you're super hot and a deliverer of orgasms. I have no defenses."

He slipped over to her with the grace of a panther and dipped down to nibble her throat, his hands sliding inside the robe, stroking tender flesh until her head tipped back and she mewled, bracing herself on the table. "I like that you're weak for me."

She made a small helpless sound. "I'm going to emerge from this an entirely different person, and I blame *you*."

"Blame accepted." He fetched her another slice of cake and a glass of milk, and remained on his best behavior while she ate it, though the smirk every time he looked at her only made her feel even more exposed.

How was she supposed to put up any kind of mental barriers against someone like him? He'd been *inside* her body—an intimacy she wasn't fully prepared to process. And she certainly wasn't prepared for how much she wanted him to be there again. The vulnerability that had been required of her and would be intensified in the coming days was too much to think about, so she didn't.

"So, you're a nurse too?"

"Mhmm. It's hard to find other work that's so compatible with being a heat helper as well. The clinic is great about managing the hours, and they're very understanding about shifts dropping last minute since they also handle the heats."

"Which do you like better?"

"I know the obvious choice is the heat helping. I like both since they're rewarding jobs, and, while being a heat helper has definite perks, it also requires me to drop things without much warning and be on call twenty-four-seven for over a week at a time."

"Oh. I guess I hadn't really thought about that."

"Most people wouldn't. I love it, but it's not an easy job."

"I'm even more work than most." Guilt slowly settled into the pit of her stomach.

He pulled her into a kiss, expertly distracting her. "Don't you dare feel guilty. I do this because I want to. I get paid well, and I'm more than happy to do what I can to make a difficult time enjoyable."

She tried to take the words to heart, but it still weighed on her. She didn't much like being a job, no matter how much he might like it.

The oven timer went off, and he pulled the bubbling tray out. Settling on the couch at his insistence, they watched a trivia show with her cuddled against him while munching her dinner. He was still a stranger in many ways, but she hadn't felt this relaxed or safe since she was a child. When she nuzzled closer, he opened his arms, and they got comfortably horizontal with her tucked between him and the couch, her arm draped over his chest.

It was so *easy*.

Why couldn't everything in her life be this easy? She couldn't remember the last time she'd relaxed like this without having to worry about an impending exam or assignment, or coordinating herself around extracurriculars and homework. It was refreshing to simply be.

"Is this all weird for you?" she asked.

"How so?"

"Well, you don't get to pick any of us, right?"

"No, but I can refuse a client if I want to, and the whole point of the scent canisters is for omegas to find someone compatible for their heat, and that goes both ways." He toyed with her hair, and she snuggled a little closer. "The hormones help too. Alphas are still affected by the ones you're throwing out, and while it's possible to fight it, I let myself be receptive to it so that I can be a better match during all this."

"That's good. I'd feel bad if this was super weird for you."

"I probably wouldn't be doing this job if it was constantly weird for me. I'd do nursing full time if that was the case."

"Right. Sorry, I'm musing and apparently not thinking clearly."

"Nah, you're fine."

After an hour of watching TV she started to get restless.

Sidney pressed his nose to her throat. "You're shifting."

Her head whipped up. "Shifting to what? Is it the heat starting?"

"Oh, you'll know when it kicks in." He tilted her face so he could look at her properly. "How do you feel?"

"A little unsettled. I don't know how to fix it."

"Let me test my theory." He patted her hip to get her to stand and then led her to the bedroom. "Have a walk around. I'll be right back."

Allie didn't want him to go, but it would be unreasonable to ask him to stay when they were still in the same house. Glancing around, her vision honed onto the laundry hamper. She allowed her instincts to guide her as she reached inside and pick out a discarded shirt. It calmed the unsettled part of her to hold it and she turned to the bed, following that little tug again that told her to tuck the shirt between the mattress and bed frame.

She turned back to the hamper and scooped out a whole armful. "I was right."

Allie screamed and hurled the whole pile to the floor. "God dammit! Don't scare me like that." She turned from his satisfied smile to the pile of clothes. It felt wrong to leave it there so she gathered it back up and went to put it back in the hamper but her arms wouldn't let go.

"Don't try to fight it. You're starting to nest. Take whatever you want from anywhere and put it wherever makes you happy."

Having his permission didn't help one bit. She remained frozen trying to deal with her rational mind telling her this was stupid and her omega side demanding she do it. Citrus and clove filled her senses, sending a tingle billowing through her that prompted her into motion.

"You did that on purpose." She pouted.

"Yep, I did." He slipped further into the room, fishing a piece of metallic mesh out of the bedside table, and fastened it around his throat.

Allie glanced up from her gathering. "What's that?"

"An alpha collar so we don't accidentally bond during all this."

"Shouldn't I have one of those too?"

He dipped towards her, mouth grazing over her throat. "Nope. You get to enjoy all this without anything in the way."

She stood, shivering in his grasp until he finally stepped back and let her continue on. With her nerves still vibrating from the attention, she turned to her task. Item by item she filled in the space between the mattress and the frame, creating a circle of scent around the bed. She plucked out the stuffed bear her mother had forced on her and added it in, but it still wasn't enough. She made a small sound of distress and slipped past him, dragging the blankets they'd used off the couch. She climbed straight into the bed with them draped over her, content as hell with her nest.

"This is so dumb. Why do we do this?"

"It creates a sense of safety being surrounded by the scent of your partner. It's a way for omegas to mitigate stress."

"Can you come in here please?"

"Of course."

He slipped under with her, and his citrus and clove filled the space and settled deep into her bones. It was a cocoon of contentment. She tried not to think about it too hard and simply let herself enjoy his proximity. Every breath was heavily laced with his scent. She never wanted to move again.

She drifted, lulled to sleep, surrounded by warmth.

Allie woke in the dark and peeked outside of her nest to see the faint light of dawn bathing the room. She climbed out of bed, careful not to wake Sidney, and trotted to the bathroom. Slick had soaked through her panties and pajama pants while she'd slept. Entirely too sweaty and gross for her liking, she stripped off her pajamas and stepped into the shower for a quick twirl to remove the worst of it, rinsing off her clothes as well and wringing them out before dropping them to the floor so she could dry herself off.

Refreshed, she gathered everything up and scampered back down the hall. A torrent of heat raced up her spine, spreading outwards. It was blisteringly hot, every nerve alive and on fire. She stopped short in the door frame and braced herself, dropping her clothing, falling to her knees. A sob tore from her throat as she curled around herself, desperately seeking some way to reduce the building tension. She grabbed at her skin, nails raking as if it would somehow diminish the sensation. Her fingers dove between her thighs, slipping into her slick-soaked cunt where the heat was most intense, desperate to banish it with the frantic thrusts.

The relief was too minimal, the heat too all-consuming, and she cried out, a scream that melted into a series of pained whimpers. Pressure against the back of her head guided her, moving her face until she was inhaling sweet citrus and clove in frenetic gulps of air. It blunted the sharpest edge of the pain, but it wasn't enough.

"I've got you." A voice reached through the haze. "Hold onto me."

Allie tried to obey, but there was no sense in her mind. She writhed, and insistent hands tugged her upright. She sobbed, begging for it all to stop, for the heat to burn itself out. The scent grew to overwhelming proportions, citrus and clove muddling her thoughts further as a warm weight pressed her into the bed. She could scarcely breathe from the pressure, but then there was friction between her thighs, and she thrust her hips wildly.

Each movement pushed back the haze a microscopic amount, but that slightest bit of relief was all she needed to prompt her. She moved with a mindless urgency, clinging to the weight above her, hips bucking, craving. Every orgasm temporarily overwhelmed the burning, throwing her over the peak of pleasure before she crashed down into the heat again, whipping back and forth between the two until she could no longer tell one from the other.

The weight kept moving, the pressure and friction between her thighs unrelenting.

It was never enough.

Chapter Three

Allie blinked.

Her vision slowly focused.

"Welcome back." Sidney looked rather ruffled and exhausted when she opened her eyes, but his smile was soft and sweet as he traced her cheeks.

"I feel like I've been run over." Every bit of her was tender. She was sweaty, exhausted, and could barely see straight.

"Not quite. You had a rough start to your heat and haven't been fully here for almost two days."

"I don't like that." She wiggled restlessly and stopped short as her muscles protested.

"No. It's not particularly pleasant. It'll get easier in the future, but right now it's all very new for your body. The lingering pain will go away shortly as well. Now that we've broken the initial haze, you should settle fairly comfortably into the rest of the heat."

"It looks like I made you put in some effort." She ran her fingers through his hair and found the roots damp with sweat.

"It was the most intense workout I've had in a while."

"Sorry." She pouted but he nipped it away, his mouth soft and demanding.

"You have *nothing* to apologize for." He pulled her close again and she nestled in to listen to the pounding cadence of his heart.

"Did you have to fuck me for two solid days? How are you even awake right now?"

"Alpha hormones can be as intense as an omega's during heats. We need the boost to satisfy when our partners are entirely insatiable. And to answer your second question, yes, basically. I had to alternate between cock, hands, and toys several times, and I am very ready for a nap, but first, do you think you're up to eating?"

She moved her legs experimentally. "I could probably make it to the kitchen."

"You can eat in here. I'll bring you something. How about a shower?"

"God, yes. I'd even be happy if you took me out back and turned the hose on me."

He laughed softly. "I need to shower, too, so I'm going to stick to hot water for now."

Sidney helped her stand, and they walked gingerly to the bathroom. She sank onto the shower bench while he got the hot water going. She barely had to move as he gently soaped her down, shampooed and conditioned her hair, dried her off, and blow dried her hair while he combed it out in long, soothing strokes.

She hummed happily as he set about applying moisturizer to her. "This is heaven."

"I aim to please." He dug his fingers into her tense muscles, and they relaxed under the attention, her mind exceedingly chill with the cloud of sweet citrus and clove that surrounded her.

When he'd attended to every inch of her, he disappeared into the kitchen while she tucked herself into the nest to wait. He served her more chocolate cake and some warmed up lasagna that she ate with ravenous excitement.

Afterward, they both tucked into the nest, and he was asleep before she'd even finished settling in.

Allie woke squirming, the edges of her awareness igniting. She rolled her hips against him with a whimper and gasped his name. *"Sidney."*

He was there instantly, gathering her in, pressing her to her back inside the nest. Their bodies slipped together without resistance, and she arched with a moan, able to appreciate the sensation properly for the first time since her heat kicked in.

The steady rhythm and the heat hormones had her shaking, each thrust shoving her up the sharp crest of pleasure and spilling over it. The expanse of skin pressed to her was still a sweet relief from the sharp heat even as it warmed her and had her sweating from the exertion. Her fingers dug into his ass cheeks, demanding more, and he accommodated, eliciting a sharp gasp from her as he drove their bodies together and flung her straight over the edge of orgasm again. There wasn't time to breathe before the next started to build.

The weight of his body and strength in his muscles was an intoxicating combination. She'd never felt quite so malleable before, like she was ready to take anything someone else could give her. Her nails dug into him as she shuddered, gasping his name. He growled in her ear and bucked forward once, twice, thrice, and then she felt the bloom of warmth inside her as he came. He sank against her, his lips brushing over her scent gland.

The scorching edge of the heat had receded, and she lay content, heart pounding, beneath him.

"I'm super annoyed that I missed out on two days of this."

He laughed against her skin. "I'm just glad you're past it. The rest of the heat is much more fun."

Sidney slid away from her and sat up, disappearing into the bathroom to bring back a warm washcloth to wipe up between her thighs.

"What now?"

"Mostly we wait for your heat to rise again. You can do whatever you want in the meantime. Although I always recommend getting as much rest as possible and eating as much as you can during the downtime."

"What if I wanted to have sex again before the next heat wave starts?"

He let out a laugh. "I'm good, but I'm not working on an infinite supply of energy. You're like marathon training."

"I was going to say you'll be so fit after all this, but you're already smokin' hot."

He broke into a delighted snicker. "It's been very fun to see you open up with all of this. Why don't you use this time to think about what you want to do with the next wave. There's certainly plenty of options."

"Like what?"

"Hmm. Well," he pulled open the trunk in the bottom of his closet, "you're welcome to any of these."

Allie climbed off the bed and kneeled, naked, before it. "Holy shit."

She stared wide-eyed at the leather implements.

"You can touch them. There's no pressure to use anything in particular. Check out anything you're curious about."

She reached for a mass of straps and buckles. "What's this one?"

"Harness. Want to try it on?"

She swallowed hard and nodded.

He crooked his finger and she inched towards him and handed it to him. "Arms out to the side, please."

Allie obeyed. He laid the straps over her shoulders and brought the cross-pieces under each breast, securing with a buckle that came down around her back. The metal was cold against her skin, setting goosebumps dancing over her.

"What do you do with it?"

He answered by grabbing hold of one of the straps, tugging her to him. "It gives a better, more controlled grip."

Her breath halted in her throat. "O-oh?"

His lips curled devilishly. "I take it you like the sound of that?"

She opened her mouth to respond, but words wouldn't make it out.

"Your scent spiked. Do you want to wear it for the next wave?"

Allie nodded slowly. "But how would it work when I'm laying like that?"

"I'd probably take you from behind instead."

She let out a squeak, warmth flooding her cheeks.

"God, you're so cute. I keep forgetting how new this all is for you besides the heat. You're doing extremely well." He kept a firm hold on the harness and threaded the fingers of his free hand into her hair. "I'm proud of you."

His words electrified her. Who knew someone being proud of her would do that?

The light pressure of the leather sent little sparks through her skin. She traced haphazard patterns across his chest, half wishing that he had a harness too for her to grab onto.

"Do you want to look at anything else?"

"The rest of the box seemed a little intimidating."

"You're just looking," he reminded her.

She hummed noncommittally and settled back in front of the trunk. There was a set of velvet lined cuffs that made her clit tingle at the thought of them.

"Pass me whatever you're looking at right now."

She handed it over with a flaring blush and went back to digging through the contents of the trunk. There was a collection of toys that turned her insides to mush, and she refused to give them to him.

The hair on the back of her neck rose when he kneeled behind her, arms crossing around her waist. His breath ghosted over her ear and she fought against the rise of heat that sparked between her thighs. "Don't be shy."

"But I *am* shy."

"Not with me. I've seen you in the rawest state you can ever be in. You have nothing to hide from me. I want to give you everything you could dream of. Any fantasy that floats into your head is fair game."

"I want to try the cuffs. Can we do that at the same time as the harness?"

"Mhmm." His fingertips danced over her ribs, and he dropped a kiss to her shoulder. Then her wrists were behind her. He braced each arm to keep in her place, pressing closer while he nipped at her earlobe.

She squirmed helplessly and felt slick glide down her thighs.

"You smell entirely edible." His teeth grazed over her scent gland and she almost came right then, shivering in his grip. He moved away and she was left untethered. "I shouldn't tease you this much between. It can trigger the next wave too soon."

"Too late." She gasped, the heat creeping hot and sharp into the edges of her awareness, nerves aflame, the craving to be touched overwhelming her thoughts.

"If you want out at any point, say so." He hoisted her back onto the bed face down and secured both wrists in the velvet cuffs, hooking them to one another. He grabbed the harness next, and her hips rose with the movement, sliding onto his waiting cock.

She groaned into the blankets and bit down with the first thrust, the bare edge of panic spiking the pleasure as she strained against the cuffs. She chanted a mantra of pleas into the fabric, lost to the devastating swell of sensation that left her with tremors of pleasure, each stronger than the last. He kept moving, the slap of their hips meeting a bright staccato to her perpetual begging *please* that was only silenced when each orgasm stole her breath entirely.

The harness pressed into her shoulders, and she followed each pull of the leather until she was screaming into the blankets. That sweet warmth bloomed between them as his thrusts turned erratic and frantic.

Allie huffed and puffed, struggling to catch her breath. She melted to the mattress. "Out, please."

The cuffs were off in a heartbeat, and he gathered her close.

He took his time massaging her from wrist to shoulder until she was relaxed against his chest.

"I gather you liked the harness and cuffs?"

"Mhmm, I did." Her heart was still pounding from it. "I didn't really know what to expect."

"Wear the harness as long as you'd like. We can take it off whenever you get tired of it." He stretched out next to her and curled around her, failing to conceal a yawn.

"You should sleep." She wiggled nearer, tucking in. "I'll wake you if I need you."

Sidney nodded slowly and pulled the blankets over them. His breath evened out so quickly Allie wondered if he'd passed out the moment his eyes had closed. She let herself relax and succumb to sleep, waking him in the morning when her heat rose again.

Chapter Four

Sidney moved in a languid and luxurious manner, tugging Allie by the ankles to the edge of the bed where he thrust inside her, her legs wrapping around his waist.

"Touch yourself."

"*What?*" The request startled her. "I can't...I don't..."

"You can and you do." He grinned wolfishly down at her. "You helped yourself along several times during the haze when you got too impatient."

A blush rolled through her body. "How do I do it?"

His gaze turned hot. "Touch and find out. You'll know when you figure out what you like best."

She whimpered, inching her fingers down her torso where they hesitated as they met the thatch of hair. It was honestly ridiculous to be self-conscious at this point, she chided herself. Sidney was literally fucking into her at this very moment.

"Should I stop to give you some motivation?" He winked and stilled his hips.

"Nooo." She whined and bucked against him, demanding more.

"The second you touch, I'll move."

She let out an especially pitiful sound and let her hand move closer, fingertips brushing her throbbing clit. He thrust back into her, making her clit graze the pads of her fingers again, and she groaned.

"Come on, little one. Show me what you like best."

His words flowed over her like lava, igniting her. She tested, one finger moving tentative strokes and circles, then two, which felt more intoxicating and kept her clit trapped, surrounded by friction. She shuddered and kept stroking, alternating patterns and pressure until she settled on firm circles, almost hard enough to be painful.

"Oh, *fuck*," she gasped.

Sidney rewarded her with a deep growl. "There's my good girl."

Allie gasped, the praise kicking her over the edge. She frantically kept up her movements, her pitching moans drawing more from him, which only made her wetter and more desperate, leaving them both growling and lost to the pleasure.

She panted as she came down from the last high and allowed him to gather her to his chest, spent cock tucked against her ass.

"How am I supposed to go back to real life after this?"

He cradled her, draped across his chest with her nose buried against his throat.

"The same way we all have to eventually." He stroked her hair gently. "You'll have other heats. At some point, you'll likely have a partner outside of them, and you can spend every day like this if you want to."

In her current position she couldn't even begin to fathom another partner. "Could I have you for my next one?"

"It's possible. Depends when it happens, but I'd be happy to do this again."

"You're not worried that I'll fall hopelessly in love with you?" She was worried, even if only a little.

He laughed softly. "Well, I don't know that it would matter even if you did. My job is really important to me and there's not a lot of people who would be comfortable with me continuing it while in a relationship, my clients included."

"Why?"

"You don't think you'd have a problem with me sleeping with multiple other omegas? Having them in my home or having to leave you at a moment's notice because someone's heat started? Potentially having to miss your own heats because I was already helping someone else?"

She bristled, stiffening at his words.

"See? Omegas and alphas get possessive. We can't help it. It would be hard for me to do my job if I were in any kind of committed relationship."

"I guess that's fair." She nosed his scent gland and inhaled deeply. "I'll just enjoy you while I have you."

"A wise choice." He resumed stroking her hair. "Someday I won't be able to keep up, and I'll have to transition to nursing only, but I'm really proud of what I do and I want to help as many omegas as I can before I'm forced out of it."

"You *should* be proud." She traced patterns on his chest, allowing herself time to gather her thoughts. "I'd been dreading this since I found out I was an omega, and you made it way better than I ever imagined."

"I'm glad." A soft rumble emanated from his chest, and she wiggled to press her ear against him, the gentle purr soothing her into a half-asleep state.

It was so much more than the sex, though she was convinced nothing else would ever compare. It was also the ease he had around her—the attentiveness, the care and compassion he showed. Not to mention that he was a pretty decent cook and a stickler for maintaining hygiene and comfort during all this which helped her relax into everything without worry. She'd never been so well cared for in her whole memory.

"How do we know when the heat is actually over?"

"You'll have a full twenty-four hours without it kicking in. That's usually the safe range. We'll hang out for a couple of days after to be sure."

"I like hanging out with you."

"Is that so?" His purr picked up in volume, and he closed his eyes.

"Mhmm. You have excellent taste in movies and you let me eat dessert first."

His laugh rumbled in her ear. "I try my best."

"What're you going to do with me after the heat is over? I can't promise to be entertaining." Allie traced patterns on his chest, channeling her worries into the mindless motion.

"You've been pretty entertaining so far," he assured.

"But there was sex involved in that entertainment. Maybe you'll think I'm super boring if we're just chilling."

"I'm pretty sure that's not possible." He chuckled softly when his words triggered her purr and held on a little tighter. "In any case, you don't need to worry about that. You're not here to entertain me."

"But I want to."

"You're doing fine. I promise I'm entirely content right now." He stroked her back in soothing motions, and the sweet citrus and clove emanated until her head spun. "Want to see a neat trick to relax an omega?"

"Absolutely. I'm a high strung individual at the best of times."

He pressed his thumb and middle finger firmly to the scent glands on either side of her throat. It turned her muscles to absolute jelly, and she sank against him with a soft mewl. He kept up the pressure and moved his fingers in gentle circular motions until her purr was like thunder rumbling in her chest and her eyes drifted shut.

"This is fucking witchcraft," she murmured, every limb like lead as she melted.

"I used it a fair bit while you were in the initial depths of the heat haze."

"Can I do it to myself?"

"You can try, but it's generally not quite as effective as having someone else doing it. Some effect is better than none, though."

"Does it work on alphas? I sort of zoned out in biology. I don't remember them mentioning if alphas had a magic chill button or not."

"It's not nearly as strong as with omegas, but it still feels nice."

"Roll over." She flopped off the side of him, staring at him until he obeyed, and then she climbed on top, straddling his waist. Her fingers danced over his neck. "Show me where."

Allie allowed him to guide her hands and then pressed against the scent glands. His purr rumbled and she grinned, validated. She traced her lips over the curve of his shoulder, dropping tiny kisses as she went, working his purr from him with focused intent.

She draped over him, resting comfortably. "It's entirely unfair I have to go back to school after all this. All my muscle knots are going to leap back into existence."

He wriggled out from under her and pulled her into his arms. "That's a problem for future Allie. Present Allie should have no such worries."

"Maybe you should distract present Allie so she doesn't have time to focus on worries."

Chapter Five

With no real schedule to adhere to, they ate, slept, and fucked according to the demands of her heat. Hours melted into days, and Allie lost count of how many times she'd been taken, how many times Sidney had made her come.

She lay draped over him, comfortably resting with his heartbeat soothing against her ear. "Do you want to knot me?"

Sidney's scent spiked, his muscles tensed beneath her.

"Sorry, is that bad? Should I not have asked?"

"You're fine." He relaxed beneath her again. "It's not usually phrased as asking if I want it and usually a demand when they're in the throes of their heat."

"Oh. Well, I was wondering. We haven't done that yet have we?" He shook his head. "I may have done some investigating on my phone while you were napping the other day. I figure there's no time like the present."

"I'd love to knot you during the next wave."

"Are you proud of me for being that bold?" She grinned.

"Always." He laughed and nipped her bottom lip. "Since you're feeling bold, go choose something else from the box."

He nudged her towards the edge of the bed until she slid off and crawled towards the trunk of hidden treasures. It felt as wildly scandalous as it had the last time she'd looked at it. She rifled through it, fingers brushing against a rainbow dildo. She paused.

"Toss it here," he called from the bed.

"You don't even know what it is."

"Doesn't matter." He held out his arm, wiggling his fingers until she sighed and snatched up the dildo, marching back to the bed. She dropped it next to his face. "Good choice."

"Yeah? What do I even need it for when I have you?"

"I assure you I can think of plenty of uses for it."

Allie blinked, heat rushing to her cheeks. "Are you going to tell me what those uses are or let me struggle to imagine?"

He grabbed her hand and pulled her onto the bed with him. "Well, I did tell you that you could handle two of me if you really wanted to."

The words turned her insides to liquid. "Jesus Christ on a cracker. How is that even possible?"

"Omega bodies are very resilient during heats."

"But that's so intimidating," she whined.

"We could use it for another first for you?" He patted her buttcheek.

"Why does that sound ominous?" She laughed and snuggled in.

"Not ominous, just new."

"So, what if I did want to explore that?"

"Then you tell me that and we play. I'm not going to pop that whole thing in from the get-go if that's what you're worried about."

"Only slightly. Barely a worry." Her cheeks flamed.

"Uh huh. Very convincing."

"You shush. It's just kinda weird, ya know? It's my butt."

That set off his laughter, and he buried his face against her skin, utterly cackling before it turned to a simmering snicker.

"It's not *that* funny." She pouted.

"It is a little." He tugged her face closer and kissed her until she was melting in his hands. "Tell me if you want to, or we can find something else."

She squirmed uncomfortably. "I might be curious."

His eyes gleamed before he reached into the nightstand and pulled out a little bottle of lube. "Then let's pursue it. Do you want the harness or cuffs for this too?"

"Could we both wear a harness?"

"Sure, let me grab one. Do you want me in the cross straps or the straight across?" He fished both out of the trunk and held them up. Her brain sparked and she forgot how to speak. He moved each one in front of his torso in turn, watching her carefully. "Straight across it is."

She let out a little squawk.

"What? Your scent spiked a little more on that one."

"I both hate and love that you know these things." She groaned, kicking her feet in a half-hearted tantrum.

"I have a lot of practice paying attention. And we're pretty tuned to one another right now. If you weren't so hopped up on heat hormones you'd notice all the little shifts with me too. Do you want to strap me in or lay there admiring me while I do it myself?"

Allie let out an indignant groan. "Shut your beautiful face."

"Only once you answer the question."

She thrust out a hand and beckoned him over.

"You're not using your words."

"Words are overrated."

"Then I'm staying right here."

Growling, she crossed her arms.

"If you're going to be stubborn, we're not going to play." He set the harness back into the trunk.

"That's not fair. You know what I want. Why do I have to say it all the time?"

"Because not everyone is going to be as good at reading you as I am. Learn to use your voice and be clear about what you want. You don't need to hide with me."

"Maybe hiding is more comfortable."

That drew a smirk from him.

"Comfortable, probably, but far less fun." He sat down next to her. "If you want the world to go your way, you have to make it clear what you desire. I want you to be able to say what you want so that you and everyone else knows for certain."

"Shouldn't I already know for certain?"

"That depends. Do you want this enough to say it out loud?"

She hummed thoughtfully and toyed with the ends of her hair. "I don't understand how you make it all so easy and so difficult at the same time."

"It's a gift." He laughed softly and tucked her hair behind her ear. "Now, do you want to experience a new pleasure or not?"

Allie puffed out her cheeks and released a frustrated sound. "Yes, I do."

"But what?"

She grabbed his face with both hands. "It's entirely unfair for someone that looks like you to be so goddamn infuriating. Yes, I want to do all the new things. I want you to wear that harness and use the toys on me and introduce me to all manner of absolute filth."

He grinned, her grip on him obscuring the expression. "Was that so hard?" He fetched the harness back and handed it to her. "Strap it on me."

She swallowed and stood on shaking legs to drape the leather over him. Her fingers fumbled the buckles when his sweet citrus and clove spiked, making her head swim. When she finally finished, she hooked both hands over the strap that stretched across his chest.

"I like this on you," she whispered.

"You should show me how much." His eyes twinkled with mirth as she yanked him closer to devour his mouth as she hoisted on tiptoe. He walked his fingertips up her back and down again, squeezing her ass. "Go get yourself comfortable on the bed, and I'll be right there."

Allie did as she was bid, snatching up one of the pillows to curl around while she watched him dig out a small box and toss it on the bed next to her. Her cheeks burst into flame when she opened it, revealing the three sizes of glass teardrop-shaped toys with flared bases. The embarrassment worsened when he grabbed her hips and hoisted them into the air. She buried her face in the pillow, unwilling to turn and witness him seeing such an intimate view.

The pop of a lid was followed by the cool drip of lube and then by the pad of his thumb moving in slow circles. She tensed and let out an incomprehensible sound at the sensation.

He kissed her lower back. "Relax."

"Easy for you to say. No one's rooting around *your* tush."

"We could swap spots if you like, but I already know I enjoy it and this is supposed to be about you."

She squawked and turned to face him. "You like getting...you know?"

"Should I not? I'm rather fond of prostate orgasms and there's only one way to get to it." He patted her buttcheek.

"I didn't think an alpha would be into that."

Sidney laughed. "Well, this alpha is into anything that feels amazing."

"Okay, I guess that's fair."

"You ready for the first one? I'm going to warm you up a little before we make use of our rainbow friend."

"I'm ready." She returned to her original position and waited.

Smooth glass slid around in the lube, and she tensed again.

"That's not relaxing." He held her hips and wiggled them until she started laughing.

Allie cuddled into the pillow, letting her back dip into an arch. The toy moved again, the tip pressing softly, gliding away to swirl through the lube and return a half dozen times that way until she was pressing back against it. He gave a final push, and it slipped straight inside. Sidney circled her clit with his thumb, coaxing her to climax. Her muscles squeezed around the plug and she gasped, her hands curling into the sheets. When his fingers joined his thumb, plunging into her pussy, she was undone in moments, a cry raking over her throat.

She melted onto the bed, breathless, as he removed the plug and his hands.

"Holy shit. What the fuck?"

Sidney chuckled. "It makes it a little more intense than usual."

"*A little?*"

"Sometimes a lot. Depends on the person. Are you ready for the next one?"

"Yes please." She didn't protest a bit when he lifted her hips and replaced the first plug with a larger one in the same manner as he'd done the first.

There was no protest in her when he flipped her over and devoured her, pumping skilled fingers and teasing an already primed clit into another orgasm. After that one she moved almost without thinking, turning and lifting her own hips. She panted, clinging to the sheets as he slid the mid-size plug free, replacing it with the largest. It took a bit more time than the first two, rotated slowly, the burgeoning pressure encouraging her body to open. It was a sensation she felt down to her toes and into her fingertips, an unexpected depth of satisfaction she hadn't experienced before.

Allie sucked in a breath, tensing everything she could on the inhale, and then exhaled slow and smooth, relaxing her muscles as best she could. Her body gave in, and the plug sank inside, leaving her shaking. She moved to tip over, but he held her in place.

"Stay up for this one." It was him who ended up on his back, sliding his face between her spread thighs, driving her to the brink with wicked lips that left her on the edge of sobbing as she came again, squeezing desperately around the plug. Black spots danced in her vision and her lungs burned; her heart pounded ferociously.

Part of her wanted to ask for a break when he sat up, but she also didn't want the sensations to abate, even as they crushed her into nothing and rebuilt her anew.

"Deep breath. In." He braced a palm on her lower back. "And out." He pulled the final plug free and set it aside with the others.

She tried to ask what was next but only whimpered instead.

"Ready for the next?"

Allie nodded helplessly.

The lid on the bottle of lube popped again, and he picked up the rainbow dildo she'd selected. More lube dropped between her cheeks, and he swirled the dildo like he had with the plugs, pressing the tip to her entrance. She arched her back and wiggled against it, craving that deep sensation, only half coherent.

"Please," she whined. The edges of her awareness blurred with encroaching warmth, heat surging through her body.

The dildo sank in, inch by gloriously torturous inch and she rocked back against it, the slight sting as she stretched dulled instantly by the growing heat. He pulled her hips back against him, cock nudging her pussy, and she thrust back against him.

"*Please.*"

She rocked desperately, and he braced a hand against her, though, if it was to keep her still, he was not successful. The glide of the toy sliding out had her whining, afraid it was going away too quickly, but then he pushed it back in and every sound froze in her throat. He grabbed onto her harness instead, which still failed to keep her still, but when he yanked back on it, she was met with the combined friction of cock and toy, the pressure flinging her straight off the edge of an orgasm as she screamed wordlessly into the sheets.

More sensation than she could handle struck her like a tsunami, and each dip and swell of the coming waves had her scarcely able to breathe past them as he thrust into her with body and toy. Allie reached a shaking hand beneath her uplifted hips and brushed a tentative finger against her clit. Pleasure lanced up her spine, all three points combining to toss her up and over another crest, and she fell, half-drowned in those waves, even as she continued to touch and he moved with a strength and finesse she didn't possess.

Her body gave out somewhere among the pleasure, held up only by Sidney's grip on the harness. He let out a gasp, a groan muffled by grinding teeth as his hips thrust forward once more, his knot swelling to trap them together. Allie's vision flared white as the orgasm sizzled through her. She lost track of how many times she came, and as the heat fell away she became aware of the rawness of her throat and the disappearance of some of the pressure as he slid the toy free and set it aside with the plugs. The huff and puff of their breathing filled the space. He pulled them both over, curling up with his face buried against her neck.

It felt like centuries before she was able to form words. "I need to sleep for a decade."

"Mhmm," he murmured against her skin. "I could go for that. A bath would be nice too."

"Carry me."

"There's no way I can carry you while we're stuck together." He sighed and kissed her hair. Every time she shifted, it sent little ripples through her, which obviously meant she had to wiggle continuously until he snared an arm around her hips and growled in her ear. "You're making it extremely difficult for me to come out of this state."

"Stay in it then."

Whatever response he'd planned dissolved when she squeezed around him. "God, I'm going to be stuck to you forever apparently."

"If I could stop doing it I would."

He nipped at her scent gland and it sparked a sensation that had her gripping the sheets. She reached around, fingers seeking out the scent glands on his throat, and gave them a firm press when she found them. He relaxed against her with a groan.

"Feel better?"

"Shh, we're cuddling. Sleep time."

She didn't have the energy to argue, so she didn't, instead succumbing to the exhaustion that pulled her under.

Chapter Six

Allie woke to the sound of the bathtub and allowed Sidney to deposit her in the hot water before he stripped the bed, washed the toys, and joined her in the bath. There was soft, languid energy to them as they lounged in the hot water, steam wafting in tendrils around them.

Sidney traced gentle fingers over her arm. "Have fun?"

"Maybe." She hummed contentedly, draped over him, fingertips tapping a slow rhythm against his skin.

"That was your first heat wave in about twenty hours, so you're almost done."

Allie grumbled and somehow snuggled closer. "I don't want to be done. I want to stay here and do nothing but eat, sleep, fuck, and cuddle forever."

He laughed, the sound vibrating in her ear. "You'll miss real life eventually. Besides, you get to indulge in all of this every year. And you can find a partner outside of your heats if you want and still do all those things."

"Shhh." She pressed a finger to his lips. "Other people don't even exist right now."

"Okay." He purred softly and twirled strands of her hair.

First Heat

When the water finally cooled and their fingertips pruned, they ventured out for food, refueling before settling on the couch to cuddle naked beneath a stack of blankets. They put on a nature documentary to keep the silence at bay and simply indulged in the nearness of one another. With the heat beginning to fade, Allie's energy levels dipped, but Sidney was ever-present, always touching and checking in with her.

She woke from a nap draped across him. Her senses were infused with his scent and she snuggled closer. "Where did the time go?"

"You may have been a bit preoccupied the last while."

"A little." She sighed. "It feels weird to be done. I don't think I want to be done yet."

She squirmed as uncomfortable thoughts flitted through her brain.

"What's going on in that head of yours?"

"So...I know we could do stuff before the heat, but what about after?"

"After like now, or after like when you're no longer a client?"

"Now. Or I guess any time before I have to leave."

"We can definitely still do stuff. I was trying to let you recover from the heat, but I suppose it would be good to make sure the heat is for sure over. If you don't have a flare, you'll be good to go."

She chewed her lip. Logically it made sense, but she wanted him to be with her because he wanted to, not as a medical check.

He lifted her chin, his soft gaze flickering over her face. "What's wrong?"

"I'm feeling a little self-conscious."

"About?"

"What if you don't want me this way? What if I'm only fun to be with when I'm in heat? What if I can't cope with being *just* a client and having this life-changing experience end with no guarantee I'll ever feel this good again?"

He kissed her softly, drowning out her questions that had grown more panicked the more she spoke. "Take a deep breath for me."

She did. Tears pricked her eyes.

"You are beautiful and perfect, and you don't need to be in heat for someone to think that. You're a client, but you're not *just* a client." Sidney traced her cheeks, rubbing away the wet, salty trails that coated them. "I'm grateful I got to go through this with you and see you become more comfortable and confident. None of that has to go away. Someone is going to be extremely lucky to have you as a partner after we part ways."

Allie sniffled.

"I want you," he insisted. "Any way you'll have me and as often as you want me while you're here."

"What if no one else wants me after this? I don't know how to be with anyone but you."

Sidney gathered her to him as the panic swelled in her chest, and she struggled to push it all down. He held her until she could breathe normally and continued to run his hand over her hair.

"You can't know the future, and now's not the time to be worrying about this sort of thing. Especially because anyone who doesn't want you is entirely incorrect. I do have an idea, though. It might help."

"Yeah?" She clung to him, not daring to look at his face. Embarrassment burned hot on her cheeks from her outburst.

"Go lay on the bed, and I'll be there in a few minutes." He patted her hip to prompt her to move.

She scampered down the hall and threw herself on the bed, bundling herself under the stack of blankets to wait. The shower turned on, and she listened to the stream, uncertain as to what was coming. She watched from a gap in her blankets as Sidney entered the room stark naked, his hair still dripping from the shower. He fished a blindfold out of the trunk and peeled open her blankets, handing it to her.

"Put this on."

She obeyed and stretched out on top of the blankets. Goosebumps decorated her skin. The prominent scent of him she'd grown accustomed to was muted, washed away for the moment. Firm hands wrapped around each of her ankles and tugged her closer. They slid up her calves, the pressure and speed fluctuating until she was shivering. Then the hands disappeared altogether.

"Sidney?"

"Shh. It's not me right now. Think of me as anyone, as a future partner, someone who's going to touch you one day."

She furrowed her brow, but nodded slowly, trying to relax. His thumb brushed over the thatch of hair at the crux of her thighs, and she squeaked. It didn't linger, touching long enough to tease her senses before moving on, digging into her hips, palms gliding against her stomach, dancing fingertips tweaking her nipples. Then the order changed again, bits of her touched at random; wrist, throat, navel, breast, thigh, a foxtrot of dextrous fingertips driving her to distraction. Every touch startled her, a little jolt of adrenaline blending with the euphoria of the sensation. Those wicked fingers dove back between her thighs, and he groaned.

"God, you're so fucking wet."

It was different from the heat high and the slick that had flowed from her. This was entirely her responding to him. Relief settled in at knowing she was capable of it.

She squirmed desperately. "Please."

He didn't set about to satisfy her though, instead returning to his teasing, now adding his mouth. He nipped along her ribs, suckling at her breast while he dug his hands into her skin, pinning her down. Those fingers trailed over her throat, wrapping just firmly enough to still her. The rapid hum of her heart beat beneath his other hand. He pulled away again, leaving her untethered in her temporary blindness.

His cock teased the lips between her thighs, sliding through the wetness, but never giving her what she craved. She whimpered, all semblance of pride vanished as he continued to glide over her clit, stopping every so often to press against her entrance until she was shaking beneath him. But still, he left her unsatisfied, switching between tantalizing her with hands, mouth, and cock.

He put his hand back between her thighs, sliding the tip of one finger in to the first knuckle and she whimpered again. She tried to rock against it, to coax it deeper, but he withdrew when she did.

"*Please*," she whined. "I need it."

Whether out of pity or indulgence, he returned his hand, sliding the single digit in all the way. Allie squeezed around it. He withdrew, retracing the path with a second finger added. She moaned and arched off the bed, panting as he pumped them at a maddeningly slow pace. He rotated them, testing the resistance, adding a third, letting them stretch her open further as she gasped and clung to the sheets.

Sidney lifted each of her legs in turn, instructing her to grab behind her knees. She obeyed and shuddered with the new angle.

"Fuck." She groaned, the word coming again, flowing in a chant off her lips. "Fuckfuckfuck. God, don't stop."

Incomprehensible sounds spilled out of her as he picked up speed, fingers thrusting into her, the pressure building as each movement battered her G spot. Every impact sent a ripple of sensation through her from head to toe, her sounds growing more desperate the harder he moved inside her until it all burst. Allie screamed, body convulsing, and she clung to her knees trying to ride out the wave of ecstasy. Her throat was raw by the time it faded and she slumped, exhausted.

Sidney slid his fingers free and rolled her over. He climbed into the bed, draping himself over her. She wiggled limp legs open, hoping he would tease her again. His cock was thick and straining against her ass, settled in the groove between her cheeks. Her lungs burned and she continued to pull in ragged breaths, face pressed to the sheets. He inched lower and teased her entrance, gliding halfway in before snapping his hips forward. She squeaked at the sudden impact of their bodies, of the delicious stretch and friction of his cock burying inside her. He withdrew again, thrust back with the same precision and force, and the surprise gave way to deep pleasure.

Allie bit the sheets, muffling the sounds that were forced out of her each time he drove into her. She wanted to touch her clit, but she was pressed down by the weight of him, unable to do anything but receive every bit of depraved pleasure. She whined, dizzy from breathing too hard, body quaking as it struggled to process.

"Harder," she moaned. It seemed impossible, given how sharp his movements already were, but the next snap of his hips shoved a guttural yelp past her lips. "Oh, God. Oh, fuck."

His mouth found her throat and brushed over her scent gland. He drove into her once more, teeth clamping down. Her vision flared white, and the cry she let out was nearly inhuman as he pressed deeper into her, warmth blooming inside. He stayed there, buried in her, tongue lapping at the bruise he'd bitten into her throat. Every bit of her felt like she was under a lead blanket, unable to move.

"Jesus *fucking* Christ on a cracker." She laughed, and it turned into a moan as he growled in her ear.

When he slid his cock free, it was a loss felt down to the marrow of her bones. She kept still, nowhere near ready to attempt moving. He lay next to her, pulling the blankets over them.

Allie woke sometime later. A soreness lingered between her thighs like a phantom to remind her of what he'd felt like. She pulled off the blindfold, squinting into the low light. A pearlescent sky glowed softly on the other side of the closed curtains, but she couldn't tell if it was dawn or dusk.

Sidney moved against her, drawing her attention back to him. She luxuriated in the sound of his breathing, the little groan when he stretched, and the way his arms tightened around her.

She still thought real life was highly overrated compared to this but had to remind herself again that real life would return whether she wanted it to or not.

"Come shower with me," Sidney murmured against her skin.

She rolled off the bed and stood on wobbly legs, clinging to him as they walked down the hall. They shared the shower bench this time, taking turns soaping and rinsing the other, washing and conditioning one another's hair, drying each other afterward. They shared a meal and settled back onto the couch.

He sighed, relaxing under her. "You're going to be a dream for someone. I'm only sorry that it can't be me."

She wasn't sure what to say in response. Her heat haze hadn't triggered, which meant she was well and truly done with her heat. Tomorrow she'd go home, and that would be that.

"You already were a dream. I couldn't have asked for anyone better for all of this." She cuddled up tighter.

They passed the night with movies and snacks, both too comfortable and exhausted to move. When morning arrived, bright and bursting with light, Allie only felt a bittersweet weight settle over her shoulders. She ate the breakfast Sidney made her, savoring each bite, and sipped her tea nestled in his lap.

The hours faded, and they indulged in a last joining, moving slow and sweet, imprinting themselves upon the body of the other, taking in the last sounds, the last tastes and touches.

Soft bliss settled into Allie, driving some of the melancholy away, even as she packed up her things and Sidney loaded her suitcase into the car. The drive back to her place seemed to pass in slow motion. She disentangled her hand from his and stared at her home. It felt different now, but then she supposed she was the different one, and not the home.

She'd gone into this with such dread.

Allie turned to find Sidney watching her, his dark eyes pensive.

"One kiss for the road?" she asked.

His mouth quirked into a smile, and he slid his fingers into her hair, tugging her toward him for the last time. She knew him now and fell into the intoxicating ebb and flow of the kiss, reluctant to pull away even though she knew she had to. Her mother was probably staring out the window watching, but she couldn't even bring herself to care.

He slipped out of the vehicle and walked around to open her door for her before fishing out her bag. She sucked in a steadying breath and clutched her suitcase handle, every step away from him and up the walk dropping a wall between them. He was back in the vehicle when she reached the door.

Sidney tossed her a wicked grin, and her phone buzzed in her pocket. He was already backing out of the driveway when she pulled it out to check the message.

Sidney:
See you next heat

A blush warmed her cheeks. She watched his vehicle until it turned off onto the main road.

Maybe being an omega wouldn't be so bad.

First Heat: Second Chances

Sidney is finally reunited with Allie during a chance encounter. She's certainly grown up in the last five years but she's as vibrant as he remembers. Now that Allie's no longer a client and Sidney has moved on from being a heat helper, he's free to pursue her. Does she want him as much as he wants her? There's only one way to find out.

Content notes: This omegaverse story is m/f and contains a spontaneous heat, knotting, nesting, purring, growling, and biting. Birth control is readily accessible in my omegaverse for all genders, sexes, and dynamics. No one is having babies unless they really want to.

There will be sex toys, light bondage, butt play, pegging and mild sensory deprivation

It's pretty fluffy so don't worry about any dark content. Just spicyness, sweetness, and a cinnamon roll alpha.

Chapter One

"Sidney?"

The scent of honeysuckle and ginger hit him a second after the sound of her voice. His memory whiplashed him back to the last time he'd encountered her. Soft breaths and hushed moans, silken hair and warm skin, the look of fire in her eyes as the heat consumed her. It sent a zing of pleasure up his spine and goosebumps broke across his skin.

"Allie?"

She was the only omega he worked with that had combined her first time and her first heat. He'd been her introduction to *everything*.

"Hey!" She bounded up to him.

Her hair had grown out, spiraling in dark coils that fell to her waist. Her face was the same though. Wide brown eyes, golden skin, and plump lips he couldn't help but remember the taste of. Her trim body was tucked into jeans and a T-shirt for a band he'd never heard of. He shoved down the surge of longing that rolled through him as she stopped in front of him.

"Hey," he said, hoping he sounded casual. "Long time no see."

"Oh my God, right? What? Five years?" Allie rattled off. "I asked for you with my next heats, but our schedules never quite synced up."

He had known, since every request was logged in the system. Each time he'd returned from helping one omega to see she'd been there and had to go with another alpha instead had been a kick in the teeth. Attachment to clients was out of the ordinary for him, so it was probably for the best that they hadn't been able to reunite while he was still working as a heat helper. That didn't mean he didn't feel the sting of those missed connections, though.

"Do you want to grab a coffee?" she asked. "But not like the '*oh we should grab coffee sometime*' kind of coffee. The kind where we actually do it and don't say the same thing when we awkwardly run into one another in another five years. Is that weird to ask?"

She scrunched up her nose and he bit back a laugh. Her energy hadn't changed a bit.

"Oh, fuck it. I'm asking anyway. So, yes? No?"

"Yes." His laugh broke free, earning him a bright smile from her. He glanced down at the shopping cart he'd entirely forgotten about. "Right now or later?"

Part of him was willing to abandon the cart in the aisle, but the other part reminded him that he needed to buy the dog food and get it home to the horde of pups waiting for their dinner.

"Later tonight? We could have dinner." Allie pulled a business card out of her wallet and handed it over. "Text me?"

Sidney nodded and watched her walk away. She turned at the last second and winked at him. The sight of it sent a thrill through him. They'd only spent a week together, but what a fucking week it had been. Watching her blossom in their time together had been a gratifying experience that had carried him through his worst days on the job. He shouldn't still be thinking about it. She'd be able to smell it on him if he let himself get too deep, and that was an embarrassment he wouldn't allow.

He turned the card over in his hand. *Allison Carmichael, Architectural Consultant* was laid out in crisp, clean letters. It was strange to think of her out in the world as a professional with a career instead of the university student he'd last known. He tucked the card into his pocket and sped through the rest of his shopping before heading back to his new house. A chorus of puppy howls greeted his arrival.

"I'm coming!"

He hauled the massive bag of food into his nursery room. A half dozen black and brown mutt puppies yipped at him, dancing at the edge of their pen for attention.

"Who's hungry?" He laughed at the yips and *arooos*.

Sidney emptied the food into the storage bucket and set out dishing up their dinner with some water and fancy additions because he liked to spoil them. He sat on the floor while they ate, showering attention upon them as they finished and came to him for love.

The business card in his pocket poked him. He fished it out and stared at it. How on earth did one approach someone who had been a client—someone who'd haunted his damn thoughts for years—that suddenly reappeared? His gaze slid to the puppies, and he snapped a picture on his phone. It was impossible to go wrong with a puppy pic. He sent it and set the phone down. His pride would have preferred he go about his day without checking it compulsively, but his pride would have to suffer.

The ping of a response sent his heart galloping.

Allie:
OH. MY. GOD.
I FORGOT YOU FOSTER PUPPIES!!!!

Relief struck him like a train. He could work with this.

Sidney:
Want to come over and meet them?
We could do dinner at my place
instead of going out

Please say yes.

Allie:
I can't believe you have to ask that question
Of course I want to meet them
Gather them in a bucket and pour them
over me as I lay down in your entryway

He snorted with laughter.

Sidney:
No need
If you get on the floor at all
you'll be swarmed

Allie:
Yessssss
Sign me the fuck UP
I'll be there at 7 to be buried in floofs

Sidney sent over his address and wandered into the kitchen to see what he could make for tonight. It may have been slightly hubristic to invite her over for dinner when he had returned from the store with nothing but dog food. As he dug through his fridge and pantry an idea struck him. Might as well bring up some nostalgia and get some brownie points. He put on some music, took a couple steaks out to thaw, and got to work making a chocolate cake.

About an hour later while the cake sat cooling he tried to read but set the book down after reading the same page four times without absorbing any of it. No TV show held his attention. He settled on cleaning and was steam mopping the puppy room when his doorbell rang.

Sidney sprinted to the door and whipped it open. She stood

there, as beautiful as this morning. She'd changed out of her jeans, he noted, opting for black leggings under knee-high leather boots, and the hem of a red shirt poked out from under her leather coat. She'd put on makeup too. Smoky eye, winged liner, and a bold, red lip.

She'd been so raw when she'd come to him last—unpainted and unprepared, sweet, eager, and perfect as she was—but she was equally stunning like this and his brain swooped into thoughts of those red lips wrapped around his—

"Hey stranger." She beamed at him and gave a little wave. "I love the new place. It's so fancy."

He pushed away the thought of her on her knees and stepped aside to let her in. She strode through the doorway, a sweet cloud of honeysuckle in her wake. His gaze followed her helplessly.

Thank God for tight jeans.

"Holy shit, it smells good in here." She inhaled deeply. "Were you baking?"

"I might have been." He grinned. "There's cake for dessert. Or as an appetizer if you prefer."

Delight flashed in her eyes.

"God, you're such a charmer." She laughed and playfully whacked him on the arm. "Baking me a cake. How are you real?"

"I'm a figment of your imagination."

"If I didn't have extremely vivid memories of how real you are, I'd be inclined to believe that."

Heat rose up his spine at the memory of her spread out beneath him. The ginger notes of her scent slipped through honeysuckle. He couldn't tell if it was responding to *him* because she was attracted to him or if it was just her omega side responding to what was probably an embarrassingly obvious alpha reaction.

She unzipped her boots and set them aside, looking at him expectantly.

"I'll take your coat," he said.

Her jacket slid down her arms revealing a cranberry red scoop-neck shirt that nipped in her waist and showed off her lean muscles.

He didn't remember her having those muscles before. Unwrapping her like a present was going to be a treat if there were all these new elements to discover... assuming she wanted to be unwrapped, that is. He hadn't asked that part yet, but her being in his house was a good start.

"Do I get a grand tour," her voice interrupted his ogling, "or are we hanging out in the foyer?"

What was the *matter* with him? He was supposed to be the cool one in these situations. She kept shutting off his brain.

"Sorry." He took her coat from her and hung up the garment in the entryway closet. "I can show you all of it, but there might be something else you want to see first."

As if on cue, a chorus of howls echoed.

Allie's head turned toward the sound, gravitating to the closed door of the puppy room.

"They're not great at letting themselves be a surprise." He laughed and ushered her into the nursery.

Her gasp of excitement when she saw the pups wasn't quite as satisfying as the ones he'd caused himself, but he was glad in either case.

"What are their names?"

"They're all named after composers. The boys are Ludwig, Johann, Wolfgang, and Franz, and the girls are Kassia and Hildegard."

She dropped to her knees in front of the pen, and Sidney closed the nursery door behind them before unhooking the gate holding the pups at bay.

They swarmed, all battling to sit in Allie's lap and lick her face at the same time. She shrieked with laughter and laid down, letting herself be utterly overwhelmed. He sat down to join her, but the puppies were far too occupied with the newcomer to pay him any mind.

His heart did some uncomfortable flips as he watched her absolute delight.

"Oh God, I got a foot in my mouth!"

Sidney hoisted one of the pups off her face. She tried to sit up but was tackled back down by another. He snatched her flailing hand, pulling her upright, and she collapsed into giggles against him.

His heart stuttered.

How was she so cute?

The puppies still scrambled to be in her lap, and he scooped up a couple to put back into their massive pen.

"You're a puppy jailer," Allie said.

"I'll let them out after dinner for some yard time, but I figured you'd want to eat first."

"Okay, I'll forgive puppy jailing since you're being logical about it."

Her hand was warm in his as he helped her up, and she didn't let go as he led her into the kitchen. He deliberately avoided looking at her so he didn't trip on the way.

"Do you want help with dinner?" she asked. "I peel a mean vegetable."

He snorted. "Sure. You can be my sous chef."

"Roger that." She beamed at him. "Give me a task, and I'll make you proud."

He shook his head with a laugh. "I'll let you wash the potatoes to start."

He dug a handful of them out of the pantry and set them in the sink for her to wash.

"How long have you been out of the nest?" Sidney asked.

"Two years now. I moved into a new apartment a few blocks from here last week."

"Ah, that explains it," he said. "I was wondering why I hadn't seen you at the store before now."

"Maybe I'm a ninja," she said, sticking her tongue out. "I still need to do a big shop. I've been grabbing frozen dinners while I get settled, so I am very excited for a real, home cooked meal."

"Well, hopefully I don't disappoint."

"I'm pretty sure that's not possible." She hip-checked him and held up a potato. "Gimme something sharp to slice these bad boys."

He passed her the chef knife from his knife block and fished a cutting board out from the lower cupboard. "You can cut them into chunks. I figure grilled potatoes go pretty great with steak."

"Goddamn, I'm going to have to marry you," she laughed. "Cake *and* steak? You're spoiling me so much tonight, and I didn't even do anything to deserve it."

He should definitely *not* be taking those words seriously. It was ludicrous to even contemplate taking *'I'm going to have to marry you'* as a remotely earnest statement. There wasn't time to psychoanalyse his thoughts about it so instead he forced out a laugh and dropped his arm over her shoulders.

"Being cute as fuck is more than enough to deserve a nice dinner."

She was so warm. Touching her was a mistake. Desire thrummed through him, and he took a deliberate step away, turning to the fridge to pull out the steaks he had marinating as an excuse to not look at her. When he turned back she was focused on chopping the potatoes. Her shoulders were slightly drooped and it tweaked at the well of guilt in his chest. He shouldn't be weird with her. It was his own fault that he couldn't stop thinking about her.

"We can cook on the grill," he said, "but if we're letting the puppies run outside I'll need you to keep an eye on them while I cook."

"Ooh. I approve of freeing puppies from jail." She smiled and looked up from cutting the final potato.

They got through the inside dinner prep without incident, wrapping the potatoes with spices in foil, and set up outside. While the grill warmed up, they outfitted the pups in tiny harnesses and took them into the backyard where they were allowed to roam free.

He watched from his post at the barbeque grill as she wandered the yard to check on each of the pups and even encouraged little Johann, the shiest of the litter, to explore, walking by his side until he went galloping along to tackle one of his siblings. Allie was just as entertaining to watch. His gaze followed her, taking in the way the breeze teased her hair, the bounce of her chest as she hopped around chasing the pups, and the flex of her muscles as she scooped them up to cuddle. He was entranced until the scent of the steaks warned him he was going to char their meal.

"Fuck." He grabbed the tongs to rescue the steaks and set them onto a plate to rest. They were a little overcooked, but hopefully she wouldn't mind.

She sat next to him while they ate outside at his patio table, both keeping an eye on the exploring puppies.

"You're good with them," he said.

"Is it possible to be bad with puppies?" she asked. "They do most of the work."

He chuckled softly. "I guess that's true. It's still cute in any case."

"Well that's a relief because it's my goal in life to be cute." She stuck her tongue out at him, and he roughly shoved away the desire to get her on her knees to make her use it.

Allie looked at him, brow raised in question. "You okay?"

"Great!" He cringed when his voice cracked.

It wasn't *fair*. He knew how to handle clients, knew what to do when it was a sure thing and a job to be done. How the fuck did he approach someone who was neither? He hadn't been on a damn date since his teen years. If they'd run into one another at a club or something more sexually-coded than a grocery store, then he might have the balls to say something. He'd grown less confident with people he wanted to sleep with that weren't clients or hookups.

It also didn't help that being so close to her was fucking with his head.

"What were your other heats like?" He mentally kicked himself. "If that's not too weird to ask."

"Nah," she said, but she speared a bite of steak and didn't answer right away. "They were good. I mean, it's hard to compare. To be honest, it's probably for the best that I didn't get to share another heat with you."

He perked up. "Oh? Why's that?"

Her mouth puckered like she'd bit into a lemon. "Truthfully, I was a bit of a mess for a long time afterwards."

Oh God.

"Did I do something wrong?" The clinic had never mentioned anything to him and she'd never filed any sort of complaint against him.

"No! God, not at all." She laughed. "If anything you did too many things right. I had no idea how to go back to my regular life. I couldn't recapture any of what I felt. I'd wake up from dreams and I'd be sweaty and desperate, completely unable to satisfy myself."

His mind churned with the image of that, fueled by his graphic memories of her. "How—how did you deal with that?"

"Not well." She pushed her plate away and sat back. "I eventually caved and bought a couple sex toys to help, but I was so paranoid over my mom finding them or hearing me use them that it made it hard to enjoy."

"Oh, yeah, I remember you mentioning that she could be invasive."

"Very. At least I'm moved out now, so I don't have that issue anymore." She winked at him and it sent a sizzle up his spine.

"A lot of the stuff with heats was...," she chewed her lip. Her scent was overpowered by the honeysuckle elements, turning thick with stress. "It's embarrassing."

He leaned back, hoping he appeared casual even though he desperately wanted to know. "How so? I've heard pretty much everything before, so I bet it's not *that* embarrassing."

She pouted her lip. "I guess I'll let you be the judge then."

"A wise choice." He grinned.

"I skipped going on suppressants right away because I didn't want to delay my next heat. Except then you weren't available, and it was too late to start them. I was ridiculously disappointed."

"I wouldn't say that's embarrassing, per se." He could scarcely breathe. "If anything, it's flattering. Who did you end up with?"

"Nick, for that one. He was honestly good, but we both knew that he wasn't my first choice. The one after that when I'd wanted to go with you again, I ended up with Carla. She was great, but not what I wanted, even though she did make me come so hard I passed out." Allie giggled. "It was intense."

Well now he was going to have to add that to his to do list.

Assuming he ever got the chance to redo their experience.

"It wasn't the same as with you," she added. "They got me through the heat fine, but…"

"What made me different?" The feedback wouldn't help him at work anymore, but he was still curious to know what put him above the others for her.

"Hard to say. Part of it was that you were my first, but also you took care of me differently." She toyed with the hem of her shirt. "It's like they could cater to me as an omega but not to me as Allie. If that makes sense."

He ruminated on her words. "So, you felt like a job to the others?"

"Sort of? It's hard to explain because I *am* a job to them. It was weird with other partners too. No one was encouraging me to explore and find what I really wanted out of the experience. I kept feeling like I was constantly brushing the edge out there." She sighed and turned her chair to face him directly. "I always tried to explain to my partners but words only do so much with someone who doesn't have the instinct to go along with it, and I didn't fully understand it myself."

Sidney wasn't sure what to do with this information. He'd never had the issue of being *too* good before.

"I wanted," she continued, "someone who could pull me under, who wanted me to see the depths, but that could also bring me back to the surface. I never knew how to get that back."

"What about non-heat partners?"

"Audacious," she laughed, "I like it. Well, I was *mildly* obsessed with you for a while after, but I did try with other people. Nothing stuck, though."

Admittedly, it was a bit of a relief to know he wasn't the only one who'd thought about their time together for an inappropriately long duration.

Ginger notes slipped into her scent again and they stared at each other with an intensity that had his muscles tensing.

"Sidney."

"Hmm?" Warmth pulsed at the base of his spine.

"I have a question," she said.

"Oh?" Thankfully his voice didn't crack this time.

She reached out and traced his thumb before setting her hand over his. "How long do I have to be here before you kiss me?"

Chapter Two

Everything froze—his heart, his breath, maybe time. Her dark eyes were like molten chocolate and lust flowed through him like lava, spurring him into motion. Sidney leaned towards her, magnetized. He slid his fingers into her hair and met her mouth with his, revelling in the soft sound she made at the contact. Ginger saturated his senses.

Allie climbed into his lap. He cupped her ass, and she slid her hands up his chest, hooking her elbow around his neck. She kissed him like she was trying to devour him, grinding her hips against him, a desperate whimper breaking free when he squeezed her. Her teeth scraped against his bottom lip, and her tongue sought out his.

The last time they'd been together, he'd been her guide, but this time it was all he could do to keep up with her. Past Allie had been exuberant but hesitant. Present Allie knew exactly what she wanted and it set his blood sizzling. She growled, and his cock strained uncomfortably against his zipper.

Sidney released an answering growl that rumbled deep in his chest. Her fingers curled into the collar of his shirt and held on like she was afraid he'd disappear. He pulled away from her mouth, diving to nip at the scent gland on her throat.

"Sweet *fuck*," she gasped out, moaning as she slid a hand into his hair.

He sucked on the sensitive patch of skin until she was shaking, her whimpers and writhing melting rational thought straight out of his brain. Every sense was saturated with honeysuckle and heat. He craved more.

Sidney hooked his hands under her thighs and lifted them off the chair. A puppy howl stopped him in his tracks.

Fuck.

"I have to bring them inside first," he murmured against her skin.

She slid down him and stayed on tiptoe, stealing another kiss before she grinned at him. "I'll help you gather the herd."

They worked quickly, scooping up wriggling pups and depositing them into the nursery before turning back to one another. Her curls were mussed and her cheeks were still flushed.

The brief reprieve from the torrent of hormones let him breathe for the moment.

He tugged her closer. Every instinct pushed him to claim her. Instincts didn't take reality into consideration with their demands, so he shoved them aside and dipped down to capture her mouth again. It was truly unfair that someone could taste as good as she did. She was sweet and spicy and perfect. Delectable enough to devour, so he did.

Sidney scooped her up and carried her to the couch, dropping her down before getting onto his knees in front of her. He slid his hands up her thighs, eliciting a tremble in her legs.

"Are you going to let me taste you," Sidney asked, "or should I get other ideas into my head?"

She let out a nervous chuckle. "God, I thought I was prepared to be with you again, but I'm a total mess."

"Not yet," he slid up, nestling between her thighs, and leaned in to kiss her, "but I intend to make sure you're a mess by the end of the night. If you let me."

Allie squirmed, rolling her hips against him, fingers clutching his shirt. "There's no way I'm not giving you permission for that."

"Good." He caged her with his arms and delighted in the look of wide-eyed desire she hit him with. "I'm going to ruin you. And this couch."

Her laugh turned into a groan as he peeled off her leggings, leaving her in a tiny black lace thong. He raised an eyebrow.

"I see you've upgraded."

"Mhmm," she shuddered as he traced his fingertips over the damp fabric. "I've upgraded a lot of things since last time."

Sidney took his time teasing her, stroking her through the lace and nipping up her thighs. She threaded her fingers into his hair and squeezed, shivering and cursing as he focused his attention there. The prick of her nails against his scalp was encouragement enough, but the longer he suckled the sensitive skin, the more she squirmed, panting and lifting her hips towards his mouth.

The lace was soaked through by the time he tugged it off. She spread her thighs eagerly, leaving her glistening cunt on display for him. He dipped down, and a wordless cry echoed through his living room, devolving into sweet little whimpers and renewed squirming. She tasted as good as she smelled, honeysuckle sweetness and ginger spicy notes coating his tongue. He licked at her clit and spread her open further with a firm hand on each thigh.

Sidney lifted his head long enough to capture her gaze. "Be good for me and keep these here."

Allie let out a shuddering breath and scooped a hand behind each knee, holding the shaking limbs in place.

He dove back down and pressed two fingers inside with a slowness that had her struggling to buck against him. "You're soaked, kitten."

Sidney leaned up to kiss her while flexing his fingers, pumping them until there was no hint of resistance. He consumed her gasp and groan when he added a third, stretching her to accommodate the intrusion. He wasn't intending to fuck her yet, but he did enjoy getting her riled up. Sliding back down, he put his tongue on her clit and worked the sensitive bud until she screamed.

Allie sank into the couch, panting and sweaty.

"You're half a mess already." He laughed softly and kissed his way up.

She laughed, and the sound melted into a sigh. "You know, *I* came here to seduce *you*."

"I'm not a mind reader, kitten. If you want me, you have to tell me."

"I thought the outfit change and putting on makeup would have been clear. You think I do up a smokey eye for just anybody?"

He chuckled and arranged her legs around his waist so he could lean close, caging her against the couch with his arms on either side of her head. "You didn't wear *any* makeup the last time I had you like this. There's no question of what's going to happen when someone hires me, but it's a different set of rules when someone is trying to pick me up outside of work."

She pulled him in by his shirt collar. "Let me be clear, then, in case the dripping cunt didn't convince you. I want you to live up to my memories and ruin me."

The surge of heat rose through his body at her words.

"And after you've done that," she whispered against his lips, "I want to ruin *you*."

His curiosity piqued. "Oh?"

She grinned. "I have some very specific things stored away in my head just for you. I've been waiting a while to try them."

"Am I allowed to know?"

"Well, you're definitely allowed to know before I try them. I'm pretty sure you have the supplies on hand."

A smile tugged at his lips. "Ah, you want something out of the treasure chest?"

"A few somethings, yes." Allie squirmed closer and traced a finger over his throat. "How does the big bad alpha feel about being taken by the omega? You said you liked it last time. Is that still the case?"

"If you're asking about fucking me in the ass, then I am more than willing to let you play."

Sidney buried his face into her throat. His instincts rose up again, pushing him to bite the scent gland. She wasn't in heat so it wouldn't bond them, but it was disconcerting. He usually had much better control and never had to contend with these urges to begin with. Indulging himself, he let his teeth press against the skin until she was gasping his name.

He sucked at the scent gland. If he couldn't bond her, he could still leave his mark. A soft growl reverberated in his chest and he pressed closer, wrapping his arms around her waist and leaning his weight on her.

Every taste of her was intoxicating.

He'd never wanted to lay and breathe someone in before. Air that didn't smell like her had no business being inhaled.

She clung to him and slid her fingers down his back to hook the hem of his shirt. He lifted his arms to aid her in removing the fabric. She tossed it aside and trailed reverent fingertips over him. Goose bumps followed their path as he shivered.

Sidney set a palm over her pounding heart and slid it up when she tilted her head back in offering. Her pulse beat under his thumb. A soft purr rumbled from her, the vibrations teasing his hand as he held her immobile with a gentle grip.

His vision blurred at the edges, hyper focusing on the way the light hit her hair, the way her pupils dilated and nearly eclipsed her irises, the rise and fall of her chest from her panting as she squirmed.

"Sidney, *please*."

He swallowed hard and spoke only when he was sure she wouldn't be able to hear the shake in his voice. "Please what?"

She let out an unsteady laugh. "I almost forgot what that felt like."

The old version of her was seeping out through the confidence. He knew how to deal with that, how to build her back up and coax all the wicked things out of her mind.

He pulled her closer and nipped her earlobe. "Use your words, kitten."

The shiver that rippled up her body was like tactile music in his hands.

Sidney smiled against her skin. "Tell me what you want."

"I want a lot of things."

"Pick one, then."

"I want," she paused to grind against him, "to beg."

Her eyes flashed with fire, and his cock strained painfully against his jeans.

"Is that so?"

If she wanted to play, he wasn't about to dissuade her.

"Mhmm." She slid off his lap and knelt between his knees. "Why don't you be fair and tell me what you want, too?"

Heat pulsed at the base of his spine. There were countless things he wanted—to do to her, her to do to him, to ask and say after five years apart.

"I want you to ruin that red lipstick."

She licked her lips. The color didn't budge so it probably wouldn't from what he had in mind but that wouldn't stop the fun of trying.

The last time they'd been together she'd been in heat and his entire existence had been about her care and satisfaction in that vulnerable, primal state. Part of him wasn't even entirely certain that he knew how to behave with a partner that didn't need that from him.

A growl climbed out of her throat as she undid his jeans and freed his cock.

"Trade places with me," she said, climbing off the couch and offering the space to him.

She touched him softly, stroking the length until he was gritting his teeth and forcing himself not to shake. Sharp exhalations betrayed him, and she smirked at him as she lowered her mouth, sucking the tip while looking him dead in the eye.

How the fuck was he supposed to maintain composure with her looking at him like that?

Allie swirled her tongue, prompting a groan from him. She gathered up her hair and picked up his hand, angling him to hold onto the silken strands so they didn't fall into her face while she sucked him.

She kissed her way up the shaft and down, making sure she had his attention before moving to the next step, the smolder in that dark gaze never wavering. Clearly her ambitions were to torture him.

Allie tugged at his pants and lifted her head. "Off."

She pouted at him until he stood and helped her drop them towards the floor. Once he was standing bare-assed in his living room she went back to work, wrapping her lips around his cock, inching forward until he hit the back of her throat. He almost came undone and fought with every ounce of his being to keep from coming down her throat. She worked him over slowly, deliberately, each infuriatingly gentle touch unravelling him.

He let out a breathless "*Fuck*" when she squeezed his ass, digging her nails into the cheeks to thrust him into her mouth. His thighs quivered, and he threaded a shaking hand into her hair.

Sidney smothered a whine when she slid off him and stood, gliding her hands up his chest before devouring his mouth. Her grin when she leaned back was all the confirmation he needed. She was definitely torturing him.

"Did you want to come?" She nipped at his lip.

"If I say yes, are you going to do anything about it?" He chuckled.

She bit her bottom lip, the picture of mischief. "I haven't decided. Maybe I want to hear you beg a little, too."

"I guess you should incentivize me a little more."

Sidney wasn't prepared for the confident hand that cupped his balls, or the other that encircled him with sure strokes as she sank down again. Her hungry mouth sucked the head of his cock.

It took everything he had to stay upright. He buried his hands in her hair and gasped out her name.

Allie pulled away, and he could have wept. Her gaze was strangely innocent considering what she'd been doing. "If you're too quiet, how will I know if I'm doing a good job?" She nuzzled his thigh. "Don't you want me to learn how to please you, alpha?"

He was so fucking doomed.

It shouldn't have made his heart jump when she called him

alpha, but it held some implicit meaning. He *was* an alpha. It was a title. But all it made him think was that she saw him as the alpha to her omega, that he was more than *an* alpha. That he was *her* alpha.

"I'm trying to keep control, and you're making it very difficult."

"That's the point." Allie gave him a smile and slid back onto his cock, her tongue stroking until he was back to cursing. She popped off again and nipped his thigh. "I can taste you getting close."

He choked back a *please*.

Allie pressed her thumbs against the scent glands on his wrists, eliciting a deep shudder that reverberated through his bones. "You can come anytime, alpha. You know what you have to do, and I'll give you what you want."

Her hands paused as well when he stayed quiet.

She darted her tongue out again. "One little word. Beg for me. Just once."

He wasn't entirely certain how he felt about this new Allie. Of course he shouldn't have assumed she'd be the exact same when she'd had five years of growing up and multiple other partners since he'd last encountered her. He would adjust, learn the new ways to tease and tempt her, to take her apart until she was blissed.

Allie's hands and wicked mouth set back to work, coaxing him until he could scarcely breathe, and then stopped.

"Fucking hell."

She giggled and looked up at him. Allie waited until his breathing had calmed and started up again, pulling him to the edge and stepping away. And again.

"Jesus *Christ*." He whimpered, and she giggled.

"On a cracker?"

That made him laugh. "I almost forgot how fucking cute you are."

"It's a gift." She teased him with another lick. "Speaking of, you're really making yourself suffer here and preventing me from giving you the lovely gift of sucking your soul out through your cock."

Her fingers stroked him with an agonizing slowness. He thought about snatching her up and turning the tables, but she was so perfect on her knees, devoting every bit of her attention to worshipping his cock, even if it did drive him to distraction.

There would be time for making her beg later.

She pushed him to sit back onto the couch and angled up his body, stroking his cock between them while she dipped her hand between her thighs. She whimpered into his ear, and the soft desperate sounds undid him more than all the confident touches.

Sidney turned his head and nudged her face until she looked up at him. He indulged in the sweetness of her mouth and devoured every little mewl she made. Tension coiled at the base of his spine, and he had no desire to let her edge him again even if he did have to break his pride a little.

"Please," he whispered.

A purr rumbled in her chest. She sank down and fastened her lips around him, sucking until the tension burst. Heat and sensation radiated through him. It took every ounce of control he possessed to not buck into her throat and hold her there until the orgasm freed him from its grip. She bobbed her head, milking him, taking him straight from pleasure into overstimulation. Her hot, slick tongue kept up its efforts. He squirmed, half desperate for more and half to give his body relief to sink into rest.

He pulled her off her endeavor and into his lap.

She looked so pleased with herself.

"Did you have fun?" He laughed when her purr started up.

"Maybe." She wiggled. "I might have thought about this a few times."

"Is that so? Did you think about anything else?" He cupped her ass and squeezed.

"Are you kidding me? I don't think I had another spare thought in my head that didn't include you for ages after that heat. Every time I learned something new I wished I'd known it then so I could have given back a fraction of what you made me feel."

The longing in her voice stirred up his own. "It's probably better that we didn't get to meet up again."

"It doesn't *feel* better."

He laughed softly. "If we had, then this right now would get me into a lot of trouble."

She quirked her head, dark curls falling like a curtain of silk. "Why?"

"It's both illegal and very against company policy for us to get involved with clients. There has to be at least two years separating any hiring before we're even allowed to consider seeing a client outside of those circumstances."

"That doesn't seem very fair." She pouted. "They go out of their way to make sure the pairings are compatible so of course that's going to come up sometimes."

"That's true but it's why the rule is in place. People in heat are not super rational, and it takes time for everything to fade. It's to protect everyone involved and prevent abuse of power if the alphas have a particularly vulnerable omega attach to them."

She snuggled in, tucking her forehead against the curve of his throat. His heart stuttered.

"Am I a particularly vulnerable omega?"

He trailed soothing fingers up and down her spine. "You would have been, yes."

"What am I now?"

"Now you're a grown woman who knows what she wants. I'm no longer a heat helper, and you haven't been a client of mine for more than enough time. If I was worried about there being an issue, I would have sidestepped on meeting with you. Although," he said, "I'm not certain that my instincts are all that correct."

She sat up and raised a questioning eyebrow. "What do you mean?"

"Well, you're not the only one who thought about our time together a lot longer than would be considered appropriate."

"You thought about me?" Soft honeysuckle radiated from her, and her purr kicked into gear again.

"I might have." He cupped her cheek. "Damn near ruined me each time you requested me and I was already committed to being with another omega."

"I hoped I was memorable," she said, "but I never dared to dream."

"I don't think it's possible for anyone to forget you after they've had you."

"You could refresh your memory." She grinned. "If you want to."

"I'm more than happy to."

"How long have you been retired?" she asked.

"About six months," he replied.

"What made you stop?"

"Heat helping is…taxing. I couldn't keep up anymore." He squirmed awkwardly. "Not that I couldn't with a single heat, but they were having to space the jobs further and further apart to accommodate my recovery time. I'm almost thirty now, and, as much as I didn't want to admit it, it wasn't something I could keep doing."

"Thirty is hardly old," she defended.

"It's not, but when you're essentially running a weeklong marathon to take care of an omega in heat, it's more than my body could continue managing. Older clients weren't too difficult since their heats had calmed down, but the younger ones with erratic needs and endless supplies of energy were…a lot."

"Ones like me, you mean?"

"Yes. You caught me at a good time in my career. A solid forty-eight hours running on next to nothing except for the hormones flooding my system is not uncommon with the first few years of heats. If you'd needed me at that level in the last year or two, I would have disappointed you."

"I don't think it's possible for you to disappoint me."

He let out a sharp laugh. "That's because you don't remember the heat haze. Trust me when I say that level of ravenousness would not have been sated by my energy levels after almost a decade on the job."

"I mean, it makes sense. I guess I never thought about the decline."

"I always compare heat helper careers to professional athletes," he said. "At a certain point you've got to step back, or the risk-to-reward ratio starts getting too skewed."

"Can I be on top?" She winked. "I've gotten much better at that since last time. Lay there and let me ride you into delirium."

His muscles tensed, pleasure rippling through him at the suggestion. "I have no opposition to that."

"I didn't think you would." She snickered

"I'm more than willing to let you have your fun."

"But?" she prompted.

"*But* I'm still intending to make you beg too."

"I don't mind taking turns." She stuck her tongue out at him. "God, how fucking surreal is my life right now? If you'd told me yesterday I'd be eating dinner with you and getting my hands on that sweet, sweet alpha dick I would have thought I was dreaming."

Sidney burst out laughing. "You're ridiculous."

He traced each of her fingers in turn, swirling circles in her palm before pressing a soft kiss to the scent gland at her wrist. Her breath stuttered, and he inhaled the sweet honeysuckle emanating from her. She was like a drug, intoxicating and alluring, and he pulled her closer.

Instead of thinking too hard about that, he slid his hands down her back and savored the way she trembled. His cock twitched to life beneath her, and she let out a little giggle. His lips curved, and he patted her butt which made her giggle more.

Too cute.

"I think I should take you to the bedroom."

Allie leaned close, brushing his ear with her lips. "Take me anywhere you like."

Sidney scooped her up and carted her to his room, dropping her onto the bed. He peeled off her shirt, savoring the sight of her breasts wrapped in black lace before he removed that too.

"Who gave you permission to be this beautiful?"

"The same people who gave you permission to be this fucking hot," she said with a satisfied grin.

"Oh, no one gave me permission. I'm breaking several international laws looking like I do."

"Hmm, I guess we'll both have to be punished, then." She bit her lip and drew him closer.

He hovered over her, and the ginger in her scent thrived with the weight of him spreading her thighs. Her eyes went dark and unfocused as she squirmed beneath him.

Perfection.

She was so soft and willing, so eager to please and to be pleased. He rocked his hips against her and kissed her, smiling against her mouth at her contented sigh that flickered into a moan. If he had his way, he would drown in her forever.

Soon enough the gentle teasing turned to her bucking against him with a whine that unlocked some deep primal part of him. He let her stoke those buried embers. Her nails bit into his scalp. She shook and panted, thrusting up against him.

He growled, low and deep and powerful. She stilled beneath him with a ragged breath.

"Sidney," she murmured.

He dipped down and licked at the scent gland on her throat, nipping at it until she filled his every sense and was an incoherent mess. Instinct wanted him to bite down, to pin her down and claim her, to thrust into her wet heat until neither of them knew their own names. As still as she was, she kept shivering, trying so hard to not move. Curiosity prodded at him. What did she see in him as he sunk deeper into his alpha state than he'd ever allowed himself to go? Did it pull her omega instincts to the surface?

The scent of her shifted. The honeysuckle and ginger still saturated everything, but her arousal permeated the air now too. He let instinct guide him, sliding down her body.

She whimpered and rocked against him. He took his time, stroking firmly with his thumb as he kissed and nipped his way from ankle to thigh on one leg, then the other. He pulled her to the edge of the bed and draped her thighs over his shoulders before diving his tongue into her cunt.

Allie cried out, arching upwards. One hand gripped the sheets and the other threaded through his hair. He flicked her clit, suckling the little bud until she was writhing in his arms. He held her hips down and drank his fill.

Nothing else existed.

She bucked against his face, cursing and squirming. Her body tensed, muscles seizing as he took her to the edge and pushed her over it. Before she stopped shaking, he pushed one finger inside, then another, and another while she squeezed around them. He thrust them slowly and kept up his focus on her clit. She came again, her muscles milking his fingers. Relentless, he continued until she begged him to pause.

He wiped his face on the edge of the blanket. Allie was spread out, eyes unfocused, and hair tousled. He slid onto the bed and nuzzled her breast, taking one stiff peak into his mouth. She bowed and flexed in his grasp.

Her scent exploded, and a wave of dizziness made him unsteady, sinking down against her. This was different. He pushed through the haze that clouded his mind. Why was it so hard to think?

Allie grew wild and restless beneath him, muttering pleas and grinding against him. Her skin was so warm. Warm...heat...*oh*.

Sidney fought against the rising tide of the alpha hormones that saturated his blood in response to her. She was in heat. But how? He took a deep breath, trying to focus, but that had him taking in more of the scent that hit him like a drug.

His head swam.

The only thing he wanted was her.

"*Please*," she whined.

His omega needed him. That was all that mattered. His craving for her consumed him, stealing his thoughts, centering even his perception of touch around what on his body made contact with her.

Her nails dug into his ass, and she rolled her hips until the tip of his cock found where it could bring them together. She dug in harder, and he moved away from the sharp pain and into the slick, waiting heat.

A shuddering growl climbed out of him as he pinned her down.

He fucked into her, setting a brutal pace, listening to her pant in his ear, to the gasps and little cries as he drove their bodies together. That was what he needed, what his instincts demanded. Those sounds needed to go on forever.

She seized under him, voice pitched and body shuddering. He kept moving. The alpha hormones kept him energized and hard, letting him carry her forward without the need for rest. All his mind kept repeating was *more*. He needed to give her whatever she asked for and more, until her mind, body, and soul broke and were remade in the aftermath of the heat.

Sidney let himself be pulled under.

Sweetness and pressure built, his gut tensing as he drove into her. He was *so* close. Allie clung to him, crying out in his ear before falling limp. Finally, his body let him join her, letting her drag him over the peak of pleasure until he melted, pouring out inside her.

Clarity flooded back in, and he sat up sharply. Allie was sprawled out, blissful and sleepy-eyed, but he wasn't the slightest bit calm. There were bruises on her wrists and hips in the shape of his fingers, and there was a fresh bond bite on her throat.

Sidney stared at his hands. He'd *never* lost control before, never sunk so deep into an alpha state that he couldn't think.

She shivered. "I feel weird."

He looked her up and down. "Weird how?"

His own body prickled with a pins and needles sensation. Everything responded, but he couldn't feel much and forming thoughts took a considerable effort.

"Like I'm in heat, but I had one two months ago." Allie stretched and sighed. "It's not as intense though. Like a baby heat."

"I...don't know what would cause that."

"Are you okay? You look kinda wigged out."

"I *am* wigged out."

She sat up and scooted over. "Talk to me."

"I lost myself with you. I hurt you," he said, tracing over the bruises on her hip.

"I can't even feel those. It's fine."

He put a hand over hers. "I'm so used to being in control. It scares me that I wasn't."

"I'm totally okay, and I trust you. You don't have to be in control all the time."

"I still need to know what caused it." He turned his face to hers, dropping a soft kiss to her lips. He glanced at the clock on the wall. "How did three hours pass?"

"Very enjoyably," Allie said, laughing. "Do you want me to sleep over?"

"Absolutely." He had wanted her to already, but there was no way he was sending her away before he figured things out. "Let me make a call."

"Okay," Allie said, getting comfortable in the blankets. "I'll be here."

Sidney located his phone and poked at the contact for his boss. She answered on the second ring.

"Hey, Dr. J, it's Sidney." He wandered out of the room so he could also check on the puppies, keeping one hand on the wall to steady himself as he went.

"I can see on the call display," she said, her tone light. "What's up?"

"I had something weird happen."

"Oh?" The lightness in her voice shifted.

"So, I've never gone into a rut before since I'm not bonded, but that's the only thing I can think of that I've ever heard with similar symptoms. Is there anything like that?" He opened the nursery to find all the pups sleeping in a pile.

"I can look into it," said Dr. James. "I'm not sure off the top of my head. Are you alright?"

"I'm fine, I think. It was just unexpected."

"Were you with someone when it happened?"

"Uh, yeah, actually. You know Allison Carmichael?"

"Oh, yes, I saw her a couple of months ago for her pre-heat check up. Interesting. Hmm. Did this happen when she was a client of yours?"

"No, but that was a different circumstance. She was a job back then, and I was in much more of a work headspace. I'm not sure if that would have any effect, though."

He heard keyboard taps over the line.

"And there was nothing different about Allie compared to other clients or experiences? What about differences in your life right now?"

Sidney hesitated, forcing all of his focus on answering the question. "Okay, I don't know if it's relevant, but she's like the only client I ever thought about much after a job was over."

"Interesting. How long did that last?"

"Um, until now? I hadn't really stopped thinking about her. She mentioned she had the same experience from when she saw me as a heat helper, and just now she said that it felt similar to being in heat."

"Come by the clinic tomorrow, and I'll have a look. In the meantime, stay safe."

They ended the call with no answers, but Sidney was hopeful that some would be forthcoming soon enough. He'd been away from Allie for too long, and his instincts screamed at him to return.

Sidney stepped back into his bedroom and found Allie curled up under the blankets, eyes closed. He slid in next to her and tucked in. She squirmed closer to him and rolled over so he could spoon her. It was exactly what he needed.

His instincts grew quiet.

"I don't know why I'm so tired," she murmured.

"We did have sex for three hours, apparently."

Allie giggled. "Okay, fair."

"Sleep while you can. I'll have to get up early for the puppies and who knows what the heck our hormones are doing in the meantime. We'll go see Dr. J after breakfast and get everything figured out."

Sidney fell asleep to her warmth and honeysuckle scent.

Chapter Three

Heat tugged at his awareness.

Sweet and potent, Allie's scent invaded his senses and roused him to wakefulness. He groaned against the back of her neck, sucking in deep lungfuls of the air saturated with her.

Allie's hips rocked against his. Her skin was damp with sweat, and she reached for him in the dark.

Sidney moved without thinking. He wrapped a hand over her hip, holding her still as she whimpered, angling himself to slide inside her warm, waiting body.

He was never prepared for the feel of her, for the sweet, silken heat of her accepting him, or the burst of ginger notes in her scent that clouded his mind. Allie shuddered. She reached back, cradling his head in her hand. Her nails dug pleasantly against his scalp, urging him onwards, each thrust punctuated with a little puff of breath that was forced out by the movement.

They rolled over as one, and she spread her thighs, letting him fuck into her, grinding her into the mattress. He hovered over her, and she turned her head, offering up her throat to him. Sidney wrapped his fingers around it, a cradle, so gentle compared to his hips or the teeth he sank into the scent gland.

All he wanted was to offer his own throat, to let her claim him in return. He'd never felt the deep, overwhelming spike of pleasure that came from a bonding bite, and he craved it with an intensity that made it hard to think. The only thing that kept him where he was was the shift in her breathing and the growing desperation of her moans. His first instinct was always to care for and satisfy. Even with the haze overtaking his thoughts, he followed that desire.

Sidney growled against her skin as her cunt squeezed him and she screamed into the sheets. He kept his pace even as she grew quiet and relaxed against the bed. It took a few moments before tension radiated from her again and she moved frantically beneath him.

Possessiveness simmered his blood. He wanted to have all of her, to give all of himself, and live in the intoxication of her nearness. She pulled him under with the sound of his own name.

He sank against her, skin sweaty, content to lay there and inhale the scent of her.

"You're squishing me."

Her voice pushed him back to the surface of clarity, and he rolled off. "Sorry."

"It's cool." She slid off the bed and disappeared into his ensuite bathroom, returning a moment later looking refreshed. "What time is it?"

He nudged his pillow to see the alarm clock on the bedside table. "Five-forty-five."

"Ugh, gross." She flopped down and rolled until she was pressed against the length of him.

"I should check on the pups," he said quietly. "I usually go on a run in the mornings too, but I'll skip it today."

"I'll come with you if you bribe me with coffee and treats."

Sidney chuckled. "Doesn't that defeat the purpose?"

"Not even a little bit. I would run for cardio. I don't care about adding cake to my waistline." She patted her belly.

He leaned down and nipped her stomach before she could react. Allie shrieked with laughter and shoved his face away.

"You can't bite me there, you weirdo. I'm ticklish."

Funny how he hadn't discovered that when they'd been together last time. He snared her waist and pulled her to lay on top of him. "Quit being adorable."

"Nope. It's impossible." She buried her face against his neck. "I have to be cute at all times, or I'll fade from existence."

"We can't have that." He cupped her ass and inched his fingers upwards, dancing up her ribs, and dangerously close to her stomach.

"Don't you fucking dare, Sidney Marino." She laughed and squirmed. "I will bite you."

"That's not a deterrent," he said. "But I won't."

She threaded her fingers into his hair and gave his scalp a thorough rub down. "That's a good boy."

Warmth flooded his chest and an involuntary squeak left his mouth.

Allie stared down at him. "What was that?"

"Um..."

"Sidney." She leaned in, her face hovering an inch from his. "Do you like being called a good boy?"

"I'm...not sure. You're the first one to ever call me that."

Allie sat up, straddling his hips. "Considering all the things you've called me, I think it's only fair that we have some kind of pet name that makes you weak. I need to level the playing field a little."

Sidney snorted. "We don't need a pet name. *You* make me weak."

"Awwww." She patted his chest. "You're the cutest sap."

"I *was* being serious."

She cupped his cheeks and kissed him softly. "You can be serious and the cutest at the same time."

He let himself indulge in her, let her nearness settle some deep and ancient part of himself he rarely acknowledged. His alpha instincts wanted her so badly, and the rest of him wasn't far behind.

"I don't want either of us in public until we know what's going on. How about some coffee on the deck?"

"There's not going to be anyone out this early," she said. "What if we took the pups for a tiny walk?"

"Okay. A very short one," he agreed. "I'll put the coffee on and get their breakfast."

Allie nodded and climbed off him, flopping onto her side and immediately closing her eyes. He left the room smiling and went about his morning business. When the pups were fed and harnessed he carried a to-go cup of coffee into the bedroom for her.

She hadn't moved an inch.

Sidney leaned down and kissed her cheek. "You can keep sleeping if you want to."

"No," she mumbled. "I'll come."

Allie rose, located her undergarments, pants, and shirt, pulling them on in turn.

"Could we stop by my place for fresh clothes? I'm a few streets over."

"Yeah, that should be short enough for the puppies."

They stepped out into the morning light, three puppy leashes each, sipping coffee as they walked side by side. He'd never had anyone take on puppy care with him before. They'd always been a draw when it came to cuteness and cuddles, but he'd always done the actual work alone.

She hummed while they walked, one arm looped through his, the other holding her coffee with the leashes around her wrist. The pups trotted along happily sniffing. He couldn't remember the last time he'd felt so relaxed with another person.

They reached her place about fifteen minutes later, and he took over the pups while she washed up, packed herself some essentials, and watered the lone plant she'd bought since moving in. He surveyed the plethora of unpacked boxes and simple furniture.

"I could help you unpack sometime if you want," he offered.

She beamed at him as she re-emerged. "Normally I'd say no, but I *hate* unpacking, so that would be fab if you actually want to."

"For sure, we'll figure out some time that coordinates with work schedules and puppy naps."

Allie bent down to pet them all, setting aside the bag slung over her shoulder. Little Johann got so excited over the attention he peed right in her entryway.

"Oh, baby, is life too exciting?" She laughed.

"I'll clean it if you watch them," he offered.

"I've got it." She hopped off to get paper towels.

He wasn't certain why he found her mopping up puppy pee while cooing at the offender so endearing.

With the clean up done, they headed back to his place.

The general populace was stirring by that time, though no one bothered them. There was only the singing birds and the happy scampering of puppies to break the morning silence.

The pups were slowing down by the time they got home again. He carted two in his arms who had sat down and refused to continue.

"This has been the cutest morning-after in my whole life," she said, giggling as she leaned down to scoop up one of her group that had been falling behind.

He tried not to think of the others. She was free to be with whoever she wanted, but it did still pick at him to know it hadn't been with him, even though he hadn't been an option.

"I can agree with that. Definitely my cutest one, too."

By the time they'd returned to his house, the pups were ready for a nap. He got them bundled away to rest and turned to making breakfast for Allie and himself. They fixed up some scrambled eggs and toast with jam before getting ready to head to the clinic.

He texted on the way, and Dr. James had Muriel take them straight in when they arrived. They sat only a minute in the exam room before the doctor joined them.

Dr. James froze, looking back and forth between the two of them. "You bonded?"

The word echoed in Sidney's head. Bonded. *Fuck.*

"I'm sorry, *what*?"

"You didn't know?" Dr. James pulled out a hand mirror from one of the drawers and passed it to Sidney. "You've both got a bond bite on your throats."

Allie snatched the mirror out of his hands and stared aghast at her neck. "We can't be *bonded*. This is our first date!"

"I wish I could change my answer," said Dr. James. "But you've got the marks. And unless you got them from other people…"

"Oh God. My mom is going to lose it." Allie dropped the mirror into her lap and buried her face in her hands. "Can we undo it? It's recent, does that help?"

Sidney sat, flabbergasted, watching her panic. He turned to the doctor. "It's permanent, isn't it?"

"I'm afraid so." Dr. James sat down across from them and opened up her laptop. "I'm sorry to rush you after that realization, but we should figure out what the situation is."

"It's weird is what it is," said Allie.

"I've input everything that Sidney already told me." She looked over at Allie. "It definitely smells like you're near a heat, which, by our records, shouldn't be happening for at least six more months."

"Yeah, that's what I thought, too." Allie groaned. "Stupid body."

"It's out of the ordinary, for sure. I did some research last night so that I could be prepared for you this morning. I'm going to venture a guess and say that the two of you are ideal mates. It would explain the prolonged focus after your initial connection and your rut symptoms, Sidney."

He listened as well as he was able, but the doctor's words were fading into the background.

"What does that mean for us?" Sidney asked.

"There's not a lot of research available, so I can't be certain. There's nothing dangerous about it so far as we know, but we can do some blood work. I'll make sure both of your birth control doses are updated, assuming the two of you aren't interested in having children at the moment."

"God, no. No babies right now. I just got settled in my career, and, no offense, but I don't know Sidney well enough to be procreating with him." The panic vibes wafting off Allie were making him twitchy. He reached over and took her hand, trying not to take her tone too personally.

Dr. James looked at him, and he could only nod. Even if he wanted children at that moment, which he didn't, he wasn't going to argue against Allie's statement.

"Fair point." Dr. James pulled out a pair of syringes and a set of vials. "Okay, let me take the samples, we'll get you a fresh dose to offset any heat concerns, and we can go from there. According to what I've read, the hormonal surge should last a day or two, but I'll send what information I have to your emails. Otherwise, you're free to go about your lives once your hormones settle."

Dr. James finished their appointment with ease and efficiency, and Sidney left the clinic feeling relieved. He didn't have all the information he wanted, but at least they knew it wasn't dangerous.

Allie was silent the whole trip back to his place.

"You okay?" he asked.

She shrugged. "Just thinking. Is that why it was weird all these years?"

"It would make sense, yeah." The shimmer of tears in her eyes sent a bolt of panic through his chest. "What's wrong?"

"I don't really know." She sniffled, sliding out of the vehicle as he parked.

He met her as quickly as he could for a hug, and she leaned into his embrace. "Want to go inside and hold some puppies while you figure it out?"

Allie nodded. Sidney moved them both inside and sat her down on the couch, returning to her a moment later with little Kassia, and set the pup in Allie's lap. The omega stroked the pups, eyes alarmingly blank.

Unsure what to do, he put the kettle on for tea and put a blanket over her shoulders, though it wasn't particularly cold. By the time the camomile tea had steeped and cooled enough to drink, Allie seemed more alert. He approached her carefully and traded her the cup for the puppy.

"How're you doing?"

"If I hadn't found you again, would everything have felt a little bit wrong forever?"

He let the words sink in. The truth of that question pressed down on his shoulders.

"I don't know," he answered honestly. "Maybe?"

"What if..."

She didn't finish the sentence, but his brain filled it in with a few questions of his own. What if they didn't like one another beyond these circumstances? What if they got together and broke up and then no one ever made him feel like she did? What if all the things he was feeling were only because they were ideal mates?

"This would have been better if we weren't anything special," she said instead. "This is too much pressure."

Sidney sighed and sat down next to her, settling Kassia in his lap. "I can't argue with that."

"I never liked how it felt weird with other people," Allie said. "There was nothing wrong with any of them, but..."

"Yeah, I get it." He fussed with Kassia's ears to give himself time to think and watched Allie sip her tea out of the corner of his eye. "We don't *have* to be together. There's no pressure from me for that."

"Don't we?" She turned to look at him, her dark eyes examining him with an intensity that made him squirm.

"I don't know what to say. I like you, a lot. Whether that's from a weird mates thing or not doesn't change that."

She nodded slowly. "I like you a lot too. I just don't know if I can trust myself, you know? Do I like you because you're amazing, or is it because the omega hormones won't let me consider otherwise?"

"I don't know, I *am* pretty amazing." That finally coaxed a smile out of her, and he wrapped an arm over her shoulders. "I think I'd like you regardless."

"It's hard to argue against that when you made me cake and let me cuddle puppies." She let out a deep sigh and sank against him.

"We could try being together. This was only our first date, and, while things got a little weird, I had the best time I've had in a long while."

"Me too."

"So, want to do that, then?"

"I'm open to it." Allie set down her empty cup and reached over to give Kassia a pat. "We still get to move at regular speed, right? Bonded and ideal mates doesn't change anything else?"

"We get to move at whatever speed we're comfortable with."

She angled up to kiss him on the cheek. "I'm glad you're as sweet as I remember. It would suck to be bonded to an asshole."

A chorus of *aroo*s echoed out of the nursery.

"I think they might be hungry. Want to supervise while I get them some brunch?"

"Absolutely I do." Allie took Kassia from him, and they went about the puppy chores.

Being surrounded by them seemed to brighten her mood, but he was still worried about her. He hadn't been planning on bonding anyone anytime soon, but he could also concede that there were worse people to be permanently stuck with.

She covered a yawn with her hand. "I might need a nap."

"Want company?"

"Only if said company is going to cuddle." Allie winked and lifted a pup off her lap.

"Go get settled, and I'll be there in a minute."

She nodded and disappeared in the direction of the bedroom while he made sure the water bowls were full and that none of their toys were missing. When he made it back, she was curled up waiting, dressed in pajamas.

"Going for the full nap experience, I see," Sidney said with a laugh.

"It's *Sunday*. I'm allowed to chill to maximum levels before I go back to work tomorrow."

Sidney stripped down to his underwear and climbed in next to her, tugging her close so he could inhale the soft scent of her. She caught his hand, lacing their fingers together.

Allie fell asleep almost immediately. He lay awake. What did *ideal* mates even mean when it only considered biology? Allie was sweet, charming, and fuckable, but those didn't necessarily make for a compatible life partner. They *helped*, but they weren't a guarantee for a happy life. Most people took bonding extremely seriously given the very permanent nature of it. While he wasn't one to concern himself with what other people thought, he knew that a lot of his family wouldn't think very highly of his situation even though neither of them were at fault.

Notes of ginger crept into her scent. He squirmed as it woke his body and fought the idea of waking her when she was exhausted. She solved the dilemma for him when she let out a long sigh that melted into a whimper and opened her eyes.

"Sidney," she whispered. "I need…"

Allie reached for him, tangling her fingers into his hair. He followed the slight pressure and leaned in to kiss her. The sweetness pulled him in deep.

He slipped his hand under her pajama bottoms and panties, finding her already wet. She rocked against him, and he devoured the moan it triggered. Keeping one hand there, he lifted her shirt with the other and fastened his mouth over the taut nipple he found. The sounds and squirming it elicited had his cock painfully hard. He focused in and stroked her clit until she was panting.

"*Please*. I need more," she whined and reached out, stroking him through his underwear.

The haze of his rut was creeping into his vision and making it difficult to think. He managed to pull off her bottom layers before he spread her thighs and plunged into her wet heat.

"Fuck," he gasped out, his hips pistoning to get the friction they both craved.

His brain shut off with each thrust. Allie locked her ankles behind him and dug her fingers into the tensed muscles of his back. He delighted in her urging him on.

Each thrust forced a little breath from her, moans and cries that became the only thing he wanted to hear. He braced himself on the headboard to get a better angle and drove into her. She pulsed around him, squeezing deliciously to drag him closer to the edge.

Allie arched beneath him, and he came with her. The rut held back on a full release, making sure he could continue attending to his omega.

"Let me on top," she murmured, pushing at him.

He rolled over at the demand, and she rose above him. There wasn't time to mourn the loss of her warmth before she sank down and enveloped him once more. She got in a few slight movements before he held her hips and fucked up into her. Allie tipped forward and braced her hands on his chest.

"*Fuck*," she gasped and cried out.

It was only when they came a second time that the rut haze had retreated enough for him to begin relaxing. Allie rocked her hips, cradling his cock inside her. He let her do as she pleased, tracing over the curves of her body, tweaking those taut nipples, and sliding up to rest a palm against her throat.

Seeing her like that, riding him while letting him possess her, was intoxicating. The ginger of her scent filled every breath. Nothing else mattered beyond her in this moment.

"So close," she whimpered.

"Touch yourself, and I'll get us to the finish line."

Obeying, she dipped her fingers to tease her clit as he began to fuck up into her again. Each gasp gratified him, and after a few moments he felt the spasms of her cunt as he came, milking his cock. This time the rut allowed him release, and he spilled inside of her. He buried himself deep, and let the wave of pleasure carry him.

When awareness trickled back in, Allie was sprawled atop him.

"We're stuck," she said when he set a hand on her back.

"Whoops." He laughed quietly. "Didn't mean to pop a knot."

She wiggled a little against him, and he groaned at the ripples of sensation. "It's cool. I like it."

He leaned up to kiss her, indulging in the softness of her mouth. The hormones were at their peak, but he couldn't help but think how easy it would be to love her. There were undoubtedly things they would both uncover that would annoy them, or differences of opinion, though it was difficult to care about those when she slid her fingers into his hair and held on like he was her anchor.

"The heat ruined my nap," she said, giggling against his mouth.

"Sleep until the knot goes down, then I'll run us a bath."

"Yes, sir."

His cock twitched at the words and that had her giggling again as she settled in. Allie tucked under his chin with a contented sigh. He pulled the blankets over them and let himself rest as well, although he didn't fall asleep.

The sound of her breathing lulled him into a state of relaxation. Having her so near settled the deep recesses where his alpha instincts were tucked away. She could draw them out or lay them to rest. But then, he could do the same to her. Alpha and omega, like the push and pull of the tides, called to one another. It was an ancient dance and one he was happy to relearn the steps to in order to be what she needed.

How many times had he thought of forever with her when he shouldn't have? It could have been because of the alpha instincts that made him consider it, but would that be so bad? Was there even a way to tell the difference?

Allie's purr rumbled gently while she slept. It was the equivalent of a hot tea and warm blanket on a cold day—deeply satisfying to his craving for comfort. Instinct or not, he knew that he wanted her and that was enough for now.

Chapter Four

The rest of their weekend passed in a similar manner—indulging themselves as the heat and rut demanded, caring for the pups, and enjoying the company of one another. On Monday morning she went to her office, and he went to the clinic for his nursing shift.

"How're you feeling?" Dr. James asked.

Sidney shrugged. "Good, I guess. It hasn't been long enough for any real sort of adjustment to the situation."

Dr. James nodded. "You're welcome to take time off to get things settled."

"I think maintaining some normalcy is better for both of us right now."

"That's fair. The offer still remains if you need it down the road."

Sidney gave her a playful nudge. "You're getting soft on me, Dr. J."

"You deserve it," she countered. "Go on to the next patient, I'll be there shortly."

He went about his day, thinking of Allie all morning.

Sidney picked up his phone as he started his lunch break and texted her.

First Heat: Second Chances

Sidney:

Are we hanging out tonight?

Allie:
You bet your sweet ass :P

Sidney:

Want me to help you unpack a little?

The typing dots appeared and disappeared several times.

Sidney:

Writing me a novel?

Allie:
Sorry :P Yeah unpacking sounds great

Sidney:

What's up?

Allie:
I dunno
For some reason I sort of expected
you to want me to move in and my
brain is doing silly things over you
wanting me settled elsewhere

Even though I don't WANT to move
in since it's only been a couple of
days and that would be weird but
also instincts and emotions are
chaos and I don't want you to
think I'm creepy :(

Sidney laughed to himself.

Sidney:
I don't think you're creepy
I just don't want you to feel pressured
Having your own space is important
and we can spend time at both

Allie:
Quit being so logical
And ok that's FAIR since I
did JUST move into my place

Feeling a little restless, he left the break room and went to pick up a treat. They both already had lunch packed from the leftovers, but he got himself a strawberry milkshake and a chocolate one for her, swinging by her work that was only a few minutes drive away according to the address on her business card.

Sidney:
Treats downstairs <3

Allie sent back a bunch of question marks and appeared off the elevator a couple of minutes later. A brilliant smile broke over her face when she saw him.

"Hey!" She bounded over and threw herself into a hug. Her obvious delight made his stomach flip, and, after kissing the top of her head, he handed her the milkshake he'd bought her.

She took a giant sip then looked up at him. "Milkshake kiss?"

He schooled his smile in time to meet her mouth. "Chocolatey."

"I'm naturally delicious." She smiled and took another sip before leaning in to whisper conspiratorially. "Want to mess around in my office?"

"You shouldn't tease me when other people are nearby," he warned.

"But it's *fun* to tease you in public." She retreated towards the elevator, looking back over her shoulder to summon him along.

He checked the time on his phone. There was enough time for a bit of play. Sidney followed, and, if there hadn't been cameras in the elevator that would have risked her job, he'd have had her pressed up against the mirrored walls in a heartbeat.

She trotted down the hallway past other offices to one tucked away, ushering him inside the small space with no windows save for the small one of frosted glass on the door.

"Welcome to my little shoebox. Sorry, it's not very glamorous, but I'm still pretty low on the totem pole here."

The corner of his mouth lifted. "I don't need glamour to take you apart in here."

Allie closed her laptop and tucked it aside before hopping up to sit on her desk. "Ready and willing to be taken apart," she said with a cheeky grin.

"Are you, now?" Sidney slunk towards her and set his milkshake down, situating himself between her knees. He traced a single fingertip down her throat. "And what if I wanted to tease you and leave? You'd spend all afternoon thinking about me and come home ready to be ruined."

"Hmm, maybe, but that sounds mean."

He tipped her chin up. "Does that imply you don't think I can be that sort of mean?"

The way she bit her bottom lip had his cock tenting his scrubs.

"I'm learning all sorts of new things about you." She toyed with the hem of his shirt and stoked her palm over the bulge of his pants. "To be clear, I can be plenty mean, too. *And* I still have extensive plans to ruin you as well."

"Good." Sidney leaned in, tangling one hand in her hair and resting the other braced behind her. He devoured her mouth until he needed to pull away to breathe, snaring just enough air to resume, moving down bit by bit to tease her scent gland.

She whimpered and pressed a hand over her mouth. Every bit

of her vibrated under his hands, the muffled sounds of her desire spurring him on. He didn't have to strip a single thing off to rile her up. It would be easy enough to tug down her pants and have his way with her on her desk, but he was enjoying her struggle to stay silent and wanted her to be soaked through her panties by the time he left.

The thought of her turning all that frustration onto him had his body burning to take her. He refrained. It would be better for both of them if he could be patient. Delaying his own pleasure for another was a skill he was well practiced in, but this time he knew it wouldn't be a long delay and that she was more than capable of making it worth his while.

He delivered a sharp nip to the scent gland and stood. Her cheeks were flushed and her breathing was shaky as she lowered her hand.

"How am I supposed to focus on work after this?" she asked.

Sidney smirked and gave her a quick peck on the lips. "That sounds like a 'you' problem."

"In a few short hours I'm going to make it a 'we' problem."

"Oh, I know. I look forward to it." Sidney pulled her in for another kiss and stroked her cheeks with his thumbs. "Your choice, kitten. I have a few more minutes before I have to head back. I'm not going to let you come, but I can give you a little more than a kiss."

"I *do* like more than kisses." Allie nipped his lip. "But I also know if you edge me my work day will be shot, and I don't have the clout at this job for that."

"A fair point."

"I thought so," she said with a grin. "When I have a corner office, I bet we could fuck and no one would think twice. But, alas, I am a lowly peon."

"Neither of our places are that far away," he said.

"You shouldn't tempt me with lunchtime sex."

"Hey, if you're tempted by the idea, that's your own problem." He laughed and pulled her up to standing. "You could come home for food and a puppy break since I'm ninety-percent sure you were working through lunch and I can't let the dark soul of capitalism ruin you like that."

Allie snorted and threw her arms around his neck. "You're such a dork."

"Embarrassing that it took you this long to notice that."

"We can't all be perfectly observant all the time."

"No, that's true. We can't all be perfect in general. It's a burden I am forced to bear."

"Oh my God." Allie laughed and covered her mouth to muffle the sound. "Quit being cute."

"Come home tomorrow. I have a craving to be domestic." Electricity fizzed between them, like static off a balloon as he pulled her closer. "I should go, but you can rest assured I'll be thinking of you all day."

"You're making me hate having a job." Allie sighed and pressed a soft kiss to his mouth. "I'm off at four."

"Five for me. Want me to bring the pups over?"

"God, yes please. I will never say no to floofs."

When they parted and Sidney was on his way back to the clinic, he had time to sit with his emotions. He knew that he'd said there was no rush or pressure and that he meant it, but he could see the future so clearly. Shared lunches, short meet ups at work when things got too busy, evenings full of foster pups and time together, nights spent unraveling one another...

Sidney squirmed in his seat. It wasn't fair to either of them to think about permanence, but that didn't stop him. It was impossible to tell what prompted the thoughts. It was equally unfair to assume it was all the bond and the hormones because he did genuinely find her to be a delight. It might always be a question, but, if they were happy, did it really matter what the answer was?

His thoughts continued swirling round and round in unanswerable circles through the rest of his work day. He focused himself with feeding the pups when he got home and seeing to their needs before packing them into his vehicle to drive to Allie's. She was visible in the window when he parked. Her apartment was on the main floor which made walking up to it with six pups wonderfully easy. He passed them through her patio doors and brought a playpen from the vehicle, along with some water bowls and toys.

"I feel like a proper mama," Allie said, gazing down at the pups. "Look at all our little babies."

Sidney snared her waist and looked down at them over her shoulder. "Six children and we're not even married."

"What can I say? We're rebels like that." Allie leaned back against him. "Do you ever think about adopting one?"

"Constantly," Sidney said with a laugh. "But if I adopted all the ones I wanted to, I wouldn't have the time or resources to help new puppies."

"I suppose that's fair. I don't know if I'd have the willpower for that."

"Luckily you can just be the cool mom, and I'll be the discipline dad who makes sure we will power everyone into forever homes."

"What if I sneaky-sneak adopted one myself?"

"I support you being a full dog mom." He could absolutely see her in that mode, and it was cute as fuck.

"You're tempting me today, and it's all over the spectrum."

"I like keeping you on your toes." He gave her a smack on the butt. "Come on, let's get some unpacking done so your apartment doesn't look so sad."

They worked through the evening with breaks for delivery pizza and a short walk with the pups. By the time she was satisfied the sun had set. Her photos were on the wall, her books on the shelves, and her dishes tucked into the cupboards. There was still more work to be done, but her apartment looked more like a home than when they'd started. Pups were passed out snoring all over her floor, which added to the homey feel, too.

"We should get the children home to bed," Allie said as she sat down on the couch.

"Want to sleepover?" Sidney asked.

"You bet your sweet ass I do." She stuck out her tongue. "I have plans for tonight that are many years in the making."

"Ominous." Sidney laughed and hoisted her back up. "Pack some things to keep at my place. You can take over the spare bedroom and bathroom as your domain if you want.”

“I do like having a domain. I only have one bathroom here, but I can keep a drawer and a shelf in the medicine cabinet free for you.” She tucked against him and kept her gaze on the floor. “That’s not moving too fast, is it?”

“For the unbonded, maybe.” He shrugged. “But I prefer to think of it more as a comfort and convenience thing rather than a relationship milestone. It’s easier to have essential supplies on hand in both our homes for whenever we end up in either place for any reason.”

Allie nodded slowly. “Okay, that’s fair. I *want* to spend more time with you, but I’m pretty sure the compulsion to make a fort out of your bed and keep you in it is the hormones talking.”

Sidney snorted and held her a little tighter. “You are one-hundred-percent permitted to make a fort out of my bed.”

“I’ll make it super stylish, I promise.” She stood on tiptoe to kiss him until one of the pups let out a yip in their sleep and stole her attention. “The babies are fussing. Okay, I’m going to pack and shower. Be right back.”

Sidney leashed up his fluffy herd and got them loaded into the back of his vehicle for the drive home.

Allie emerged shortly after with damp hair and a small rolling suitcase in tow. “I think I got everything. I’ll have to do a bit of a shop to acquire doubles of some things, but I’m all set for now.”

They took separate vehicles back to accommodate work schedules, and Sidney set about getting the pups settled in their nursery for the night while Allie unpacked some things into the spare room. He hopped into the shower to wash the day away when he’d finished with the pups, and when he emerged he found Allie waiting for him on the foot of his bed in red lingerie and a little black silk robe that hung open to expose the red lace.

A ripple of lust rolled through him. “Sweet fuck. You’re going to give me a heart attack, surprising me with an outfit like that.”

She grinned adorably wide. “That’s the reaction I like. You

should put on something spicy, too."

"I have a few things. Any preferences?"

"Nope. Surprise me." She propped one foot up on the bed as she watched him. Her slender fingers sliding down her body to stroke over the lace guarding her clit held him in rapt attention until she giggled and broke the trance. "The sooner you get dressed, the sooner you can touch."

It took considerable effort to tear his gaze away and step into the closet. He stripped down and replaced his clothing with leather pants and the strappy harness he knew she loved. A pair of leather cuffs with detachable ropes and the strap-on she'd hinted at were selected in addition to a bottle of lube. He stepped back out into the room and was greeted with a desperate groan of appreciation.

"Jesus Christ on a cracker. Who the fuck gave you permission to look that good?" Allie slipped off the bed and glided towards him. "I've never seen you in leather pants before."

"You like them?"

She hooked her fingers into the waistband and yanked him closer. "Maybe."

Her gaze slid to the assortment in his hands, and she picked up the strap-on with a wicked gleam in her eyes. The attached dildo was slimmer than he could take, but he was too impatient to work up to his maximum tonight.

"I haven't done this in real life," she said. "I've done extensive research, though."

"Uh huh, what kind of *research* was this?"

Her cheeks flushed. "Okay, *some* of it was valid proper research. The rest was porn, but *still*."

"Well, I'm available to answer questions if your research left any gaps."

"Help me put it on?" Allie asked.

Sidney set down the rest of his supplies, held out the straps for her to step in, and tightened them until it fit snugly around her hips. He gave her ass a little smack while he was down there for good measure. "Perfect."

"I'm kinda nervous but also really fucking excited." Allie shifted from foot to foot.

"You're going to do great. Now, how about you cuff me to the bed and have your wicked way with me?"

A small, desperate sound escaped her mouth. "God, *yes.*"

She'd already cleared off the blanket and pillows from the bed, but he grabbed a towel to spare his bedding before she hooked his cuffs to the wrought iron frame.

"Has anyone ever told you how goddamn delicious you look tied up?"

"Just wait for the day you have me trussed up and helpless." He flashed a grin at her as she squeaked and fumbled the last hook.

"We'll work up to that." She slid a hand down his bare back, nails lightly scratching on the return journey. "I'm happy to take turns with it down the road."

"Good to know." He tugged on the cuffs and found himself sufficiently secured. Sidney let himself relax, sinking down against the soft sheets. Allie stroked down the curve of his back and over his shoulders, kneading muscles on the way.

She dropped a kiss onto one shoulder and tugged gently on his hair until his face was up high enough for her to kiss him. Her grip was steady, guiding him. As much as he was used to taking control with clients, he sometimes craved the relaxation of not being in charge. Partners he trusted enough to do this with were few and far between. It might only be the bonding that allowed him to relax with Allie, but whatever the reason was he was grateful for it.

Allie took her time, exploring his body with a patience that had him relaxing onto the bed. Her hands were surprisingly strong as she dug into the tense muscles of his calves through the leather. She located knots he didn't know he had and worked them loose.

"I'm going to hire you as my permanent massage therapist," he murmured as she kneaded his scalp.

"I'm just buttering you up before I get my hands on that ass. I want you relaxed."

"Everything about me is relaxed except for my cock."

Allie snickered. "That'll get attended to in time."

Her fingertips walked over the seam of his pants and she pulled away. "Is there a secret zipper on these?"

"Mhmm. Easy access."

"So fancy! I love it." She crawled behind him. "Ready?"

"Mhmm." He adjusted himself, lifting his hips into the air while she carefully managed the zipper, laying him bare while the leather stayed on his waist and legs.

"You have such a great butt," she mused, patting each cheek in turn.

"It's one of my best features, I'm told," he said.

"Ten out of ten." She moved behind him and he settled in with his eyes closed.

The lube bottle popped open and the slick liquid dripped between his cheeks. Soft pressure slowly introduced it inside, with more being added every so often. Then the firm, slippery shaft of the strap-on nudged his entrance, testing the receptiveness. His cock was hard to the point of discomfort and he itched to reach down and take care of it, but his hands were bound, forcing him to be patient.

Sidney groaned as the strap-on inched its way inside. It was on par with sliding into a warm, wet cunt, but with the indulgence of surrender added on top. After each miniscule movement, Allie would pull out and add more lube until it was gliding freely.

Allie laid her hands on his hips and gave an experimental thrust.

"Oh, *fuck*," he gasped.

"Is that a good 'oh, fuck', or a bad one?"

"Good one. Keep going."

Following the instruction she moved again. The satisfying glide was punctuated by the tip of the strap-on prodding his prostate and sending little sparks of pleasure rippling outwards from the impact. She held on tighter and moved with greater confidence. Murmured curses disappeared into the sheets, and he held onto the headboard, knuckles white on the wrought iron.

"Don't stop." Sidney tried to angle to give him more distance to reach for his cock, but the straps binding his wrists didn't allow for it. He whimpered.

"I said your cock would get attention in time," Allie said behind him, her hips burying the strap-on deep inside him. "So little patience."

She slowed down her pace as if to taunt him. He tempted her into retaliation by moving his hips, trying to speed things up again. She reacted exactly as he'd wanted, delivering a quick smack to his ass cheek.

"Excuse you." Allie pulled back, the dildo leaving his ass entirely. "If you're going to be naughty, I can drag this out a lot longer."

"Maybe I like being naughty." He turned his head and stuck his tongue out at her. "Guess you'll have to tame me."

With a low growl and satisfied smile, Allie climbed over him and got her teeth on a scent gland. He nearly came from that and was panting desperately as he arched his back, letting her get the dildo back into his ass. Her growl had the hairs on the back of his neck standing up. A soft, wet tongue lapped at the bite as her hips fucked against him.

So close.

His groan pitched deeper with each thrust. He squirmed, trying his best to stay still, teasing the head of his cock against the bedding. The sensitized tip leaked onto the towels. Allie moved in a steady rhythm, letting the dildo tease his prostate until he was breathless, sweat prickling on his brow.

Sparks of pleasure radiated through his body. He could hear himself begging but didn't have the coherency to rein it in. He just wanted to come. The next thrust undid him, hitting perfectly to unravel the threads that held him together. Heat rushed over him. The coiling pressure of sensation burst and rolled through every inch of him, filling him with energy before draining away—a wave against the shore, pulled away to rejoin the ocean.

When he resurfaced, he was laid out flat and face down against the sheets. He was too relaxed to move. Allie rolled him over, and he lay there staring at her with still-fuzzy vision as everything settled.

"Sounds like someone had fun." She pressed a soft kiss to his mouth and disappeared, returning a moment later with a warm cloth to tidy the mess he'd made on himself.

"Mhmm."

The back of his mind reminded him that she still needed to come, too. When she'd taken the bed towel and cloth to the laundry and returned without the strap-on, he tugged at the restraints.

"You're cute tied up. If you were still hard, I'd climb on top and ride you into the mattress."

Sidney stretched luxuriously. "My mouth is perfectly rideable."

"You're so correct."

Allie grinned and undid his cuffs before setting a knee down on either side of his face. One eager hand grabbed his hair. The rush of her scent overwhelmed his senses, coating his tongue as he licked up into her. His hands found her waist and pulled her down.

He revelled in the sound of her moans. The deep and impatient melody of her was intoxicating as her cunt ground against his mouth. Her other hand braced against the headboard, giving her additional purchase to ride him.

She fed the craving in him, the bone-deep want. The bounce of her chest drew his eye and the sway of her dark curls, her mouth parted sweetly with blazing red lips. Perfect.

His tongue dipped inside her and back up to flick her clit, suckling the sensitive bud until she was writhing above him.

"Sidney," she gasped out. Her fingers tightened in his hair. She bucked against his mouth, seeking that gratifying friction she needed, and he let her take her pleasure from him.

He slid his hands up her back in a smooth motion to gather up her long hair around his fist. She let out a groan as he tugged and fucked his face with a growing ferocity.

The dam burst.

There was no chance to react as she rocked against his mouth, driving down as she came. The wetness of her slipped down his cheeks and coated his chin. She slowed in increments, gentling her pace and flopping over next to him, breathless.

"I almost pulled a muscle at the end there," Allie said with a laugh. "Don't let me skip leg day anymore."

Sidney rolled over and snared her close. "Fucking me can count as a workout."

"I accept this."

He curled around her, inhaling deeply of the honeysuckle sweetness as her scent mellowed. "You smell so good. Now you can never leave." He held her tighter and buried his face against her throat as she laughed and squirmed in his grasp.

"Nooo, my freedom!"

Sidney rolled on top of her, squishing her into the mattress. "Oh nooo, you're trapped. A tragedy. We'll have to stay in bed forever."

"You're such a dork." Allie giggled, relaxing beneath him.

Sidney kissed her cheek. "Want to have a bath before bed?"

"With bubbles and wine?"

"I can arrange for both of those."

"Hell yes."

"Red or white, kitten?"

"Red, please." Allie wiggled again. "I can't help if you don't let me up."

"You rest. It'll only take me a minute." Sidney hopped off the bed and got the bath water running while he rummaged through the kitchen for wine options. He picked out a nice smooth pinot and poured two small glasses before returning to check on the bath's progress, adding a splash of bubble bath after setting the wine glasses down. The water frothed, whipping up a rose scented foam.

"Bubbles!" Allie skipped into the room, naked and grinning. "I'm going to get so spoiled staying here."

"Eh, I wouldn't say going beyond the bare minimum to be spoiling. You deserve nice things, and I intend to give them to you," he said.

Allie locked her hands behind his neck and pulled him down for a lingering kiss he felt down into his toes. "I'm going to have to up my 'nice things' game."

Sidney scooped her up by the back of her thighs and held her close. "I won't be complaining about that. Hop in the bath, and I'll join you."

He stepped back to give her space and let her sink into the fragrant water. Once she was settled, he followed her in, getting comfortable in the jacuzzi tub and pulling her to lean against his chest.

"I haven't taken advantage of this bath nearly as much as I should."

"Really?" Allie traced her fingertips along his arm. "I'd be in this thing every night."

"It's all yours whenever you want it."

"Sweet indulgence." Allie's purr came out as she relaxed against him.

They sipped wine and soaked until the water lost its warmth. Afterwards he toweled them both off and watched her blow dry her long hair. It shouldn't have been as endearing as it was. Stray strands whipped out of place, and she tucked them back over and over until the curls were dry and fluffy.

"Remind me to grab my diffuser attachment next time so I don't look like a pom pom," Allie said, setting down the blow dryer.

"You look cute. Voluminous, like when a cat gets startled."

She rolled her eyes. "You shush. It'll calm down by morning."

He checked on the pups before climbing into bed and spooning her. "Goodnight, kitten."

"Sweet dreams."

Chapter Five

Sidney stepped out of the shower after his run, finding the scent of coffee wafting into the bedroom. Allie appeared in the doorway a moment later, dressed in leggings and a short denim dress.

"Morning, handsome." She passed over a steaming cup prepared how he liked, in the same manner as every morning over the past not-quite two weeks.

"Good morning." He stole a sip before leaning in to kiss her. "Pancakes okay for breakfast?"

"Music to my ears." She beamed and settled down on the edge of the bed while he got dressed.

It was a rhythm they'd worked out since bonding. After his run and their coffees, he made breakfast while she fed the pups and packed their work lunches. Evenings were shared meals followed by movies, cuddles, or sex depending on the mood. It was...bliss, for lack of a better word. Aside from her inexplicable disdain for olives and constantly missing the hamper with at least one sock, there was nothing he'd noticed that caused even the vaguest irritation. The more time he spent with her, the more he wanted to spend. She sank into his bones, slotting herself into the empty spaces of his life he hadn't realized were bare.

Sidney turned around with the plated pancakes and found the kitchen empty. "Where'd you go?" he called out.

"With the babies!" Her answer came from the nursery. He set down the plates and wandered over to see Allie curled up on the floor covered in puppies.

"Getting in some cuddles before their new parents get here?"

"I can't believe they're old enough to be adopted. They're still little babies."

"They're going to be fine in their new homes," Sidney said, squatting down next to her.

"I hate that my apartment limits dogs by size." Allie sighed. "These floofs have paws too big to risk."

Sidney smiled to himself as she cupped Ludwig's face in her hands and kissed his forehead.

"You have to be *so* good for your new parents because I'm bummed I'm not your new mom."

Ludwig wriggled and licked her face.

"Be brave, my almost son." She snorted when his tongue went up her nose, and Sidney couldn't help laughing.

"The upside of the pups getting families is that we can start having sleepovers at your place, too."

"Oh," she said. "That's true. I hadn't thought of that. Though my apartment is going to feel small and sad after chilling at your house."

"Maybe, but it's *yours*. If you decide you don't want it when your lease is up we can figure out a plan, but might as well use it while you have it, right?"

"Okay, but we have to save the really freaky stuff for your place because my neighbours are going to hate me otherwise."

Sidney laughed and sat down, pulling her and Ludwig onto his lap. "I don't think that'll be a problem."

The doorbell rang and Allie let out a small sound of distress. "The puppy thieves are here."

"Puppy *parents*," he reminded her. "Scooch off."

She did so, reluctantly, and he went to answer the door. A couple stood waiting with another handful of people coming up the walkway.

"Welcome, come on inside, and I'll get each of you your new family members."

Adoption day was always bittersweet for Sidney. He tried not to get too attached to the animals he raised but always failed. For now, he put on a happy face.

He fetched each pup in turn and presented them to their new family, relieved and gratified at how excited everyone seemed to be. When they'd all gone, the house felt oppressively quiet. Allie snuck her arms around his waist and nestled against him. Soft fingers wiped away the wetness on his cheeks.

"You did good," she said. "All those babies have homes because of you."

Sidney nodded, still silent. His heart broke a little each time even though it was good and important for the fosters to move on to forever homes so he could help more.

"You wanna drown your sorrows in some cuddles and ice cream?"

He smiled despite himself.

"We could go over to my place so you don't have to see the empty nursery tonight," she offered. Allie squeezed him tightly. "I'll even distract you with orgasms later."

Sidney laughed and swung an arm over her shoulders. "Sounds perfect."

She needed to stop fitting his life so well or he was going to slip and start thinking about 'L' words he shouldn't be contemplating so early on. He pushed the thought aside and packed himself an overnight bag to stay at her place.

The trip over was short, and her apartment was just as he'd last seen it. But then she had hardly spent a moment in her own home since they'd met again. Part of him wondered if he should feel guilty for monopolizing her so much, but he didn't hear any complaints.

"I told my friends about you," said Allie. She stood at the stove stirring spaghetti sauce.

"Oh?"

"Well, we're practically velcroed together, so it seemed weird to not mention it." She checked the noodles and carted them over to the sink to drain. "To be fair, they already knew about you in general, but now they know we're attempting togetherness."

"Do they know we're bonded?" he asked. At some point he'd have to tell people, but he liked having this all to himself.

"Not yet," Allie said.

Sidney dished up their dinners, and they sat at her little kitchen table. "If I tell my parents I have a partner, they're going to insist on meeting you. They can be a lot, so I'll leave them in the dark for a while if you don't mind?"

"I'm content to avoid parents for a while. God knows my mom is going to be up my ass about babies the second I tell her we're together. Doubly so if I tell her we're bonded."

The mental image of her with their fictional children, carrying one in her arms and one in her belly, slugged him in the gut and stole his breath. She was already beautiful, but he knew without a doubt that she'd be exquisite as a mother. He shouldn't be thinking about it. They hadn't even had a conversation about what she might want but now it was branded into his thoughts.

"You okay?" Allie asked. "Your face is doing a thing."

"Yeah!" He cringed as his voice cracked. "Do you even want kids?"

She shrugged. "Not at the moment. A few years down the road? Sure."

Her words did absolutely nothing to dispel his mental image.

"You'd be a good mom."

"You think so?" Her eyes glimmered with mischief as she asked. "Well, I can't get pregnant until an unregulated heat, but we could spend considerable time practicing for that day."

His cock tented beneath the table. "Sweet fuck, woman. Are you *trying* to give me a heart attack?"

She slid from her seat and over onto his lap. "Does that mean you don't want to breed your little omega?" Her mouth descended onto his, her leg swinging to the other side of him so she straddled him in his chair.

The warmth and weight of her flipped whatever rational switch kept his brain in check. He held onto her hips and pressed her down against his aching cock. "You shouldn't tease me."

"Why not?" she asked, nipping his earlobe. "Are you going to punish me for it?"

He groaned, deep and needy. "You said nothing like that at your place."

"Hmm, I lied. I don't know my neighbours yet. I don't need to befriend them." She attended to the other ear, all the while rocking her hips. "If I'm loud enough, maybe one will knock on the door and they could join us."

The bolt of lust up his spine at the suggestion almost made him come in his pants. "Eager to share me already?"

"It would have to be a really cute neighbour." Allie laughed and slid off him. "I'll keep you to myself for the moment. Leave the spaghetti, we'll warm it later. I want to break in my new bed."

"Yes, ma'am."

Sidney followed her to the bedroom and tossed her down onto her fresh sheets, taking a moment to appreciate her spread out and ready. She was already wriggling out of her pants.

"Impatient, are we?"

"If you don't like it, you can discipline me." Allie stuck out her tongue.

He climbed into the bed and held her hands above her head. "I can go for a *very* long time even without the heat hormones helping me along. If you want to play this game I can make you come until you forget your own name and need help to stand."

"Oh nooo. However shall I survive such a punishment?"

"Kitten, you're going to eat those words." He let his weight sink against her, devouring her mouth and pinning her in place.

She melted beneath him with a hot fervor. Sidney snuck his hand between them and into her panties, stroking the already wet folds as he fastened his mouth onto the scent gland on her throat. The eagerness of her body---its willing malleability---all fueled him. His fingers sank into her cunt and her moan filled his senses. He craved that sound.

Sidney moved relentlessly, spurred on by her rocking hips and panting in his ear. She came hard and fast, her cunt squeezing his fingers. Before she could catch her breath, he had her climbing the crest of another. He swallowed up the cry and kept on, changing hands for the third and fourth orgasm.

Allie lay limp as he sat up and pulled off her pants. The wetness was easily visible and he knelt before her like a supplicant. He dragged her to the edge of the bed, dipping his face down to feast. She was an altar he would never grow tired of worshipping at.

The trembles that ran through her invigorated him. She squirmed in his grasp, her voice already hoarse as she cried out again. His cock throbbed as he worked her into a frenzy.

"Sidney, *please*." She whimpered and fisted her hands in his hair. "I ne—"

Her words choked off as she came again.

"*Fuck*." Allie moaned and lay motionless as he rose up again.

He took his time stripping off the rest of her clothing and teasing the flesh he uncovered. The goosebumps that decorated her delighted him. He traced patterns on her skin and alternated teasing her breasts with his mouth and her cunt with his hand. She clung to him, her body growing fatigued as the moments passed.

"How're you doing, kitten?"

"Not quite ready to eat my words. You'll have to work a little harder."

"You picked a more difficult challenge when I don't have access to the treasure chest, but I'll do my best. Want to bring in some of the toys you have?"

"Ooh, yes, please." She rolled over and grabbed out her small collection as well as a bottle of lube. "We love a man who views sex toys as team members and not competition."

"That's always been my philosophy," he said, picking up a slim butt plug. "Booty up."

Allie giggled and lifted her hips, wiggling her ass playfully.

Sidney set his palm against one of the plump cheeks. "Is that a request?"

"It might be."

He delivered a sharp smack to her ass, revelling in the little yelp that turned into a groan as he massaged the skin. Sidney tended to the other cheek for the sake of symmetry and to indulge himself.

"Beautiful," he murmured.

Sidney added some lube and rolled the toy in it before slowly inching it inside of her. It was a small one and the resistance was minimal as it slipped in. Taking advantage of her position he set about eating out her cunt until she was shaking. He kept her pinned with one arm over the back of her waist and the other keeping her folds spread.

With her face buried in the sheets he could hardly hear the sounds it elicited, but the tremble of her thighs and the bursts of sweet ginger scent betrayed any attempt at muffling her reaction.

Allie snatched up her pillow, shoving her face into the fabric as the scream left her. She tried to inch away as she came down from the high, but Sidney held her ensnared, tonguing her clit until even the pillow couldn't hide the whimpers.

He pulled away and flipped her over. Allie sprawled on the bed, hair askew, skin flushed and sweating. His face was wet, and he wiped it with the back of his hand before catching both of her ankles and bringing them up to rest on each side of her head.

"Flexible." He smirked. "Never going to get tired of that."

"You're going to have to keep them there." Allie sucked in a deep breath and let her legs relax in his grasp. "I'm not strong enough after all that."

"Don't worry, kitten. I'll take perfect care of you."

"Facts." She laughed softly. "That's one thing I've never doubted."

Sidney slid his cock over the wet warmth of her folds, teasing them both. The slick friction sent ripples of pleasure through him, and he held off joining their bodies for the sake of keeping her like this a little longer. He adored the little squirms and frustrated pout as she tried to rock her hips from her current position. It was all but impossible, though he still felt her muscles flex in the attempt.

"Relax," he murmured.

She gave an impatient whine.

"Okay, okay." Angling his hips, Sidney pressed the tip of his cock into her cunt, inch by scintillating inch.

The heat enveloped him, a groan falling from his lips to match the one that sprang from her.

"Fuck, you're so tight." Sidney closed his eyes.

"It's practice," she said, panting. "Gotta keep those muscles strong."

He briefly freed one of her ankles to grab her egg vibrator. Pressing the button on the bottom, he placed it against her clit. The spasm of her cunt cut off his next breath, and he almost pulled the vibrator away to spare himself the temptation to come.

"Keep this here. You'll come as often as you need to until I'm done." His voice came out a low growl as he fought for control. She felt far too incredible and looked too perfect spread open for him.

Allie placed one trembling hand onto the vibrator. Once she was settled, he returned his hold on her ankle and fucked into her in earnest. The sensation of gliding inside of her was almost on par with the satisfaction of forcing a dark, guttural sound from her throat.

Each stroke was heaven. Sweet, hot, glistening heaven where her body welcomed him over and over again. Any attempts at silence vanished as she made her enjoyment known with overlapping gasps, whimpers, and moans. Coherence fell away. His growl rumbled in his chest, a sound that she responded to with gleaming eyes as her omega instincts slid to the forefront.

He fucked into her, holding steady as she came, breathing while she pulsed around him.

"Jesus *Christ*." Sidney held tight to her ankles.

As soon as the pulsing began to slow he began again. The craving for her overwhelmed him, and he flexed his muscles, burying himself to the hilt as the vibrator tipped her over the edge once more.

The *pulse, pulse, pulse* caressed his cock, coaxing him to follow her to the edge.

Soon.

Sweat prickled his skin, and the sound of her coming undone filled his senses.

"Oh, *God*. Sidney." Allie's squirming renewed. "Please, it's too much."

He wouldn't last through another wave. "One more, kitten. You can handle it."

She whimpered and nodded, dropping her head back to the mattress.

"Good girl," he growled. Sidney renewed his pace, allowing himself to relax and let the coiling pressure build.

This time when her muscles seized and the pulsing milked his cock, he let go. She pulled him over the edge with her.

A myriad of curses fell from his lips as his vision turned black in the peak of the pleasure. His lungs burned. Her body eased in increments, and, with it, his own body slowly returned to normal. He released her ankles and sank down on top of her, hovering on his forearms to keep from crushing her.

"I think my legs are made of jelly now." Allie laughed and ran her fingers through his sweaty hair. The vibrator lay discarded to the side, turned off, and he reached down to slide the plug out of her as well.

Her kiss caught him by surprise when he sprawled out next to her. He matched her eagerness despite the exhaustion creeping in, rolling over to bring her on top of him.

"Did you have fun?" she asked.

"Mhmm." He nodded and nipped her lip. "You?"

"So much fun I'm not going to be able to look my neighbours in the eye."

"Luckily, I have no neighbours to overhear anything."

Her gaze turned soft, and she traced his cheek with her fingertips. "My lease is for a year."

"Sublet," he said before he could consider otherwise. He kept going before his brain would properly catch up with him. "I know we said go slow so I wouldn't ask you to get rid of your place, but I'm saying it anyway. I want you to stay."

She kissed him with a fiery intensity that warmed him down to his toes. "You're not saying that because we had incredible sex?"

"It might have turned my inhibitions off a little, but the sentiment is real," he promised. "I like you. More than I've liked anyone, and I swear it's not just because we're bonded or ideal mates or whatever. You were adorably perfect from the moment I met you, and now that I've found you again I want to keep you."

"I know that logically a lot of this *is* because we're bonded, but it's hard to care. I want you to keep me. Really, really badly."

"Okay," he said softly, threading his fingers into her hair and pressing a kiss to her lips. "So we keep each other, for as long as that makes us both happy."

"Was that your nefarious plan?" she asked, eyes glinting with mischief. "Give me orgasms until my brain turned off and I'd realize how much I never wanted this to end?"

"I wouldn't say *nefarious*." He grinned and kissed her again. "That's just a fortunate byproduct."

Allie snorted and collapsed against him giggling. "You're such a dork."

"Excuse you. I'm *your* dork."

She laughed again. "Of course. You're my everything whether you like it or not."

Peace settled into his bones and he traced her cheek with his thumb. "I do like it, kitten." He kissed her fiercely. "I do."

First Heat: Bonus Story

Sidney and Allie get naughty at work.

Content notes: This story is m/f and contains sex toys, butt stuff, and inappropriate behaviour in an office.

Bonus

"Oh shit."

Allie gripped the edge of her desk as a zing of pleasure pulsed through her. The hum of the remote control vibrator tucked inside her while she was at work was, in all likelihood, one of her worst ideas. It was hard to care about that as it buzzed against her G spot. Her asshole squeezed around the plug that Sidney had slipped into her along with the vibe that morning.

The vibrations disappeared and she sank down, resting her elbows on her desk. "Fuck."

"Allison?"

Reality crashed over her.

"Oh God, I'm so sorry. I got a leg cramp," she lied. She fished out her cell phone and opened the app that controlled the vibrator buried equally deep inside Sidney and jacked it up to full power for a few seconds in revenge. "Anyway, let's continue?"

Her client got back on topic as they discussed the design of their new home.

Allie's phone pinged.

Sidney:
I spilled my coffee because of you :(

Allie:

Tough cookies :P

I was on a call with a client

The vibrations came back with a vengeance and she slapped a hand over her mouth to muffle herself as her client happily chattered away. Allie counted down the seconds to the end of the call, squirming in her seat and hoping desperately that it wasn't obvious she was getting close to the edge.

"That all sounds great," she squeaked out. "I'll get the forms done up and have them sent over to you by end of day."

"Perfect. Talk to you later."

Relief poured over Allie as the call ended. Every bit of her hummed and she longed to dip her fingers under her skirt and push herself over the peak. But that wasn't the agreement. Her orgasms today depended on Sidney's goodwill, just as his depended on hers.

Sidney:

Downstairs!

Ready for lunch?

Allie:

Ready for a lot of things ;)

The vibrations toned down enough that she could comfortably stand. She grabbed her purse and headed to the elevators to meet Sidney for their lunch date. Allie kept the app open, and as she stepped into the lobby she pushed his vibe to max power as soon as he came into view. She giggled to herself as he fumbled his drink, but managed to save it from tumbling to the floor.

"Hey stranger." Allie stood on tiptoe and kissed him quickly. Her job wasn't big on PDA so she'd save that for later.

"You're evil," he said. "Sexy, but evil."

"Don't pretend you don't love it."

His gaze darkened and he dropped an arm around her waist. "Come on, kitten. I've got more on the agenda than a meal."

She slipped into the front seat of his car so they could drive to their chosen restaurant—a little walk-in Thai place with the best pad Thai in the city. He turned her vibe up midway before starting the car.

"You can marinate for a little bit and think about what you did."

She shuddered. "You're lucky I care about road safety or I'd make you come on the way."

"You only have to care for about five minutes." He laughed and set a hand on the bare skin of her knee.

Allie closed her eyes and laced her fingers together to keep herself from nudging his fingers closer. He must have read her thoughts, though, because he inched his hand up and she let her thighs fall apart. Her skin buzzed with anticipation. A whine climbed out of her throat as he stroked his pinky against her panties. It wasn't nearly enough, but when she pressed her hips toward his hand he retreated.

"Nope. You come when I say you can come and trying to push for more is going to make this take a hell of a lot longer than you want it to."

They pulled into a parking spot facing away from the restaurant. Allie undid her seatbelt and reached over, snaring Sidney by the collar of his shirt. He popped his own seatbelt, leaning toward her, their mouths meeting in the middle. She craved his touch, wanting him to pull her into his lap and let her grind him in the parking lot.

While he didn't do that, he did snake a hand to hold the back of her neck, applying pressure to her scent glands as he devoured her mouth. Warmth prickled her skin and she balanced herself with a hand on his thigh. Her fingers dug into his muscle as she whined into his mouth.

Sidney pulled back, his dark eyes sparkling with amusement. "You can touch if you need to, but you can't come."

"You're cruel," Allie said, even as she slid her hand under her skirt to stroke her clit. She'd been wet all day, from the time he'd fingered her that morning before slipping the toy inside, through each torturous buzz, and now as she brought herself to the edge.

Sidney grabbed her hand and nipped her bottom lip. "Naughty kitten. That orgasm belongs to me."

Allie whimpered and fumbled opening up his fly. With a soft chuckle, he assisted in undoing the button so she could free his cock. She bent towards it, wrapping her lips around the head, fully aware that her skirt-clad ass would be clearly visible through the window to anyone who looked towards their car. Let them watch.

He gathered her hair up into one hand and gripped the steering wheel with the other like a lifeline. Sidney wriggled beneath her attention, shuddering with every eager suck and sweep of her tongue.

Allie popped her head up and gave him a grin. "Good luck making that inconspicuous while we pick up lunch."

His eyes narrowed. "Someone's got brat vibes today."

"*Maybe*," Allie said, pulling her hand from under her skirt. She licked one finger slowly, keeping eye contact with him as she did so. "Do you like it?"

Sidney snatched up her hand and stuck the remaining shining finger into his mouth, tongue wrapping around the digit to clean off her wetness. He nipped the fingertip before letting her have her hand back. "I might."

She waited for him to maneuver his cock back into his pants, giggling as she watched the struggle.

"You're getting way too much enjoyment out of this," he murmured as he finally fastened the button and pulled up the zipper.

"Really? I think I'm enjoying it the *perfect* amount."

They slipped out of the car and Allie noticed a person in a car the next row over, staring at them slack-jawed. She winked as they walked by and hooked her arm through Sidney's.

The line up inside was a dozen people long as they took their spot. Sidney turned the vibration of her toy off and looped an arm around her waist. She glanced up at him, one eyebrow raised curiously.

Instead of answering, he leaned down for a chaste kiss. "Ordering your usual or branching out?"

"I'm a creature of habit. At least with food." Allie grinned and tucked her hand into his back pocket. She teasingly pressed her wrist against the plug buried in his ass and he shot her a dangerous look.

They moved their way slowly up the line. Allie opened the toy app on her phone and casually increased the intensity of his toy, one notch for every step forward. His grip on her waist tightened. She kept her gaze forward, enjoying the uptick of his breathing and his fingers digging into her.

Finally they were at the front of the line.

"What can I get started for you today?" the cashier asked.

"Hi! I'll get the—" Pleasure zinged full force through her and her knees buckled. It was only Sidney's grip that kept her upright. She braced her hands on the counter and forced down a groan. "The… chicken pad thai, please," Allie managed.

"Thai beef bowl for me," said Sidney.

"Is she okay?" the cashier asked.

"Yep," Allie said. "Just *super* hungry."

Sidney paid for their food and they stood to the side to wait. He used her as a shield, tucking her ass against his jeans so he could wrap his arms around her waist. The pressure nudged the buttplug inside her, a teasing sensation that had her grinding back against him as inconspicuously as possible. Allie played with the app, swirling the controls with no rhyme or reason. Sidney pressed his mouth to her hair, his arms tightening around her.

His whole body was trembling against her by the time their order was called. Having mercy on him, she turned the vibrations down and grabbed the to-go containers, leading him out of the restaurant.

"Struggling?" she asked with a wink.

"Not as much as you're going to when we get back to the office." He slapped her ass before circling the vehicle to get in. The words and impact sent a thrill through her.

She opted to behave herself on the short drive back to her work, suspicious that he kept the vibe off as they navigated her building.

Allie waved to some coworkers they passed who were eating in their offices. After sequestering herself and Sidney in her own office, she set the food down on the desk and turned to look at him. His gaze smoldered and held her immobile.

"Hands on the wall, kitten." His voice was a low rumble that had her shivering.

She spun and set both palms on the back wall. The vibrator buzzed inside her, a slow rolling wave that had her whimpering with each swell. His body pressed against her, fingers hooking under the hem of her skirt to pull it up around her waist.

"I've been thinking about having you like this all day." He kissed her throat. "I know you can't be quiet, so I'm going to help you with that. Okay?"

Allie nodded, trembling in place.

Sidney dropped down into a squat and pulled her panties down to her ankles, freeing them from each foot. He stood again, holding the panties in front of her face.

"Open up, kitten."

Her mouth popped open obediently. The taste of her filled her senses as she bit down on the fabric.

"There's my good girl." He traced teasing fingers over her, goosebumps following each lingering touch as he made his way to her hips.

She held as still as she could as he wiggled the buttplug out of her ass and set it aside on a napkin. He kept foil packets of lube in his wallet for "emergencies" that they'd made use of on more than one occasion. She heard his zipper slide open, and the lube packet rip. Slick liquid was added to what had already been used for the plug that morning. A moment later his cock nudged her asshole.

Allie took a deep breath and relaxed as he inched forward, his hands holding her hips steady. She groaned around her gag, craving the stretch and glide of him sinking into her body.

"Vibes on, kitten." He passed her phone over and she blearily managed to turn his up to max, yelping when he did the same to hers.

"*Fuck*," he whispered, and then laughed quietly. "I need an extra pair of those panties for myself. You feel too good."

Sidney moved experimentally and when the motion was smooth and fluid, he fucked into her hard. Allie panted and squirmed as he reached one hand around to tease her clit while the other pressed over her mouth to silence her further. His harsh breathing was loud in her ear, a puff of air warming her skin with each thrust. Heat simmered in her blood and her thoughts clouded.

The world around them fell away. He satiated every craving, filling her body and her senses with him. The only thing that would make it better is if he could have stripped her down and tied her up, but you can't have everything when you're doing illicit work quickies.

He didn't last particularly long between the vibrator in his ass and his cock buried in hers, but he didn't need to. Sidney's growl was muffled against her skin and she savored the sting of his teeth on her throat. His fingers worked a steady rhythm on her clit and she followed him tumbling down that peak of pleasure a moment later. He'd been right to use the gag. Even with his hand over her mouth her office neighbours would have heard her scream without it.

They stayed like that, him supporting her shaking body against the wall, the vibrators still buzzing away cheerfully. Sidney kept teasing her clit and kept her pinned in place. She struggled with the order to keep her hands on the wall, scratching her nails on the drab paint.

Her cunt pulsed and squeezed the vibe, hips bucking between his cock and his hand as he undid her again. Her legs were jelly and she'd have slid to the floor without him holding her.

"Mercy?" he whispered in her ear.

Allie nodded and he took his time turning off both of their vibrators and sliding his cock out of her ass. He tidied her up, wiping away the slickness that had dripped out of her cunt before replacing the plug in her ass and returning her panties to their proper place. She was dizzy from the taste of her still lingering on her tongue. He cleaned himself up as well, looking like an absolute snack in her completely unbiased opinion.

Sidney kissed her, slow and deep, pressing her back against the wall.

"Eat your lunch, kitten. I don't want you passing out before dinner." He kissed her again and picked up his takeout container. "I have to get back to the clinic."

"Text me when you get back so I don't turn on your vibe while you're driving." She winked.

"Will do." Sidney laughed and gave her one more quick kiss before turning to leave. "You be a good girl until I get to play with you tonight."

Conference Confidential

Abby and Leo don't like each other. In fact, they've despised each other since the day they met. Unfortunately for them, their company has decided they have to attend a conference together and make some new connections to elevate the business. A screw up in the reservations forces them to share a room and brings their belligerent sexual tension to a head when a spontaneous heat takes them both by surprise. With their jobs on the line they have a lot to navigate—the demands of the conference, the demands of Abby's heat, and the fallout of stepping over lines that can't be uncrossed.

Content notes: This omegaverse story is m/f and contains a spontaneous heat, knotting, nesting, purring, growling, biting, and bonding. There is belligerent sexual tension, workplace rivals to lovers, and only one bed.

There will be public play and cranky sexy shenanigans.

Friday

Abigail Dresden stared at the receptionist at the hotel, trying her damndest to not take out her bubbling fury on them. She practiced her breathing techniques instead.

Inhale.

Exhale.

Breathe in the peace.

Breathe out the rage.

Inha—

Leo dropped his arm around her shoulders and she stuffed down the urge to kick the back of his knees and send him to the floor. At least he didn't use her head as an armrest like he had on their first meeting.

"Remove. Your. Arm," she growled.

"Come on, Abbs. You have to get used to me being close."

"You do *not* have permission to call me that." She seethed and shook off his offending limb.

"Aw, Dresden, you're so cute when you want to eviscerate me." Leo laughed and patted her head. "How about you check your attitude so the lovely receptionist doesn't have to feel those hate beams coming out your eyes?"

It took all her willpower to not suckerpunch him in the balls. She forcibly turned away from him and focused back on the staff. "I'll take literally any other room. I don't care how small or undesirable.

You can't make me share a room with him."

"Ma'am, we're really sorry but there's nothing available. We're booked solid for the conference." The young beta offered an apologetic smile. "Could we offer you a complimentary dinner?"

Leo nudged Abby before she could snap.

"You bet you can," he said. "We'd love a free dinner, wouldn't we, Drez?"

"You know I don't like my last name shortened," she said.

He ignored her and continued talking to the beta. "Enough for both of us for each night we're here to make up for her sharing a room with me."

"Of course, let me apply the credits to your room." The beta tapped away at her computer before handing them two room keys. "Sorry again for the booking confusion. Have a wonderful time at the conference!"

Abby snatched up her key and marched toward the elevator, rolling suitcase in tow.

Fuck.

She already despised having to work with Leo, and now she had to share a hotel room, too? Some god had to be laughing at her. Stupid arrogant prick. If he wasn't so good at his job she'd have convinced their boss to toss him out. Why did he have to be such a goddamn asset?

Abby had already been stressed after making the arduous drive down to the conference. She'd had perfect evening plans involving sex toys, a long hot shower followed by room service, and a solid sleep. But no. There would be no stress relief sharing a room with him.

Leo pushed the elevator button as he rolled up next to her. She'd never been particularly bothered by her shorter stature, but, every time she was around Leo, she was made uncomfortably aware of it. She wasn't intimidated—just the opposite. She was annoyingly *attracted* to tall people, and she was almost certain that he knew it. It also didn't help that he was conventionally attractive with dark brown eyes, equally dark hair with a slight wave, and sun-kissed skin.

If his personality didn't make her want to throat-punch him on a regular basis, she'd have already hooked up with him.

"Hey, Drezzy." He was looking at her with a satisfied smirk on his full lips. "How much do you want to toss me out a window right now?"

Neither of them had ever made their dislike for one another a secret. It didn't affect their work, so no one was in the habit of telling them to shut up and get along.

She ground her teeth as the elevator arrived, and they stepped on together. "A little more with every word. Can you at least pick one nickname I hate and stick to it?"

"Hmm, I *could*, but I know the inconsistency pisses you off, so..." he shrugged.

Abby shoved her thumb several times against the button for their floor, urging the elevator to hurry.

She could survive a three day conference with him. Her career depended on it.

"I'm not going to deliberately fuck with you," he said. "Not much, anyway. If that's what you were worried about. I can be good for a conference."

"You've never been good a day in your life."

The elevator pinged as it arrived onto their floor.

"That's not true. I'm just never good around *you*."

Abby took another deep breath as she stepped into the hallway. A mistake. At the office everything was so efficiently ventilated that she never had to reconcile that someone she couldn't stand smelled so fucking alluring. It was truly unfortunate that people had evolved the need to breathe. Unfair, really. Maybe she could inhale through her mouth instead...

"Move your ass, Abbs."

Abby blinked, having frozen herself in indecisive panic right in front of their door. She didn't respond and instead swiped her card to get inside.

There was only one bed because of course. The universe was obviously conspiring against her. He sprawled out on the bed.

"Order a cot from the front desk," she said. "We are *not* sharing a bed."

"You'd rather sleep on a shitty cot than a king-sized bed?"

"Oh, *no*." She spun around to glare at him. "*You're* sleeping on the cot. Where's your goddamn sense of chivalry?"

"Fuck that." He rolled his eyes and whipped one of the pillows at her. It beaned her in the face before she could fully catch it. "I'm sleeping on that bed. You do whatever the fuck you want."

Abby grumbled. Leo sat up and glared at her. Lightning bolted up her spine when he peeled off his shirt.

"Leo, what the sweet fuck do you think you're doing?"

"Going to shower?" He raised an eyebrow. "It was a long trip. I want to clean up before dinner."

"Strip in the bathroom, you animal." She forced her gaze to the ceiling even though part of her wanted to follow the magnetized journey back to staring at his bare chest. A whimper tried to sneak out, but she smothered it ruthlessly down.

He hopped up, rustled through his suitcase to acquire shower supplies, and came to a stop directly in front of her. The earthy scent of petrichor radiated off of him, like he was carrying around his own personal thunderstorm. Cantankerous and enigmatic, just like his personality. She'd always loved storms, watching them from her window or immersing herself in the rain when the weather was warm enough for it. If she had less pride, she'd ask him to ruin her, to pour himself over her until nothing else existed in the world.

Why was he standing so close? The rebellious part of her wanted to reach out, to step nearer and breathe in that scent until she could taste it. Heat pooled between her thighs and rose up her spine.

"You're blocking the bathroom," he said.

She stepped aside awkwardly, hating herself for wanting him.

When he closed the door behind him, she hurled herself onto the bed and screamed into the pillow. She'd been kidding herself. Surviving a whole weekend in the same room with him would be the end of her.

As she lay there face down, she wondered if there was enough time to rub one out before he left the bathroom again. Nervous fingers slipped under her hips, ears perked to listen for the water turning off. She just needed a bit of satisfaction to get through the weekend. If she waited, she might never get the chance, and then she'd implode with the frustration.

Abby snuck her hand into her panties, rocking her hips. She was already wet and more than a little desperate. Ordinarily, she would luxuriate in the sensations and take her time, but she had no idea how fast Leo showered. There was no way in hell she could live down the mortification if he caught her.

She stroked her clit, grinding her hips downward, urging her body to scale the peak of pleasure as quickly as possible. Abby moaned into the pillow. She tried not to think about how incredible it would feel for Leo to slide his fingers into her, for him to catch her like this and fuck her into the mattress. Each time her brain flung thoughts of Leo at her, she pushed it down. She had her pride and wasn't willing to give it up.

Abby squirmed. She'd need to find a fuck buddy at the conference to keep her head on straight. It was usually easier to ignore these kinds of thoughts about him. But now, with him naked on the other side of a door, and her fucking her own fingers, they were much harder to drown out.

Maybe it would be fine. He'd never know if he was the one she thought about like this. She certainly wasn't going to tell him. So she continued, imagining that door swinging open, imagining him pulling her hand free, fingers soaked and slick, replacing them with his own.

"Sweet *fuck*." Tingles rippled through her. She was so close.

The water turned off. Abby had barely enough wherewithal to whip her hand out of her panties before the door swung open. She bolted up, hiding her dripping fingers behind her to wipe them on the blanket.

Leo paused in the doorway, towel slung around his hips. His nostrils flared. He looked at her with an expression she'd never seen on his face before. Something dark and potent stirred in his eyes before he shoved his gaze towards his suitcase. He didn't speak as he pulled out a fresh set of clothes and retreated back into the bathroom.

Abby collapsed back with a whimper.

Fucking hell.

Now she was definitely going to have to find someone. Without pausing to change her outfit or wait for Leo, she snatched her purse and room key and fled. She pulled her hair out of its tight bun as she rode the elevator upwards, letting the long, silken strands fall down her back. Abby beelined for the hotel bar the second she got off at the rooftop lounge. The night air was cool, a welcome relief against her flushed skin.

The space was crowded with others there for the conference. It would be easy enough to find someone to satisfy her. The people at these events were always eager to break up the monotony and have a fun story to take home. She went to the bar and ordered a shot of rum, tipping it back with ease before asking for a sea breeze cocktail she could sip while scoping out her options.

Abby slipped through the throng of people. A good half were in their business attire like her. The rest were dressed in clothing that straddled the line between casual and bedroom-chic. The bartender was plenty cute, but their shift had probably started recently. Tonight was not the night for patience.

An older alpha rose from his spot against the viewing glass, whisky on the rocks tinkling in his hand as he walked over. His hair and beard were black with salted streaks scattered throughout. He had a medium build, an overwhelming aura of confidence, and the strong scent of smoked cherries.

"Michael," he said, holding out his hand.

She placed hers into it and gave it a firm shake. "Abby."

"Are you here for business," he asked, "or for pleasure?"

"Always both." She winked and took a sip of her cocktail. "The pleasure makes the business much more bearable."

"That it does." Michael stepped closer, scooping up her free hand to press a kiss to her knuckles.

She was already worked up, and the simple contact had her clit pulsing. Abby glanced past him, the reckless part of her wondering if she could get away with being fingered up against the glass without alerting the entire lounge.

Michael tugged her towards him, sliding his hand up her arm, over her shoulder, to rest against the curve of her throat. Goosebumps broke over her skin, and she shivered.

"Come to my room," he said.

Annoyance battled with desire. He'd known her all of ten seconds and was already inviting her to his room. Not that she didn't want to go, but she did still like to be wooed before being propositioned. He could at least *pretend* that she wasn't a sure thing.

"You've got to work harder than that."

He smirked and rubbed her chin with his thumb. "Hmm, no, I don't think I do. Your scent already told me you want to. Anything now is wasteful theatrics."

She bristled. "Maybe I *like* the wasteful theatrics."

Michael leaned in, inhaling deeply. "Perhaps, but I know if I reached between those thighs, I'd find you wet and ready. Why make us wait? We both know you came up here to find someone to take you."

Abby stepped away, but he dug his fingers into her shoulder so she didn't get far. "Yeah, maybe I did, but that doesn't mean it's going to be you. Let go."

He frowned but kept his hand where it was.

"Buddy, if you don't stop touching me right now, I will bite your hand off at the wrist."

Michael only smiled. "You're a feisty little omega. I'll enjoy taming you tonight."

Petrichor flooded her senses, and a ripple of excitement flowed through her.

"You heard the lady." Leo's voice sounded behind her. She didn't turn but felt the heat of him as he moved to stand near. "Back off."

"We were having a conversation," said Michael, glaring at Leo.

"No, we weren't," Abby snapped.

Michael took a long sip of his whisky and then sighed. "Suit yourself."

Leo didn't move an inch until Michael was ensconced in a conversation on the other side of the lounge. Abby stood frozen, waiting for some kind of reprimand, but Leo stayed quiet so long that she turned to face him.

"Are you okay?" he asked.

"Yep." It didn't sound truthful in her ears.

"Abbs..."

"I'm *fine*." She took a gulp of her cocktail. "You don't need to babysit me."

"Oh, I am well aware of that."

"Then why are you up here? How did you even know I was here?"

"You were wound pretty tightly, I figured you'd want a drink to chill out. I'm allowed to want the same thing. I just happened to come by in time to save you from potential assault charges."

She rolled her eyes.

"Don't make that face at me. We both know you'd have clocked him within the next minute if I hadn't shown up."

"Okay. Fair." She took another sip.

"I'm getting a drink. Are you going to run off on me again if I turn my back?"

Embarrassment warmed her cheeks. "I didn't *run off*."

"If you say so." Leo stepped over to the bar and returned a minute later with something clear and fizzy with a lemon twist set atop the ice cubes. "Sit with me?"

She raised an inquisitive eyebrow. "Why?"

"Because it might be nice to see if you're as annoying outside of work as you are at the office."

"Oh, *fuck you*."

"Fuck me yourself." He took a casual sip, moving to sit at one of the small tables near the viewing glass.

She followed, not entirely sure what else to do and unwilling to let the conversation end there. "What's that supposed to mean?"

Abby sank down into the chair opposite him.

"It means exactly what I said."

"Why would I want to sleep with *you*?"

"I dunno." He shrugged. "You tell me. I'm not the one who made our room smell like sex."

Heat zinged up her spine as embarrassment flooded her cheeks. She stuffed all her annoyance to the forefront to keep herself from gaping like a fish. The last thing she needed was to let him know he'd gotten to her.

Abby huffed. "I can be aroused by people that aren't you."

"Mhmm." He took a slow drink and fixed those dark brown eyes on her. "So you didn't want me to catch you?"

Abby narrowed her eyes. "If I wanted you to catch me, I'd have sat on the end of the bed facing the bathroom with my cunt out."

He choked on his drink, and she waited for him to collect himself, simmering in self-satisfaction.

"Why are you bringing this up?" she asked. "You're either trying to embarrass me, or you want to get in on it. So which is it?"

When he recovered, he leveled his gaze on her. She straightened her spine, refusing to give an indication that her stomach was clenching, excited for the potential of what his answer would bring.

"We don't like each other, right?"

"Correct."

"But we're sharing a room, and you came up here to find a stranger. If you wanted to fuck someone you don't even like, I'm right here."

Abby sipped some more sea breeze. "That's making a lot of assumptions about me being able to stomach your presence long enough to come."

Leo chuckled softly. "I think you could manage, Dresden. Besides that, I think it would be good for us."

"Oh, really?" She lounged back in her chair, eyeing him curiously. "How so?"

"We could work out our frustration with one another. I'm man enough to admit that I want you."

A thrill zipped up her spine.

"Plus, we're always conveniently located. Shitty day at the office? Meet up in the exec bathroom and blow off a little steam."

She couldn't answer right away, despite her eagerness to find out what sleeping with him would be like. Abby paused, letting him believe she was taking the time to consider, rather than giving him the satisfaction of an immediate agreement.

"Alright," she said slowly. "I'm willing to give it a go, but, if you're a bad fuck, I'm telling the entire office, so you'd better impress me."

"I'm not worried." He sighed and leaned back. "Let's go get some dinner. You'll need to fuel up for later."

Abby rolled her eyes even as her pussy clenched at the thought of what was to come. "If you can wear me out, I'll be surprised."

They finished their drinks and rode the elevator down to the hotel restaurant. The trip seemed to take forever. Abby's body trembled being so close to him, his scent saturating every molecule of air. At least he looked equally unsettled next to her.

"I wonder if we should get room service instead," he said. "You're wandering around smelling like a flower shop on steroids. Everyone is going to know you're itching to get upstairs with me."

"God, Leo, can you *please* shut the fuck up for once? You think people can't smell *you*? You're not exactly subtle."

"The fact that you can pick up my scent at all says a lot considering I use a scent-neutralizing body wash."

"Well, it's not working, so I don't know what to tell you. Maybe you just stink." She crossed her arms and refused to look at him as they stepped into the lobby.

Petrichor infused her senses. She shivered, biting back a moan. Abby startled when his hot breath ghosted over her ear.

"Nah, you like it. You can't hide that from me."

"If you want to play this game, we can fucking play, and I can make it very uncomfortable for you." Abby steeled herself and turned, snaring the collar of his shirt with both hands so he couldn't escape.

She exhaled softly in his ear, letting it turn into a moan. "*Leo, please.*"

The surge of petrichor was instant. He backed her up against the nearest wall with a low growl that sent her nerves fluttering. Panic and lust swirled in an intoxicating cocktail that left her drunk with desire as he caged her in.

"Leo," she squeaked out. "Everyone is looking at us."

"Good."

Every ounce of her being wanted him to toss her over his shoulder and take her back upstairs, but her pride kept her from giving in so easily.

"I already *know* you're an animal, Leo, but you don't have to prove it to everyone else."

He took a slow, deep breath. His pupils were so large that they nearly eclipsed the irises, making him look like some wild demon come to claim her. Leo straightened in increments, bringing himself back under control except for the telltale bulge in his pants and the roiling petrichor scent that clung to him.

"Playing is dangerous, Drez." His voice was rougher than usual. Abby knew whatever frustration she built up in him would be given back once they were upstairs, but part of her craved it. She wanted to provoke him, to give him a reason to ruin her once she finally got her hands on him.

They walked awkwardly to the restaurant, and Leo asked for a booth near the back.

"A party just left one. Give us a moment to get it cleaned up for you," the host said.

They waited in silence until the server came to collect them. Leo slid into the booth next to her and they ordered their drinks. They were out of sight for the majority of the occupants, and those who might look over were too blitzed to notice them.

"We should lay down some ground rules," said Leo.

"Like what?"

"Like not fucking with me where everyone can see unless you want me to flip you over my knee and smack your ass in front of them."

She swallowed hard.

"And," he said, "if I do something you don't want, you give me an indicator. Same for if I do something you like. I might think you're a little shit, but I'm not about to make you genuinely miserable."

"Okay, that's fair. What indicator?"

"I'm flexible. A green light. A nod or a yes, and I'll move forward. If you make it clear you don't want something, you do the opposite, and I'll stop."

She nodded slowly. "What if I don't know if I like it?"

"Then you tell me that. And I'll tell you. I'm capable of listening and paying attention. Plus I'm very interested in having an office fuck buddy, so I'm rather invested in making sure you enjoy yourself enough to do this again."

The server returned with their drinks, the same as they'd been drinking at the rooftop lounge, and took their dinner orders—steak for Abby and lobster for Leo since the hotel was comping them.

Usually when they were stuck together they would bury themselves in work or their phones to avoid talking, but that wasn't an option now. So, while they waited for their meals, they had their first real conversation since they'd started working together four years ago.

"Tell me something about you I don't know," said Leo.

Abby started with the basics. "I have an older sister, Natalie. I'm not sure if that's interesting enough."

"Is she as annoying as you?"

"Worse," Abby said, smiling into her drink. "Natalie would drive you up the wall inside of five minutes. Smart as a whip, ultra-competitive, top of her class in *everything*. God, she was exhausting. My parents *adore* her, of course. Nat's the kiss-assiest kiss-ass to ever kiss an ass."

Leo snorted. "Sounds like my brother. Don is a straight up dick. You'd hate him."

An idea sparked. Leo... Don...

"Wait, wait, *wait*. What is Don short for?"

Abby watched as the light faded from Leo's eyes. "Donatello."

She burst into laughter and choked on the sip she'd taken. "Your parents were such nerds. Is it just the two of you or do they have the full set of Renaissance masters?"

"I can't believe *you're* such a nerd that you thought of the Renaissance before you thought of the turtles." Leo shrank in his seat. "And, just the two, but my aunt also has two boys…"

"*No.*"

"I'm afraid so." Leo took a gulp of his drink. "Raph and Mike. None of us go by our full names. Also, Donatello isn't *technically* a Renaissance master, but my brother is the baby of all of us, and my dad is both a history nerd *and* a fan of the turtles so that's how that happened."

"Your dad is my new hero."

"Don't tell him that. He'll rope you into a three-hour lecture about whatever he happens to be learning about at the time."

"Are we sure your dad and my mom aren't the same person?" asked Abby.

"We can never allow them to meet. They'll destroy the fabric of space-time."

"How did I not know you had all these nerdy tendencies?"

He shrugged. "I'm full of surprises. You still haven't surprised me yet, though."

"Okay. I've got something you wouldn't expect. I was almost a professional soccer player."

"Yeah?"

"Yep. I even got scouted, but then I tore my ACL."

"Yikes." Leo cringed. "That's shitty."

"Very," she agreed. "I was out of the game for so long that I lost my scholarship. So I transitioned to a business degree, and the rest is history."

"Why didn't you go back to soccer?"

"Between surgery and months of physio, I was not particularly eager to risk going through that again. I still play for fun sometimes, but I was so good at business that I wasn't too upset about how things turned out."

"What about dating?" Leo asked.

"What about it?"

"I've never heard anything through the office grapevine of you being attached to anyone."

"I dunno if you know this fabulously well-kept secret, but a lot of people are intimidated by confident and successful women. As soon as people find out how much I make, they either get freaked out that it's way more than their income, or they start looking at me with dollar signs in their eyes."

"You're trying to date the wrong people then."

Abby rolled her eyes. "I have too much taking up my time to worry about that. I get what I need through heat services, and if I don't mention my job, then people are happy to fuck. It works well."

"That's a sad life, Abbs."

"You can't lecture me about this. Aren't you in the same position?"

"Yeah, that's how I know it's sad."

She wasn't entirely certain how to respond to that, but luckily the server arrived with their plates.

Once they were left alone again to eat, Leo's expression shifted. He set his hand on Abby's thigh under the table. She stared at him, glancing around at the few inebriated patrons near them. The heat of him sank into her skin and made her stomach flip.

"Yes or no?" he asked quietly.

"Yes," she whispered.

"Open." His fingertips tapped her opposite thigh and she spread them enough for him to press against her aching core and tease her clit with the seam of her pants. "If you're not quiet, everyone will know."

She bit back the moan that climbed up her throat and forced herself to keep as silent as possible. Abby let her head fall back, resting against the booth, eyes closed as Leo touched her. It was a light stroke, enough to awaken but nowhere near enough to satisfy.

Abby dropped her hand to his thigh as well and dug in. "Yes or no, Leo?"

"Yes."

He was so close to her ear when he said it that it set goosebumps free on her skin, a shiver skittering up her back. She let her fingers wander. The slight hiss and hitch of his breath was the only indication she had that he was being affected. She moved higher up and traced the outline of his cock.

"You're getting dangerous again," he said, whispering the warning.

"Why can you touch but I can't?"

"Because only one of us has something obvious for people to look at. I can do whatever I like to you, and no one would know you were a dripping mess for me unless they got you to spread your legs."

"Just don't stand up for a while," she said, continuing to tease him. "By the time you finish eating you'll be fine, unless you get yourself worked up by what you do to me."

Leo turned his dark, dangerous eyes to her and slid his hand to the small of her back. Abby froze, not entirely sure what he intended.

"I want to get my hands on your cunt. Do I have your permission for that?"

Abby stared at him. "*How*?" She couldn't quite fathom how he'd manage without the entire restaurant knowing what was happening.

"Yes or no?"

She huffed. "Okay, yes, but I don't understand how you—"

His hand snaked right down the back of her pants. She jumped, startled, and ended up giving him enough room to complete the journey. When she settled back down his fingers were pressed flat against her.

"Sweet fuck, *Leo*." She braced her elbows on the table and buried her face into her hands.

He leaned in and licked the scent gland on her throat. Abby pressed her palms tightly over her mouth to muffle the desperate sound she made. His fingertips moved gently, curling upwards as she squirmed, shifting to allow more access until he sank into her. Abby whimpered into her hands.

"You've been ready for me this whole time," he murmured,

growling softly in her ear. "Wet and waiting."

Abby shivered, pushing down the surge of heat that pulsed at the base of her spine. Sweat prickled at her temples. There was no way to move that didn't make her distractingly aware of the fact that he was inside of her.

"Your lobster will get cold," she managed to say, still not looking up from her current position. She heard the sound of his fork hitting his plate and turned to glance at him. "Are you seriously eating your whole meal with one hand so you can tease me?"

"Would you prefer I remove my hand?"

She didn't respond to the words, instead focusing on not shivering as he slowly moved his fingers, the warmth of his hand pressing against her most intimate places.

"Abby?"

She shook her head and turned to him. "Keep it there. I'll enjoy watching you try to navigate a lobster one-handed."

Leo smirked. "I guess we'll both enjoy watching the other struggle, then."

He wiggled his fingertips, and she clenched around him with a gasp. Her pride could keep a straight expression on her face, but there was nothing she could do about the wetness dripping into his palm or the twitch of her muscles as he teased deeper.

She sliced off a chunk of her steak and popped it into her mouth. He only had lobster tails to contend with, so it wouldn't be as entertaining to watch as if he'd had to fight with a whole lobster. Nevertheless, watching him pick and choose his bites was satisfying.

Abby tried to eat strategically, but he seemed to wait until she had a bite before curling his fingers each time. It was an exercise in restraint to make it through the meal. When the server had come by to check on them, she'd smiled too wide, thanked her too loudly, and gulped her drink when they were alone again. Embarrassment fought with the rush of excitement at having his hands on her.

The food satisfied one hunger, but by the time she'd finished eating, another type of hunger was overwhelming. It clouded her thoughts. She wanted nothing more than to get back to their room and let him fuck her until she couldn't move.

"Can I get you any dessert?" The server asked as she arrived for her final check on them.

"No, thank you," said Leo. "Just the cheque, please."

"Of course, how will you be paying?"

"The front desk is giving us free dinners to make up for losing one of our reservations, so you can just charge it to our room."

The server nodded and had him fill out the room number on the receipt before leaving them alone. Once she'd turned her back, Leo slid his fingers out of Abby and wiped them thoroughly with the napkin.

Abby followed him out of the booth and back towards the elevators. She held onto his arm as they walked, feeling unsettled. Her blood hummed.

Inside the elevator, he leaned against the wall, tugging her to join him with her ass pressed against his cock. She was drowsy leaning against him but also jittery and too horny to think.

Abby bolted when they arrived on their floor and swiped her card before he caught up.

Leo closed his hand over hers on the handle. Part of her wanted him to press her to the door, to grind on her until she was breathless. They tumbled into the room, and Leo kicked the door shut behind them.

His low growl had goosebumps springing up all over her body, nipples tightening, and clit pulsing. An answering growl rose up, and she turned, yanking him in for a kiss. She broke away long enough to jump up. He caught the underside of her thighs as she wrapped her legs around his waist and devoured his mouth. It was truly unfair how good he felt.

He carried her across the room and dropped them both onto the bed, pressing her into the mattress. The weight and proximity were exactly what she craved. Abby rocked her hips, desperate for more contact.

"Hurry up," she whined. "I don't need more foreplay."

"Impatient." Leo laughed quietly and untangled himself from her grasp. He peeled off his shirt, letting it drop to the floor before doing the same with his pants, then hers. She wrestled off her own shirt while he stripped off her panties. Once they were down to their final layers, she let herself look at him. Tall, toned, and ready for her. Perfect.

"Get on the bed," she demanded.

"Someone's pushy today."

"Shut up. We're here to fuck, and you're delaying." Abby sat up and unhooked her bra, tossing it to the floor. She caught him staring and snapped her fingers. "You can admire my tits after you get me off."

Leo rolled his eyes even as he chuckled, pulling off his boxer briefs. Abby crawled into his lap as he settled against the headboard.

She was too impatient to savor much, guiding his cock straight to her entrance and sinking down slowly with a groan. Abby whimpered. She dug her nails into his shoulders, enjoying the hiss and muttered cursing from him as she took him in. Leo was thick, fitting her perfectly, satiating the bone-deep craving she'd had for him since they met. She didn't even care how pitiful her little murmurs and whimpers were, she just wanted more.

He grabbed onto her hips, his breathing sharp as she moved. Abby rocked at first and then rose up until she was nearly free of him before gliding back down. She rode him hard and frantic, squeezing around him.

His scent drew her in, and she buried her face against his throat. They should make a perfume of him. She could spritz it onto her pillow to bathe in the scent of rain. It heightened every sensation, and she inhaled it in deep gulps like she'd been drowning.

"Abbs," he gasped out." You're going to end this too quickly if you don't slow the fuck down."

She clapped a hand over his mouth and continued her pace. "Shut up, you're ruining it."

If she could come, she could shake off the insistent need that infused her blood. He needed to stop talking and let her fuck him into oblivion.

Leo pushed her off to climb over her. She squawked, indignant as she flopped onto her back.

"Calm down for a half second. You're not the only one involved in this."

She was too warm to calm down. Sweat prickled over her skin, and her cunt throbbed.

Abby shook her head. "Please."

He slid his fingers over her clit until she squirmed.

"It's not enough." Abby whimpered and hoisted her hips up, demanding more.

"Okay, okay." Leo plunged three fingers into her. She arched with a moan. He fucked her like that, quick thrusts, and worked her clit with his other hand until she was panting.

"Fuck." She groaned. "*Fuck.*"

Her cunt grabbed onto his fingers, and she cried out, bucking against his hands to get even more friction. She didn't settle as the sensation abated. Heat roared up her spine like a torrent and infused every cell. The warmth turned to a burning. She pulled Leo in, writhing in discomfort.

"Make it *stop.*"

His nostrils flared, his eyes widening as he stared down at her. "Did you just fucking go into *heat*? You came to a conference when you were due?"

"I didn't." She shook her head frantically. "I don't know. I just—help, please. Please, please, please."

"Okay." He sank against her, inhaling deeply at the scent gland on her throat. His own scent erupted, filling the room. "Christ. You smell so good. It's so hard to think."

Leo scraped his teeth against her throat, and Abby arched against him, pleasure spiraling out from the soft bite.

"Harder," she begged.

He indulged her, biting down, holding her immobile as her nerves fizzed with sensation. She spread her thighs beneath him, wiggling until his cock was pressed against her. He fucked into her with a smooth thrust that stole her breath. She wrapped her legs around his waist and let him take over.

Nothing mattered except for the friction and pressure of his body driving into hers. She lifted her head to fasten her mouth onto the scent gland on his throat, reveling in the taste of the storm on her tongue. The room fell away, and fog filled her thoughts as the heat haze dragged her under.

Her only awareness was the weight of him, the nip of his teeth, his growls in her ear, and the delicious pleasure of their bodies joining.

When Abby surfaced, Leo was still there. Pleasure broke over her. She held onto him, riding the wave of it until the strength melted from her limbs and she lay limply beneath him.

Every inch of her hummed. Leo sank against her, still for the moment.

"Leo," she murmured softly.

"Oh, thank fuck."

"What happened?"

He groaned quietly. The pressure between her thighs sent little ripples of sensation through her. She sorted through her hazy brain, trying to find why it felt different than usual but also familiar.

"Did you *knot* me?" Abby asked, pushing against his chest. The slightest shift had her shuddering as it pressed against her G spot. He didn't budge, and an experimental wiggle of her hips proved her suspicion correct.

"Mhmm," Leo murmured quietly. "I didn't mean to. Don't move and maybe it'll go away."

She settled back onto the mattress. The weight of him was soothing but the edges of panic poked at her.

"I'm pretty sure you're in heat," he said, interrupting her thoughts. "You have to be. I shouldn't be able to knot anyone outside of a heat. God. I feel so high I don't even know where all of my body is right now."

"But…I can't be. I take suppressants. I'm not due to go off them for months."

"Well then I have no idea what the fuck is going on, but it sure as hell seems like a heat to me."

The pressure of his knot released slowly, and he rolled off of her, panting. Her body immediately protested the separation, so she turned over, tucking her face against his throat.

"Where's my phone?" she asked. "I'll look up what it could be."

He sat up slowly and glanced around. "Your purse is on the floor by the bathroom."

She didn't want to move. In fact, she wasn't even certain if she *could*. "Get it for me."

He looked like he wanted to tell her to fuck off and get it herself, but he didn't. Leo got up with a grumble, crawled towards her purse, and tossed her phone to her when he fished it out of her bag.

She patted the bed, summoning him back since her body was getting jittery without him there. He stretched out, and she backed up until her ass touched him before opening up her search engine app.

Spontaneous heat, she typed in.

The first few results were a smattering of scientific studies and medical websites all highlighting the same thing.

Ideal mates.

She made a sound of disgust, and he hovered over her shoulder. "What?"

Abby turned the screen so he could read it.

"What the fuck is that?"

"Not sure." She blinked rapidly to clear her vision. "You're not close enough."

He tucked even tighter against her.

She clicked into the first article, scanning the information to read it aloud for Leo's benefit. "'Ideal mates are rare alpha and omega pairings that have the maximum biological compatibility possible. A spontaneous heat can be induced in the omega portion of this pair if they spend either a considerable amount of time with the alpha or if they engage in various forms of sexual activity.' Aw, fuck."

"Okay, sex may have been a bad idea," he said, murmuring against her skin.

Abby continued reading. "'Spontaneous heats of this nature tend to be short lived and less intense than traditional heats, but the risks can be greater because they seem to occur without warning so little preparation is involved. In response, the alpha will enter a pseudo-rut which will make it more difficult for them to control themselves or think clearly.'"

She read further, and cold engulfed her body. "'Due to the lack of preparation and mental acuity of both partners during a spontaneous heat, the chances of pregnancy and unplanned permanent bonding are much higher than usual.'"

Abby whipped around and shoved his head to the side. Her bonding bite was an angry red over his scent gland. She leapt up on unsteady legs, dashing into the bathroom where she pulled aside her hair and stared at her throat in horror.

"FUCK!"

Leo appeared behind her. He paled. "Did we..."

"You bet your fucking ass we did." Abby sank to the floor and held her face in her hands. "God, this is worse than a drunk wedding. I can't get an annulment on a bond. This isn't fair. I don't want to be bonded to you."

"It's not exactly my first choice either." He sat next to her, resting his head against the wall. What a pair they must look: naked and distressed on a hotel bathroom floor.

"What now?" he asked.

She shrugged. "I wish I had an answer."

Leo set a tentative hand on her back. The simple contact had her blood sizzling as the heat crept back in.

"*Leo.*"

"Oh, shit. Did I start it up again?"

"Yep."

He scooped her up and took her to the bed. She squirmed in his arms as the heat fever demanded attention.

Leo set her down. Abby stretched out, shoving a pillow under her hips to raise her ass. He draped over her and sank into her dripping cunt. Groaning pitifully into the bed covers, she hooked her ankles around his calves. His growl reverberated through her, and she whined, grinding back into him. He dropped his head, inhaling her as he nipped her scent gland, sending a spiral of pleasure searing through her.

"Sweet fuck, you make it so hard to think." He caged her with his arms, keeping the bulk of his weight from crushing her as he moved. "Every time I breathe, I feel like I'm getting a drug hit."

Leo nuzzled the mark he'd left on her, licking over it until she was panting.

"Bite it," she demanded.

He sank his teeth against the gland as he continued fucking her, a sizzling spike of pleasure bolting through her blood. Leo growled, keeping her pinned in place as the friction drove her up the peak and tossed her over the edge. The heat hormones made her pliant, and they kept him energized and hard far past an alpha's usual abilities. Every cell in her body felt primed, riding out each wave with him driving her onward. She lost track after the fifth time she came. So little of the world existed outside of Leo. Only he and the bed beneath her kept her anchored.

Abby scaled one more peak of pleasure, and his groan melted into a whimper as her cunt squeezed his cock, milking him until he relaxed his weight against her back.

Leo stayed where he was, huffing and puffing in her ear.

"More." She wriggled beneath him. How she could possibly want more was beyond her understanding. She could barely move, yet she was still unsatisfied.

Stupid heat.

Leo let out a whine and rolled to the side, tucking her hips against him. His fingers dipped between her thighs to stroke her clit with a quick, relentless precision that had her shaking. Everything faded away again as she lost herself in him.

When she surfaced again, she unlatched her fingers from his hair. "It's cold."

"I've got it." Leo tugged the blanket over both of them.

He sighed against her skin and tucked her close.

The sky outside of their window had gone dark, the city lit with a blaze of neon to push back the night. They lay quietly, neither moving, both breathing heavily. She was so tired. The bone-deep craving for him had turned to exhaustion, and she succumbed before she could open her eyes to blink again.

Saturday Morning

"I have to pee," Leo said in her ear. "You're laying on my arm."

Abby let out a groan of protest and peeled open burning eyes. The sky had lightened, tinged softly with orange.

"You're supposed to hold it like a gentleman."

"Yeah, that's not happening. Unless you want me to piss all over you, you have to move."

"Fine." Abby grumbled, using what little energy she possessed to roll over. She debated whether or not she wanted to attempt getting up to pee as well. It seemed like so much effort when she could just hold it and fall back asleep.

He poked her leg, and she opened one annoyed eye to look at him.

"*What?*"

"Get up so I can take this nasty blanket off the bed."

"Help me."

"You can walk. I believe in you."

Abby contemplated a small tantrum, but the energy reserves weren't there. Instead, she staggered into the bathroom to relieve herself and rinse her face. She collapsed back onto the sheets, and Leo pulled her against him.

Sleep lured her back instantly. When she woke again it was to a knock on the door.

Why didn't anyone want her to sleep? She groaned and buried her face.

The scent of bacon and coffee was enough to break through the fog and she turned to see Leo half-dressed, wheeling a cart further into the room.

"What's happening?"

"It's conference time."

"Oh. Well, fuck." The hotel wall clock told her it was nearly seven. "How the hell am I getting through a conference while I'm in heat?"

"I've already got you covered. I had them send a few extra things up with breakfast." He sat in one of the chairs and pulled out a black bottle. "Got some scent-neutralizing wash and some weird gel they had to help mask bond bites. They also had an omega emergency pack. I have no idea if the birth control tablets in there will be effective, but take them anyway. I already took my own."

"How do you have the brain power for all of this after last night?"

"Turns out huffing those Abby fumes is great for energy, and once you fell asleep your scent calmed down a lot, so it no longer felt like my brain was melting out of my ears. I ordered a bunch of stuff from the front desk before I fell asleep."

"Oh. Uh, thanks?" She sat up all the way and scooted to the end of the bed. Leo poured her some coffee from the carafe, dropped a cube of sugar into it and passed over the steaming cup, being careful not to touch her.

Abby stared at the cup for a moment, lifting one eyebrow in question.

He shrugged. "You think I've worked with you for four years and never noticed how you like your coffee?"

"I never thought you'd care to notice," she said simply, taking a sip.

"Observation isn't the same as caring," he pointed out. "But it proves useful sometimes. Does that mean you don't know how I take mine?"

Her cheeks flushed. "Two creams, one sugar. But if you're bringing something in, I'm pretty sure it's a cinnamon dolce."

A soft smile tugged at the corner of his mouth. "See, proximity breeds familiarity."

Leo dropped the contraceptives onto the saucer for her, and she stuck them under her tongue to let them dissolve.

"I don't want to do the conference. What if I start up again?"

"You'll probably get fired if you skip out," said Leo, "and I'm not willing to let that happen. You're a pain in my ass, but no one is as good at your job as you and it wouldn't be fair for you or the company to suffer over something you can't help."

"You're being...surprisingly reasonable."

"Sometimes I'm like that." He poured himself some coffee, added the cream and sugar, and lifted the cover on their plates. "I have no idea what you eat for breakfast, so I got the basics. I figured we could both use the calories."

Abby stabbed a forkful of scrambled eggs and scarfed them down. "Why're you being so nice to me?"

"It's only fun to piss you off when you're at the top of your game," Leo said. "I'm not a complete monster that'll kick you when you're down."

At least that meant she could relax a bit. "What do we do if another wave gets triggered while I'm in public?"

"Then we find a secluded place, and I'll fuck you until it passes." He plucked up a strip of bacon and shoved it into his mouth.

She smothered down her body's unhelpfully excited reaction to those words. "God, today is going to be a nightmare."

"Undoubtedly." Leo nodded, biting into a piece of toast. "I'll stick close to you. There's no way I'm letting you wander around unattended, even with precautions."

She wasn't sure what to say. She'd never expected him to be accommodating to her needs or to want to look out for her. "Thank you."

"Thank me if we pull this off. Hurry up and eat so you can go wash me off of you."

They plowed through the food—blueberry pancakes, eggs, bacon, toast, and fruit salad—and she sucked back three cups of coffee before hauling herself into the shower.

The neutralizing wash did nothing to soothe her anxiety nor did masking the bond bite and carefully covering it with foundation so no one would ask about the fresh mark. She did her makeup, got dressed, and stood in front of the mirror wondering how easily people would be able to tell she was a few seconds off panicking.

"Keep it together, Dresden." Leo chided, fixing his tie in the mirror behind her.

"Easy for you to say."

"Oh, it's not easy at all. The second you cave, I'm getting roped in. We're bonded now, right? So, I'm painfully aware of you whether we like it or not, and I'm just praying I won't have a raging hard-on the whole day."

Abby smoothed down her pencil skirt and took a deep breath. "Let's get this hell day over with."

They walked down to the main hall where the various talks would be held and meetings would take place. Leo walked a step ahead of her, parting the sea of people so none of them touched her. She paid extra close attention to keep from walking into Leo. They'd avoided touching in case it triggered another wave, but Abby's anxiety was through the roof.

She *needed* to be able to focus, or she was going to be screwed with the company. Sure, there were laws in place to protect her as an omega—for needing time off for heats—but they could cite something else, make up an excuse to remove her if she fucked up this weekend. There were too many important people here.

Ordinarily, she loved conferences. It was always nice to speak to people with a passion for business, but today it was the last thing she wanted. Abby moved slowly and deliberately, missing the confidence that let her strut into any room, but it was hard to feel like a badass when she was stewing in a hormone soup that made her feel vulnerable. It was honestly too bad it wouldn't be socially acceptable for her to wander around with a blanket draped over her shoulders.

Fuck.

Her omega instincts were trying to make her nest.

"Leo," she whispered. He slowed and turned to face her. "I'm feeling freaked out."

"I don't know what I'm supposed to do about that."

"Well, I don't know either, but I have no one else to tell."

There were too many people. Too many alphas in the crowd. So much noise and enough scents to make her head spin. Nausea and anxiety churned her gut.

"Hey, okay, you look like you're about to pass out." Leo reached out and hooked an arm around her shoulders, guiding her to a quiet corner. As quiet as an alcove with thousands nearby could be, at least. "What do you need?"

Since she couldn't go back to their room, she wasn't entirely certain what would help. She curled her fingers around his lapels and tugged him in until she was sandwiched between him and the wall behind her. With him standing there, the throngs of people were blocked out. It settled the growing panic. If he hadn't been wearing the scent-neutralizing products, she'd have asked to breathe him in for a few moments, but this would have to do. She squashed down the part of herself that wanted to ask to hold his hand so that she could have a solid anchor point.

Her hands shook, and he set his own over them. "Deep breaths."

She tried. Abby used all her focus to stay steady. If anyone found out she was in heat, she'd have to leave the conference. She *needed* to figure out a way to get back into her bad bitch mentality, or she would be utterly fucked.

"I don't know if I can do this," she whispered.

"You *can*," Leo insisted. "Fuck, Abby, you're a goddamn force of nature. I've seen you cow the most confident people in the business. I know you can make it through this."

She nodded and closed her eyes, savoring a few more moments of the feeling of safety.

"I'll get you back to the room at every opportunity to rest, okay?"

"Okay." Abby straightened up, fighting against every instinct, and stepped out from the protective wall of his body.

Be a badass. Easy peasy.

She got through the first two talks, not absorbing a single word, but at least Leo had the forethought to record the audio for her. Next on the agenda was a long, and likely painful, lunch with some people they were supposed to schmooze to get on favorable terms for a contract.

Leo stopped short in front of her, and she walked straight into his back. Warmth rippled through her, and her lips parted in a soft gasp.

God*dammit.*

"Leo." She squeezed her thighs together and shivered at the pressure on her clit.

Abby bit down on the whimper that formed in her throat.

He turned to face her, realization sparking in his gaze the second he looked at her. "Aw, shit. Alright, let's see what we can find." Leo hooked his arm through hers and tugged her along.

They passed a dozen occupied rooms before finally finding an empty meeting room. Leo pushed her inside, swung the door shut behind them and dragged a couple chairs in front to block anyone from entering. It did little to calm her nerves. Anyone could still get in with a bit of force.

"Focus on me," Leo said. "I can't use scent to chill you out, so I need you to look at me."

He traced her body through her clothes, igniting the needy embers that burned beneath her skin. She held still. Leo kept eye contact, his dark eyes holding her captive as he peeled off her jacket and tossed it over the table. His breathing turned rough and his grip got stronger. He undid the buttons of her blouse with an agonizing slowness, his growl rumbling in his chest with each new inch of skin he uncovered. The shirt stayed on, hanging open to reveal the cream-colored lace beneath.

Leo dropped to his knees before her and unhooked the front clasp of her bra. He kept watching her as he took a nipple into his mouth, flicking with his tongue, the wet warmth enveloping her. Abby gasped and bit her lip, lifting her hands to cradle his head. Her nails dug into his scalp as she trembled, trying to stay silent.

She set her palm on the table to combat the wave of lightheadedness that overwhelmed her.

Leo lifted his head. "Keep looking at me. You're okay."

Abby fastened her gaze back onto him, a soft groan escaping as he went back to work, sucking at the stiff peak until she was vibrating in his arms.

"Leo," she whispered as he switched to her other breast. "Please, for the love of God."

He paused, giving a final flick with his tongue before he stood. Abby looked up at him, waiting for whatever came next. Leo took her face in his hands and kissed her. It was a slow, deep devouring that made her tingle down to her toes. Abby let herself fall into it, sinking into the warmth and taste of him, until she was drunk on that even without the petrichor to infuse her senses.

She whined into his mouth and pressed against him as he hiked up her skirt and kicked the rolling chairs aside.

"You'll be good for me, right?" Leo slid his hand up her chest until his palm sat against her throat.

She tipped her head back, following her instincts to give over control. "Yes."

"Turn around."

Abby was loath to lose contact, but she obeyed the instruction anyway. A firm hand on the back of her neck pushed until she was face down against the table. Her omega instincts had her squirming with excitement. The cool wood was a balm against the heat that simmered her blood even as it chilled her to the bone.

Leo pulled back to tug down her panties and undo his pants.

"Hurry *up*," she whined. Abby stood a little higher on her toes and held her breath, keeping her face resting on the table.

He yanked her hips closer, sinking into her already wet cunt. She grabbed onto the table with a moan, and he clapped a hand over her mouth.

"No one can catch us. We'll get thrown out."

Right.

She had to be quiet.

He took hold of her hips, setting a punishing pace that unraveled her. Abby cursed quietly, using one hand to brace herself and the other to keep herself muffled, a struggle considering how strong Leo was and how insistent his hips seemed to be to ruin her as quickly as possible. Each stroke undid her further. He kept his hand firm on the back of her neck as she squirmed and wriggled desperately.

Abby bit down on her fingers. Her thighs were going to bruise, but she found herself unable to care. She missed the overwhelming scent of petrichor to soothe her omega senses, but the touch was there, the heat and friction and ferocity that drove her to unrivaled heights.

Nothing mattered or existed beyond the hard table and Leo behind her. She couldn't even count how many times she'd imagined this exact scenario over the years. She'd wondered on countless occasions if it were possible to annoy him enough that he would silence her this way. Part of her had had it in mind every time they'd fought, each time she took it further, provoking as much passion from him as she could.

Her body seized as the first orgasm hit her.

Her vision filled with white, and she stuffed her clothed wrist into her mouth. Leo kept up his pace, and it took all her fortitude to smother down the sounds she wanted to make.

The world turned on its axis as he flipped her over, rolling her torso on the table, pulled off her panties entirely, and stepped between her thighs. She'd imagined this, too. Although, in her fantasies it had been one of their desks, everything shoved carelessly to the floor, rather than an empty conference room table.

She flicked off her heels using his ass to scoot them off her feet and dragged him in even closer. Abby reached down to stroke her clit, forgetting herself for a moment as she whimpered between the sharp sensation of pleasure and the deep satisfaction of him fucking into her.

"Open your mouth," Leo hissed. "Since you can't keep silent."

Abby did, confused until he stuffed the damp fabric of her discarded panties into them. She bit down. He cursed when she came again, her cunt gripping his cock, ensnaring him from within so that his pace faltered.

"*Fuck.*" He stared up at the ceiling before he began once more, putting his thumb to her clit in her stead until she was limp and exhausted beneath him.

Abby sighed when he finally slowed to a stop. Every bit of her felt like it was vibrating. She laid still, unable to summon the energy it would take to sit up. The blurred edges of heat in her vision receded, and she knew that—for the moment—the wave was over.

Leo leaned over her, plucking the fabric from her mouth and pressing a kiss there instead. He chuckled softly. "Who knew the best way to shut you up was also the hottest?"

She heaved another sigh, letting her body relax entirely.

"We only have five minutes until our lunch meeting, and you look thoroughly ravaged."

Abby remained unmoving, breathing slowly as she came down off the heat high. Hopefully it would satiate her for a few hours.

"Thank you," she murmured.

"Eh, you're welcome. Don't go getting soft on me about it."

Leo helped her sit up and tucked himself back into his pants. They smoothed each other out, fixing hair and clothing until they were presentable enough to risk being in public once more.

He moved the chairs from in front of the doors to do a cursory check outside before waving for her to join him. They were running slightly late for their lunch, but hopefully the people they were meeting wouldn't mind.

Abby asked about their reservation when they arrived at the restaurant, and the server took them to a crowded table near the windows. It was full of men in suits, most looking to be in their late forties or early fifties.

She froze, recognizing one face among the crowd.

Michael.

Leo stopped short, and Abby glanced to see if he recognized him as well. She couldn't tell, but he brushed off his initial reaction, greeting the group with a smile. The lot of them welcomed Leo like they'd been friends for years while barely giving her a second glance. Abby bristled. She didn't know if it was because she was a woman or because she was an omega—or even some other prejudice they kept tucked away in their shitty bigoted brains.

There was no reason for them to ignore her. She had an excellent reputation for her competence in the industry.

Abby and Leo sat at the two remaining chairs. Michael was staring at her.

"You're late," he said. "Unprofessional."

"Sorry about that," Leo replied. "We got a bit turned around on the way here. Have you all ordered?"

The ones nearest to them nodded. "Just the drinks," one said. "We're still waiting on food."

"Shall we get started with shop talk in the meantime?" Abby asked.

"No," Michael said tersely. "Whatever business you personally bring, I'd like nothing to do with it."

The group turned to him. "What's the point of the meeting if you've already decided that?" someone asked.

"I hadn't decided until I saw their faces." Michael sipped his water. "I met them both yesterday and have no desire to work with a company that has representatives so poorly behaved."

Leo opened his mouth, but Abby put a hand on his wrist.

"Michael," she said. "I'm surprised you understand the meaning of the word 'no.' You were so keen to ignore it when I used it last night."

He frowned. His colleagues glanced between the two of them.

Abby blatantly ignored Michael and looked at each of the others in turn. "Can I persuade any of the rest of you, or does your recalcitrant friend hold the power here?"

The alpha nearest to them cringed. "He's the CEO and has veto power."

"I see." Abby stood, and Leo followed suit. "Well, gentleman, I'm truly sorry that my bodily autonomy got in the way of business. Please do reach out to me or our company in the future when you get a CEO that possesses an ounce of respect for women and omegas. Have a wonderful day."

She managed to fend off trembling as she stalked away, Leo only a few steps behind her. When they turned the corner, she sucked in a panicked breath.

"God, I'm so fucked. I'm going to get fired."

"You won't. I was there when that asshole harassed you last night. I'll tell the president everything."

"It won't matter."

"It *will*," Leo insisted. "They can't expect you to make a deal with someone who cuts the whole thing because you wouldn't fuck him."

"I really think you're overestimating the amount of compassion our company president has. He likes me but not enough to overlook my being the reason we lost this deal."

Leo grabbed her hand and pulled her to a stop. "If he pulls that garbage I'll quit, too."

"*What?*"

"You might be a pain in the ass, but you're *my* pain in the ass now. We're bonded, and I'm not going to let douchebags treat you poorly."

Abby snorted. "Does that include you?"

"I'm trying to do the right thing here, and you're not making it easy."

"I've never intended to make your life easy, Leo, and you've never given an inch before this weekend to make things easier on me."

"Listen," he huffed. "I might give you a hard time when you're being an asshole, but I know you're damn good at your job and you deserve to have it. I'm not willing to work with or for a company that would fire you over this. Got it?"

She stared at him for a long moment before finally nodding. His integrity was sneaking to the surface. "Got it."

"Good."

They walked in silence back to the elevators and to their room. Abby paused inside as Leo closed the door.

"I'm sorry I freaked out."

"Don't be," said Leo. "I wanted to deck him. I can only imagine how you felt."

"Not great." Abby sighed and sat down. "This weekend feels like it's lasted for a year already."

"Are you feeling up to the rest of the conference?"

"Honestly, I'm not sure. I'm pretty certain I'm getting my ass handed to me on Monday. It's difficult to muster up the energy when I already feel like trash."

"Okay." Leo walked around to the other side of the bed and pulled back the blankets.

"What're you doing?"

"Making you rest." He stripped out of his suit before climbing under the sheets and patting the spot next to him. "Get in."

Abby hesitated but still took her clothing off as well. She slipped into the bathroom before joining him, using a washcloth to scrub away the residue of the protective patch on her scent gland, and to rub away the remnants of the scent-neutralizing body wash. Abby tossed him a cloth and he did the same before she stretched out next to him. Her omega senses were over the goddamn moon that she was finally laying down in bed with her alpha.

"Bodies are stupid." Abby dragged one of the pillows over and held it against her chest, relaxing into Leo. "Who the fuck let evolution come up with this bullshit? *Ideal* mates? There's nothing ideal about us together."

He laughed quietly, burying his nose against her throat. Petrichor filled the air around her, and she lounged comfortably.

"I dunno. You're not the person I ever thought I'd have attached to me, but we make a decent enough team."

"The perfect work rivals bonded pair. God, we're a disaster. We can't be together, Leo."

"No, and we won't be," Leo said. "We'd drive each other to homicide if we attempted an actual relationship. But we're still bonded. Permanently."

"We're going to be the laughing stock of the office. Who the hell accidentally does a permanent bond in this day and age?”

“We are *not* telling anyone. The company gets weird about relationships, and we’re both on track for the VP position. We’re not giving them an opportunity to get rid of us for some idiotic policy.”

“Oh, right.” She pouted. “I forgot about that rule.”

“It’s a power grab. There’s no reason to prevent mates from working at the same company, but that’s just my opinion.”

“How the fuck are we navigating this going forward?” Abby asked.

“Elaborate, please.”

“Well, I certainly don’t intend to remain single for the rest of my life, and there’s no way in hell I’m marrying you.”

“Agreed on all counts,” he said.

“How do you date when you’re permanently bonded?”

“People can bond to more than one person. If they want to. There’s multiple scent glands that can be used for it. The throat is just the most common.”

“So, we...carry on?” she asked.

“I’m not sure what else we would do. We can meet up for your heats if you want to, but the rest is life as usual.”

Abby contemplated in silence. Leo was far too irritating to consider living with, but a heat partner would at least make her insurance company happy about not having to put out cash for a heat service. She wasn’t too keen on seeing what it would be like to try now that she was bonded anyway.

“Go to sleep, Abby,” Leo ordered. “No big decisions until your heat is over.”

She grumbled and settled in. Her omega side was pleased as punch and pulled her into the shadows of sleep almost instantly.

Saturday Evening

"Hey, Abbs," Leo's voice nudged her awake.

"What?" She yawned and stretched luxuriously.

"There's still time for the cocktail evening, if you want to go."

"Not really, but I did pack a nice dress. It would be a shame to waste it."

"Should we test how close a new wave is?" Leo asked.

"How? I'm already stretched out naked next to you."

Leo tucked in close to her throat, licking over the scent gland before giving it a sharp nip.

"Sweet *fuck*," Abby gasped. The rise of heat didn't come, only the pleasure of the bite. Relief sank into her bones. "I think we're clear."

"Good to know." He patted her butt. "Get your ass out of bed, and get dressed."

Moving seemed like a task and a half, but she rolled away from him and shuffled into the bathroom.

She pulled her red dress out of the garment bag and slipped it on. It clung to every inch of her, cutting off just above the knee and hooking around her neck in a thick-collared halter. Now that her heat seemed to be over, she could skip the protective patch, focusing instead on her hair and makeup touch-ups. Leo appeared behind her in a sharp black suit.

"You should wear that more often," said Abby. She was doomed if he did because sweet *fuck* he looked incredible. "It looks good."

She noticed the barest hint of pink flush on his cheeks.

"Only if you wear more red to the office."

If it would make him blush in public, then she was certainly willing to do it.

"Consider it done." She added a swipe of lipstick, and they went together down to the main event in the ballroom.

It was crowded and loud, but that was where Abby thrived when she didn't feel like she'd been run over. She strode in with confidence and immediately spotted people she knew. Leo went to the bar, and she went to socialize, mingling her way around the vast room over the next couple of hours. Old friends from university and previous jobs were happy to catch up and make plans for coffee, dinners, and business meetings.

She kissed her old college roommate on the cheek, parting with the promise to get together next month.

"Abigail Dresden?"

Abby turned to see Michael standing there, signature whisky in hand. "What?"

"I looked into you," he said, his gaze sweeping her head to toe.

"And?"

"You have an exemplary career, top marks at your university, top internships during and afterward."

She eyed him with suspicion. "You don't have to recite my own CV to me."

"I'm merely reminding you of what you'd be throwing away by making an enemy out of me."

"*Excuse me*? Me, make an enemy of you? You're the harasser here."

"It shouldn't have come to that." He tapped the rim of his glass. "A good omega knows their place."

"Guess I'm a shitty omega then." Abby's hackles rose. "And I don't know where you got these fucked up ideas, but there is no *place* for me to be put into."

"I—and other alphas like me—would disagree."

"Then I'll pray to never meet another one like you."

"I can avoid telling your employer how abhorrently you behaved towards me at lunch and how poorly you're treating their potential business partner now, if you come to my room tonight."

"Fuck you."

Michael sighed. "You know I take no pleasure in ruining your career."

"Then *don't*." Abby's heart thundered in her chest. "There's literally nothing forcing you to do anything."

"Oh, my dear, that's simply not true. *You* force me."

Abby steadied herself, all of her instincts telling her to strike or flee, but neither would work here. Someone like him was too used to power.

"Listen, I'm really sorry that you've never made a partner come in your life, but you need to tone down your misplaced anger."

Michael frowned, looking very much like he'd never had anyone speak to him with anything but the utmost respect. He bared his teeth. "Well, now I think I'll rather enjoy taking you down a few pegs."

"Good luck with that, asshole."

Michael grabbed her wrist when she tried to step past him. A growl rose in her chest, but, before she had a chance to react, Leo's hand locked around Michael's arm.

"You take your fucking hands off my mate *now*." Leo brought himself up to his full height and stepped between them as Michael let go of Abby.

Michael shook him off, looking between them, amused. "Mates, is it? You were so eager to avoid me that you bound yourself to the next alpha you saw?"

"Don't think so highly of yourself," Abby snapped. "You're such a jackass, ruining a nice evening. I will *never* fuck you, but you can bet your sweet ass I'm going to fuck *him*," she gestured to Leo, "so enjoy the thought of what you'll never get your hands on, you misogynistic omegist prick."

She was seething by the time she got out of the ballroom and whirled around to see Leo right behind her.

"Want me to break his nose?" Leo asked. "I would *really* love to break his nose."

"No, it's fine. I don't want you to get arrested." Abby paused out of sight. "You didn't have to defend me."

"Only *I* am allowed to give you a hard time. Everyone else can meet my fist or my lawyer."

Abby bit her lip to contain a smile. "Well, thank you."

"It's cool." Leo shrugged. "Now we're *both* getting fired."

"We're a bit doomed," Abby agreed. "I'm half-tempted to leave this stupid conference tonight."

"We could if you want to. It's only a three hour drive home."

"You don't think that's taking the coward's way out?"

"Doesn't matter if it is. We'll have a shitshow on our hands come Monday regardless of whether we stay or not."

"Okay, that's true," said Abby. "What if we left in the morning instead? We can get expensive room service and have a last fuck before we return to real life and the smoldering remains of our futures."

Leo laughed. "I like the way you think. Let's do that."

They put in the order when they arrived back in their room.

"I feel like I got dressed up for nothing," she said, twirling in front of the hotel mirror.

"Nah, not for nothing," said Leo. "Everyone got to see how smokin' hot you are, *and* you get to peel yourself out of that while I watch. Win-win."

She spun one of the chairs and sat down. "You first. Strip for me. I've been too distracted to properly enjoy what you look like."

His eyes smoldered. "Yes, ma'am."

Leo removed his suit jacket and set it aside with care. He took his time undoing his shirt buttons, his eyes never leaving hers.

Easy confidence radiated off of him. He flicked the shirt open when he reached the last button and moved to his belt. It was hard to appreciate the visage of each new bit of skin he revealed when she couldn't seem to look away from his face. She bit her lip as he slipped the belt free.

By the time he was bare, she was squirming in her seat. He braced a hand on each arm of her chair and leaned in, inhaling her scent as he nipped her throat.

"You are entirely too dressed."

How had she gone the last four years without this? "I am, aren't I? You should fix it."

Leo flashed a wicked smile, sinking down in front of her. "Stand."

His hands snaked up her legs as she stood, lifting the bottom of her dress. He toyed with her garters and pulled her panties down, letting her step out of them. She'd worn them overtop so they'd be easier to remove without undoing the garters.

Leo pulled down her zipper slowly and rose up, bringing the rest of the dress with him, leaving her only in bra, garters, and stockings. She shivered at the sudden rush of cool air on her body.

"Get on the bed, Leo."

"Make me," he said with a smirk.

Abby walked him backwards and pushed. Leo toppled back with a whoosh of air. She tossed her bra and heels aside but kept the stockings and garters as she climbed into his lap. He inched them further onto the bed and held her hips, guiding her onto his waiting cock.

She groaned, riding him slowly, enjoying the leisurely pace now that the last heatwave had passed. When she opened her eyes, he was watching her with a smug smile on his lips, his head pillowed by one folded arm.

"What?" she asked, pausing.

"Just admiring. You told me I could after I got you off, but then you were too rushed so I didn't get to enjoy."

"Oh." A blush warmed her cheeks, and she resumed the slow undulations that had her sighing. "Carry on, then."

"I intend to." He slid a hand up her torso and cupped her breast, thumb teasing the nipple. "You're a nice view."

"You're not so bad yourself." She leaned forward, bracing both hands on his chest, her hair falling around her.

"I know." Leo laughed when she threw him a withering glare.

"Modesty is not one of my virtues, and I know it's not one of yours either. I'm not going to pretend to be humble."

She squeezed his cock with her cunt and earned a stuttering groan from him. It was a sound she'd grown rather fond of over the course of the weekend. Abby fucked him slowly until his muscles seized and he cried out, pressing his hips up into her.

He nudged her by her ass until she was kneeling over his face. Leo pressed down on her thighs and buried his face in her cunt with a voracious tongue until she was shaking and panting. He held firm, never letting her squirm away, stroking her clit with his tongue like it was his one job in life.

Abby held his hair in a tight fist. Her other hand braced on the wall was the only thing keeping her upright. She came hard and fast with a desperate sob and rocked her hips as briskly as her exhausted limbs would allow.

She flopped to the side when he finally let her free. Leo rolled, tucking himself around her.

"We should go to conferences more often," he said, laughing.

Abby groaned and whacked him with one of the pillows. "Shut up, Leo."

Two Weeks Later

"It's negative," said Abby, holding up the pregnancy test. "Now, can we please get back to business?"

"Hold on." Leo held up his hand, waiting. Abby rolled her eyes and smacked her hand against his in a high five. "The dream team remains a twosome!"

"It does, and will forever. Now let's get back to the business plan, so we're not moldering on the streets six months from now."

"Okay, okay." Leo grinned and turned his computer screen toward her. "I came up with the best idea to spite-ruin Michael's company once we get off the ground."

She read over what he'd written out, growing more impressed with each line. "This is really good."

"I know." He smirked. "Being fired has only made me smarter and more determined to ruin all those fuckers."

"God," Abby murmured, "we are way too alike."

"Don't pretend you don't love it."

"Couldn't if I tried."

Abby sipped at her coffee. Nothing seemed real anymore. Had it only been two weeks since she'd gotten herself bonded to her rival and set her career on fire? Everything had changed. Leo might be a pain in the ass, but dammit, he was her pain in the ass. And they were going to take the world by storm.

Heat Play Love

Gray

Heats make him desperate and that's the opposite of what he needs to be with his mate out of town. Their alpha roommate is too tempting, and all too willing to give Gray everything he shouldn't be asking for.

Lyall

His best friend's mate shouldn't be on his radar. But when Gray's heat starts early and Mateo is away at a conference, it's all too easy for Lyall to imagine what it would be like for the omega to give in. He would do anything for Gray, and maybe that's exactly what Mateo wants.

Mateo

He knows that Gray is in good hands with Lyall while he's away. His mate going into heat wasn't in the plan and nothing short of disaster would stop him from getting home to Gray. Will he arrive in time? Or will Gray end up with two alphas?

Content notes: This omegaverse story is m/m/m and contains a spontaneous heat, knotting, nesting, purring, growling, and biting. Birth control is readily accessible in my omegaverse for all genders, sexes, and dynamics. No one is having babies unless they really want to.

There will be phone/video sex, light bondage, sex toys, butt play, threesomes, masturbation and mild sensory deprivation It's pretty fluffy so don't worry about any dark content. Just spicyness, sweetness, and a cinnamon roll alpha.

Chapter One

"Don't go." Gray clung to his mate in the entryway. The omega tucked perfectly under his mate's chin, his fingers curled in the soft cashmere Mateo wore.

"I don't want to." Mateo dropped his weekend bag to the floor and kissed the top of Gray's head. "I have to."

Gray stepped back to look at his mate, even though Mateo was already burned into his soul. He memorized each of Mateo's black curls, the stubble set into deep bronze skin, and the flash of mischief in dark chocolate eyes. Gray sighed. Mateo was simply too beautiful.

"I know you have to leave." He buried his face against Mateo's throat, inhaling the faint scent of ginger and juniper. "But I hate it."

"This could get me a promotion which would mean I wouldn't have to travel so much." Mateo held Gray so tightly the omega could barely breathe. "We really need the money with both you and Lyall out of work now. I'll be home in five days. A conference, a couple days of client meetings, and then I'll be back."

Gray knew all these things objectively, but it made Mateo's impending absence no easier to deal with. If anything, it made him feel even guiltier for being fired. While he knew it wasn't technically his fault, his guilt didn't respond to logic.

"You have company, at least," Mateo reminded Gray.

The omega tried not to pout. As much as he liked Lyall, he

wasn't Mateo, and Gray had been extra needy with his mate going to the conference.

Lyall had hung back, but he was visible out of the corner of Gray's vision. The other alpha hovered near the kitchen so that he wouldn't intrude on the mates' goodbye. He was a little taller and leaner than Mateo, with golden skin, strawberry blond hair, and bright blue eyes. Both alphas were beautiful, but Mateo was his safe space. Lyall had been friends with them for years, a lover on occasion, and now a roommate since getting laid off last month.

"Babe," Mateo murmured. "I'm going to be late if I don't leave. There's a work dinner tonight."

"Okay, okay." Gray stepped back, trying to rein in the riot of emotions that sang in his blood. It was simply *wrong* for Mateo to be leaving. The flood of apprehension he experienced was easy to attribute to the stress he'd been dealing with lately, and it wore down his defenses. He'd been all over the place since he'd gotten fired and he craved security to subdue his anxiety.

"I'll call you when I arrive." Mateo gave Gray a last kiss and slipped away.

Despair fell over the omega. He leaned against the door and tried not to cry.

"You want some hot chocolate?"

He turned towards the voice. Lyall was watching him from the kitchen entryway.

"Yes, please," said Gray.

Sugar was his crutch in times of hardship and their roommate seemed more than willing to indulge him.

"Hug, too?" Lyall asked. "Or treat only?"

Gray had never been one to turn down physical affection. "Hug, too, please."

The alpha met him in a few strides, moving with a lithe grace that Gray had always admired. He never felt particularly graceful but felt even less so when his roommate was moving around the house like some sort of majestic panther.

Gray sank into the waiting embrace and he couldn't help but make comparisons to Mateo. Lyall's scent was balsam fir and honey, a complement to Mateo's juniper and ginger. Similar enough to be comforting but not close enough to soothe Gray in the same way. Lyall's heart beat a steady pace beneath lean muscle. The omega curled his fingers into the back of Lyall's shirt, squeezing until his hands trembled.

The alpha puffed out an *oof* and a grunt. "You're crushing me."

Gray leapt back, embarrassed. "Sorry."

Lyall chuckled softly. "It's okay. Come on, let's get you that treat. I'll add extra marshmallows."

Ordinarily, extra marshmallows would have improved Gray's mood, but Mateo leaving was still too fresh. "Is it okay if I sit for a little bit?"

Lyall's gaze searched Gray's face and curled a soft hand into his hair. "Whatever you need."

The omega shivered.

He slid to the floor as the alpha disappeared into the kitchen. The entryway was chilly, the cold providing a helpful anchor to keep Gray from spiralling. He occupied himself with tracing the delicate dips and ridges in the stone tile, grounding himself in the repetitive, mindless motion while listening to Lyall fussing around in the kitchen with the hot chocolate.

Lyall returned as Gray continued to wallow, passing him a cup topped with whipped cream. Gray accepted the cup and absently licked off the cream in delicate laps to make the confection last. He plucked off each marshmallow one by one to savor them, letting each melt on his tongue. Marshmallows were the food of the gods. He sucked the sweet cream off each of them before sipping at the drink portion.

Gray became hyper-aware of Lyall watching him, unsure if it was curiosity, concern, or...something else that prompted the attention. The alpha's gaze had been fixated on his every movement. Gray continued to lick his fingers clean, sliding each into his mouth in turn, lips puckering softly as he sucked off the sticky bits.

Lyall continued to sit next to him without speaking. Gray tried not to notice how the alpha's breathing shifted.

By the time Gray finished the drink he was settled, if a lot more conscious of Lyall's proximity to him and the low warmth that thrummed at the base of his own spine.

"Are you doing okay?" Lyall asked.

"As okay as can be expected," said Gray. "The sugar worked some of its magic, though. Thank you for the treat."

"Anything for you, sweetheart." Lyall winked.

Gray's cheeks flushed at the endearment. It was hardly new for it to be used, but it usually only came out during more intimate moments.

"I should accomplish things," Gray mused. He stretched out and wiggled his toes. There was no shortage of chores to be done—and he hated having tasks incomplete—but it would take time to gather the energy needed to finish anything.

Lyall frowned. "But you're sad."

"I can be sad and accomplish things at the same time." Gray held his hands out. "Help me up?"

"Will you at least take it easy? I worry about your stress making you sick."

If the concern hadn't been so heavy in Lyall's voice, then Gray would have rolled his eyes, but he checked the reaction. "I won't do a lot, but I want to get some chores done. It's the only time I feel useful lately."

Despite being untethered when he was home all day with no clear direction, Gray supposed it was still better than the work environment he'd left. He never figured out why that beta and his friends had hated him, but they'd made the workplace so hostile that Gray had frequently called Mateo on his lunch break in tears. Being fired had been kind of a relief, even with the financial burden he knew it would bring.

The alpha took Gray's hands and hoisted him up.

"You know, you don't have to be *useful*. You're allowed to just be."

Gray chewed his lip. "Logically, yes, I know that. *However*, I can't stop feeling otherwise so you're going to have to let me do my thing."

Lyall wrapped him in a hug.

Every nerve in Gray's body flew to attention, and he clapped a hand over his mouth to smother the moan that climbed up his throat. His vision wavered, black spots dancing and swirling so much he needed to hold onto Lyall to remain upright. The alpha supported him until he was steady again.

"I think I should go lay down." Gray's voice sounded foreign to his own ears. "I must be more stressed than I realized."

Lyall didn't outwardly question the decision, but the omega saw the curiosity plain as day on his face. Gray turned away and retreated upstairs to the room he shared with Mateo. He threw himself onto the bed, burying his head under one of the pillows. His heart pounded, a drum in his ears, choking choked off his air with the force of each beat. Gray squeezed his eyes shut. He forced in sweet lungfuls of air that still smelled like his mate, shivering as he tucked himself under the blankets.

The omega fell into a fitful sleep and woke in the night. His head ached, and his mouth felt like he'd been sucking on cotton. Sliding gingerly out of bed, he padded down the stairs in search of water. The entire house was dark. He moved as quietly as he could manage, navigating by the glimpses of street lights through the windows until he arrived in the kitchen.

His ears perked to every sound. The gentle creak of the floorboards, the hum of the refrigerator, the...moan?

Gray froze.

It sounded again, emanating through the door to the basement. He stared at it, warmth infusing his blood. He palmed the front of his pants where his cock stood erect against the fabric. The omega whined, biting his sleeve to muffle the sound. He inched closer to the door and pressed his ear against it.

Gray pushed down the waistband of his pants and wrapped his hand around his cock, stroking it softly while he listened to Lyall likely doing the same. The alpha groaned and muttered something

Gray couldn't discern. Gray bucked his hips, thrusting through his fist while he laid his forehead against the door, panting.

He moaned.

What was the matter with him? Mateo had only been gone for a few hours, and his self control was usually so much better than this. Images flooded his brain. Flickering memories of Mateo. Of Lyall. When they'd all been naked and he'd been deliciously at their mercy. It only made things worse that he knew what Lyall felt like, how he tasted, how he shuddered when Gray had wrapped lips around his sweet cock...

He growled and cursed as he came sharply, spilling over the door and dripping onto the floor.

Gray stared at the mess, half dazed.

"Fuck."

The omega pulled off his sweater and frantically wiped everything, stumbling back when the door swung open. He landed with an *oomph* on the floor, panic lancing through him. A spear of light from the stairway illuminated Gray. Embarrassment overwhelmed him. He knew what he must look like—hair tousled, cheeks flushed, dick out with a cum-smeared sweater tossed haphazardly to the floor.

"Gray? What..." Lyall trailed off. His pupils blew wide and his nostrils flared.

Alarm spurred Gray on, snatching up the sweater, dashing up the stairs as quickly as he could manage. He slammed the bedroom door shut behind him and sank to the floor.

"Fuck. Fuck. *Fuck!*" He tugged at his hair, breaking into a sob.

A few minutes later there was a soft knock. "Sweetheart, are you alright?"

No.

He curled up even smaller, wrapping his arms around his knees.

Lyall knocked again. "Can I come in?"

Gray hiccuped.

"Please?" Lyall asked. "I want to make sure you're okay."

The omega scooted away from the door and put himself somewhat back together. He tucked himself back into his pants and threw the sweater under the bed so Lyall wouldn't see it.

"Come—" Gray croaked. "Come in."

The door opened slowly and Lyall peeked inside. "Sweets, what's wrong?"

"I don't know." Gray swiped at his wet eyes. "I think I might be sick. I don't feel like me. Nothing feels right."

"What about a heat?" Lyall asked softly. "Would that make you sick?"

"Maybe? My symptoms aren't usually that bad leading up to things, and I'm always so regular. I'm not due for another month and a half."

"Okay. Maybe it *is* stress or a flu or something." Lyall nodded sympathetically. "Let's get you into bed."

Gray flinched at the wording.

"Just sleeping. I'm going to go back downstairs to let you rest once you're settled."

Lyall moved slowly and easily, letting his hand hover for a moment before touching Gray, giving the omega the chance to move away. He held still. The alpha scooped him up and set him onto the bed. The covers were still kicked back from when Gray had climbed out. Lyall tucked him in with a tenderness that undid Gray.

The omega burst into tears. "I'm sorry."

Lyall raised a curious eyebrow. "For?"

"I didn't mean to..." Gray trailed off and Lyall hushed him.

"Stress does weird things to the body and mind. Don't worry about it."

Gray nestled in, tugging the blanket up to his nose. "Thank you."

"I'll get you some water." Lyall disappeared while Gray stewed in his discomfort. The alpha returned, setting the glass on the bedside table. "Mateo arrived safely. He called while you were asleep and phoned me to make sure you were okay. I imagine he's gone to bed already, but you can phone him tomorrow."

Misery spread through Gray. He sniffled. He'd missed Mateo's call when he needed his mate the most.

"You good, sweetheart?"

"I guess." Gray pouted. He was lonely and craving touch, but he didn't dare ask Lyall to stay with him when he was feeling so erratic. "You can go. I'll be fine."

Lyall hesitated but finally nodded. "Okay. Let me know if you need anything."

Gray tucked fully under the blanket, too embarrassed to say anything else.

When the silence assured him he was entirely alone, he kicked the blanket off and stared at the ceiling in the darkness. Shadows danced across it as cars on the street drove past, their headlights bursting through the small gaps in the curtains.

Restless, Gray squirmed.

He climbed out of bed to pace the room. Back and forth and back and forth. His whole body felt like a shaken champagne bottle, and no amount of movement seemed to diminish the energy.

Gray picked up his phone to text Mateo.

Gray:
Are you awake?

Mateo:
I can be
What's up?

Gray pressed the video call button. Mateo answered on the first ring. "Babe?"

"I need you." Gray's voice came out with more whine than intended.

Mateo's breath stuttered, setting goosebumps rolling over Gray's skin. "I'm here. What do you need?"

"I need my brain to shut off. I can't fall asleep again, and I wanted to see you."

"You're really making me regret going on this work trip." Mateo chuckled softly. "If I were there I know exactly what we could do to shut off that brain."

Gray gazed pleadingly at the screen. His cock was back at full attention, his whole body quivering at the smolder in his mate's eyes. "We could pretend."

A low purr rumbled through the speakers, and it gratified him to know the idea pleased his partner.

"Go get whatever you like from the supplies then come back," Mateo ordered.

Gray scampered off to root around in the box under the sink. He pulled out a suction cup dildo, grabbed a bottle of lube from the medicine cabinet, and trotted back to the bed.

"What did you get?"

"The white one." Gray held it aloft so Mateo could see. "I figured the suction cup would help with the illusion."

"Put on the leather harness, too. The full body one."

Gray nodded and fished it out from the closet, laying the complicated net of black leather over his pale skin. He settled back onto the bed, setting his phone on the bedside table and kneeling so everything was visible.

Mateo growled low. "Touch yourself for me."

Breathless with wanting, Gray asked, "Where?"

"We'll go top to bottom, get you all riled up by the time we get to where you're wanting attention."

Gray tipped his head back, an offering that displayed his throat to his alpha. The omega quivered as he traced his fingertips down the sensitive skin, turning one way, then the other, dragging his nails gently over the scent glands in his neck. He followed the pattern of the leather, sliding off course to tweak his nipples.

Mateo growled again. Gray looked at the screen to see his mate already attending to his own waiting cock. Mateo looked at Gray as though he were a snack to be devoured.

"Stay there," said Mateo.

Gray bit his lip and toyed with the stiff peaks under his mate's watchful gaze. The omega squirmed, each brush and pinch sending a spiral of sensation straight to his cock, an arc of electricity that had him panting.

"So perfect." Mateo groaned. "A little harder now."

Gray pinched both nipples in tandem. A gasp left his lips, and he whimpered as he squeezed tighter, panting and squirming against the intensity of it.

"Hold." Mateo's voice was gravelly, laced with power.

Shivers wracked Gray's body as he obeyed.

"Release."

The omega dropped his hands and sucked in sharp lungfuls of air. His cock strained, the head weeping, beading pearlescent liquid at the tip.

"Keep going, babe, but I don't want you giving that sweet cock any attention yet."

Gray whined but still obeyed, sliding his palms over his stomach until his hands diverged and slid down each thigh, dragging back up with his nails scraping when he hit the knee.

"Mateo, *please*."

The alpha laughed. Goosebumps broke over Gray's skin at the sound.

"Impatient and desperate is my favorite."

The dark flash in his mate's eyes had Gray trembling with need.

"Where's your collar?"

"Bedside table." Gray grabbed it and fastened the thick leather around his throat. It comfortably fit two fingers beneath it, but if he angled his head just right it felt like Mateo's hand wrapped around him.

"There's my perfect little omega. So well behaved for me." Mateo smiled, lazily, dangerously. "Have you been good?"

Gray flinched. He *hadn't* been good. He shook his head.

Mateo clucked his tongue. "I see. Get the clamps, too, then. I'm in the mood to tease you for a while."

A thrill danced up Gray's spine as he located the clamps with silver bells dangling from them.

"Now?" He asked.

"Mhmm," Mateo purred. "One at a time. Nice and slow."

Gray teased one nipple to attention again and applied the clamp. His cock twitched as the nerves fired. He did the same to the other and panted desperately to keep his composure. The bells danced, providing a cheerful song to his divine misery.

"Touch your cock for me. But," said Mateo, "no coming. You can touch only with two fingertips and only as long as I say."

The omega nodded and rubbed the weeping tip with his middle and pointer fingers. It took all of his will to not buck against his hand. He revelled in the feel, even as unsatisfactory as it was when he wanted to wrap his fist around himself and thrust into it until he came undone.

"Stop." The smooth baritone was like a rich whiskey, beautiful and potent as it denied Gray his release. The omega shook as he pulled his hand away.

"Hmm," Mateo mused. "Present for me."

A deep, primal longing fizzed in Gray's blood as he turned, pressed his face to the bed and lifted his ass into the air. The alpha groaned and the slickness of him fucking his lubed fist was audible as Gray lay there, waiting for further instruction.

"Fuck, you're beautiful. I wish I wasn't so far away. I could ruin you until you forget your own name."

Gray trembled and moaned into the sheets.

"Get the lube. Start prepping yourself."

The omega squeezed a dollop of lube onto his fingers and stroked them between his ass cheeks from his prone position. He slipped in the first finger,meeting no resistance. Gray bit the sheets. He moved the finger in slow circles, plunging in and out methodically before adding another lubed finger. Mateo's pitching groans emanating from the phone. Gray thrust his fingers agonizingly slowly, listening to his mate.

"Another," Mateo growled.

Gray added a third finger and pressed back against his hand, chanting his mate's name.

"Get the dildo. Lube it up," said Mateo. "I want to watch it sink into you before you start fucking yourself on it.

The omega did as he was told, positioning the tip to push inside of him. Mateo started counting backward from twenty and Gray followed the beats, inching it inward, gasping as it spread him open and filled him up. He pushed until the base hit his ass and waited.

"*Fucking* hell. I already regret having to leave, but you're going to make me despise being away."

"Please," murmured Gray. "I need you."

"Get the dildo on the headboard, babe."

Gray mewled as he removed it from his ass and then slammed the dildo against the headboard so it stuck.

"Get yourself on that cock."

Mateo's voice sent a ripple of lust straight down the omega's spine. Gray backed up, angling the toy until he could feel the pressure he craved.

The alpha groaned. Gray looked over at the screen to see Mateo teasing the tip of his cock. "Come on, babe. Let me in."

Gray shuddered and pressed back, letting the toy stretch him open while he muttered incoherently into the sheets. When he hit the base he paused and tried to catch his breath. His blood felt like it was vibrating and he mewled.

"Keep going," Mateo ordered. "Fuck yourself on it so I can watch you come undone."

Gray slid off and thrust back. The bells of his nipple clamps jingled. He did it again while Mateo muttered encouragement. Each time he got too fast, too excitable, Mateo would slow him down again, prolonging the sweet torture until Gray's brain couldn't hold a single coherent thought.

The soundtrack of dancing bells, slick skin, and ragged gasping punctuated the quiet of the night. He drowned in the friction, fighting against the rising tide of pleasure at Mateo's behest, eager to obey his alpha but desperate for permission to let himself be pulled under.

Gray buried his face in the sheets, biting them to muffle the strongest of his moans as he rocked his hips.

"Go ahead, babe." Mateo's voice broke through the haze in Gray's mind. "I'm so close."

The omega lost himself to the sensation, slamming his hips into the toy, each thrust spreading him open and striking the sensitive spot buried inside him. Every movement forced incoherent sounds out of him. Mateo growled, low and deep, and the sound electrified Gray as much as the slapping sound of Mateo fucking his own fist.

Gray slammed back once more, wrapping a shaking hand around his cock. His vision turned white. His muscles squeezed around the toy until he could barely breathe.

He collapsed to the bed, sweaty and satisfied, little ripples of pleasure ricocheting through his body. He turned to the screen and found that Mateo had already come. He'd missed it in the depths of his own orgasm.

"Fuck, I wish I could have been there." Mateo settled back, mopping himself up with cheap hotel tissues.

Gray nuzzled the sheets and brought the phone closer to his face. "It's okay. I know your work is important. And you're here like this which is better than nothing."

"I assume you're feeling better? Lyall said you were fast asleep when I called earlier."

"Mhmm. Much better, thank you." Gray puffed out a sigh, utterly content. The fizzing sensation that had aggravated him before had calmed, and he stretched out, relaxed with his alpha's voice in his ear. "I just needed you, I guess."

Mateo laughed softly. "I'm always happy to give you whatever you need."

"I know. I love you."

"I love you, too." Mateo yawned. "Make sure you clean yourself up before you fall asleep. Call me if you need anything, okay?"

"I will. Goodnight."

"Night."

Gray ended the call and took his time gathering everything up. He rinsed himself clean in the shower and washed the toy as well, before climbing into bed, his thoughts laden with filth that no amount of water could remove.

Chapter Two

Gray woke far more settled than the previous day, but he still dreaded going downstairs. How was he supposed to look Lyall in the eye after he'd been caught? The omega kicked his feet and rolled over, grumbling into the sheets.

His phone buzzed.

Mateo:
Morning <3
How're you feeling today?

Gray:
Better <3
Thank you for last night
I miss you :(

Mateo:
Only three more nights
I'll call you when I have a break
Love you <3

Gray:
I shall await
Love you too <3 <3 <3

Gray got ready for the day slowly, steadfastly refusing to think about what might await him downstairs. Instead, he indulged in a long shower before starting on some chores. After an hour of Gray rustling around and scrubbing the bathroom, Lyall knocked on the bedroom door.

"I hope you're not skipping breakfast because of me."

The omega's cheeks flared with warmth. "Nope. Definitely not."

"Uh huh. Super convincing." Lyall parked himself on the bed. "You don't have to be weird. It's not the first time I've seen you in that state."

Gray squeaked and scrubbed harder at the bathtub. "That's not the point."

"Okay, well, if you're going to be embarrassed and avoid me, then you have to at least eat while you do that. I'm going to go out to run some errands so you have some space and don't feel the need to hide up here all day."

Gray waited, frozen in silence, until he was certain Lyall had left the room. He padded out and paused at the top of the stairs, listening intently for any sign of the alpha. Hearing none, he raced downstairs and dove straight into the fridge where he found a plate of scrambled eggs and bacon waiting for him.

Sighing, he pulled out his phone.

Gray:

Thank you for making me breakfast

Lyall:

Anytime sweetheart

Eat up

I'll be back around dinner

He popped the plate in the microwave and sat on the counter to wait for it. His gaze kept drifting to the basement door. He shivered and hopped down, venturing towards it. There were still vague traces of his shame, so he fished out some sanitizing wipes to scrub it all down until he was satisfied there were no remnants left.

The microwave beeped, and Gray sat down to his meal. He puzzled over his emotions while he ate. Stress always made him particularly needy. Usually Mateo was his source of comfort, but, apparently, with his mate away, his body didn't know how to process anything.

He just had to manage for a few more days, and then everything would be okay again.

The house felt eerie with no one else in it. Silence roared in his ears so loud that he was tempted to text Lyall and ask him to come back, just so there would be the sounds of someone else there. He didn't trust himself to do that, though. Instead, he turned on the TV for companionate sound and set about getting the home in order so it would be perfect by the time Mateo arrived home.

He made his way through the dishes, the sweeping, the mopping. Each time he passed Lyall's door, his curiosity piqued. He hadn't been down there since Lyall moved in. Doing so now felt like a breach of privacy.

But he had planned to do laundry, he reasoned. Maybe Lyall would be fine with it if Gray did all of their bed laundry at the same time.

He pulled the door open. A wave of balsam fir and honey hit him like a wall as he stepped into Lyall's space. The omega whined. Lyall's scent was never this intense. The last time Gray had been overwhelmed by it was when they'd all been in bed and he'd buried his nose against the alpha's throat. Even when Lyall typically emerged, sweeping his scent onto the main floor in the rush of air when the door opened, Gray had never noticed such an intensity. Was it always that strong and he'd somehow never noticed?

He sat down on the stairs. His legs shook and his palms were uncomfortably moist. Gray pressed a hand to his head and willed away the sensation.

It didn't work.

The universe was probably telling him to not be such a snoop. But where was the fun in that? He inched down the stairs one at a time until he reached the bottom. Each step pulled him deeper.

Lyall's scent saturated everything—every particle of air—and Gray breathed him in.

When he reached the bottom he paused. It looked…unexpected. There were boxes lining a whole wall. Everything seemed so impermanent. But then, he supposed, Lyall hadn't been planning on staying forever, so it made sense that he wouldn't unpack everything and get too comfortable. Somehow the idea made Gray melancholy. Although he hadn't imagined Lyall being a forever feature in their home, the thought of him leaving or not feeling like he belonged here didn't sit right with Gray.

Guilt sank into him. He'd let Lyall leave today rather than addressing things like an adult. What if he left for good because he thought Gray wasn't comfortable around him?

He gravitated toward the bedside table where a framed photo of the three of them sat. They were hugging and laughing, shirtless and sunburnt, a remnant from a vacation they'd taken to the ocean. Gray traced the frame.

He laid back on the bed. The mattress wasn't particularly comfortable, at least not compared to his own. Gray made a note that they should replace it for Lyall when they were a little more financially stable. There was a stain on the ceiling tile from a pipe leak last year. Gray frowned up at it. They should replace that too. Neither he nor Mateo had put a ton of thought into the basement when they'd bought the house. Hell, if the previous owners hadn't outfitted a bathroom down there and finished up the floors, they likely wouldn't have gotten around to it at all and wouldn't have been in a great position to help Lyall out.

They would do better, Gray resolved. Lyall deserved more than they'd been able to give him. With a sigh, he heaved up and set about stripping the bed so he could make it fresh for Lyall's return as a gesture that he wanted him to be there.

"Come off!" Gray gave a firm tug to the fitted sheet and the corner let loose, whipping the entire thing towards him. He huffed and slapped it down, tossing it into the hamper with the rest of the bedding.

He scooped the basket up, propping it on his hip as he marched off to the laundry room feeling pleased with himself. Gray hummed as he dumped the sheets and quilt into the machine, sprinkling in the soap.

By the time everything was washed and dried, he was antsy for Lyall to get back. He was spreading out the fresh bedding in Lyall's room when the front door opened. Gray sprinted up the stairs. He skidded into the entryway before Lyall had even closed the door behind him.

"You're back." Gray was breathing heavily and pressed a hand to his chest.

"Why were you running? What's wrong?" Lyall dropped his groceries and crossed the short distance to him . Lyall cupped the omega's cheeks and scrutinized his face, searching for the source of his panic.

"I made your bed for you." Gray locked his fingers into Lyall's shirt.

"You...made my bed?"

"I didn't mean to make you feel like you had to leave today." Gray fidgeted, the nearness of Lyall amplifying the balsam and honey scent that seemed to pour off of him. "I want you to want to be here. To feel like this is your home."

Lyall smiled indulgently and gathered him into his arms. "You didn't chase me out."

Gray let himself sink into the warmth of Lyall's embrace. The alpha's physique was discernible even through his sweatshirt, and Gray tried not to remember what every inch of him looked like when he was stripped bare. He cursed his apparently photographic memory and shoved the imagery away before he embarrassed himself.

Lyall shifted and dug his fingers into the omega. "Are you sure you're feeling okay?"

"Better than yesterday. Why?"

The alpha tucked a curled finger under Gray's chin and forced him to look up. He held eye contact for so long Gray started to fidget.

"What?"

"I dunno." Lyall shook his head and let him go. "Come on, let's get these groceries put away."

Relieved to not be under scrutiny, he dashed over to pick up several bags and cart them to the kitchen. The two worked as a unit and ate a simple dinner before Gray suggested they watch a movie together as an additional gesture to prove he wanted Lyall around.

Lyall picked out an action movie that Gray had only a passing interest in, but the omega didn't mind if it made him happy. Gray stretched out and rested his head on a pillow in Lyall's lap while they watched.

Every inhalation was infused with Lyall's scent. Gray tucked the blanket up to his chin even though he was already sweltering in his sweats. He squirmed this way and that trying to get comfortable, but it seemed that there was no solution to his discomfort. He couldn't kick off the blanket because his cock was tented against his pants. He was curled up so it wouldn't be *too* obvious, but without the blanket there was no guarantee that Lyall wouldn't notice. It would be awkward all over again.

When Mateo got home, he was going to have to ask his mate to rail him until he couldn't think or move, then keep doing that until his brain remembered he only had *one* alpha, and it was not the one that he was draped over right now. He rustled around again, trying to expel his nervous energy.

Lyall stroked a soothing hand over Gray's hair, teasing the strands in a slow, rhythmic fashion. Gray shoved a bit of the blanket into his mouth and tried to breathe normally as each fingertip felt like sparklers going off on his scalp.

Sweet fuck.

Touching was bad. Touching made him *feel* things.

Gray ground his teeth as Lyall traced those recalcitrant fingertips down the back of his neck, sliding back up, threading through the blond strands to massage his scalp. He chanced a look at the alpha and blessedly found his attention entirely focused on the television screen. A relief because he felt entirely too high strung to deal with those beautiful blue eyes focused on him.

Lyall raked his hand through Gray's hair again, and the omega moaned.

They both froze.

Gray hastily tugged the blanket's edge from his mouth. "Sorry. My scalp is really sensitive."

"It's okay." Lyall paused and pulled his hand away. "Do you want me to stop?"

The answer was a profound *no*, but Gray didn't know what to actually say out loud. There wasn't anything overtly sexual about Lyall touching his hair while they watched a movie, but it stoked a quiet ember in his chest that slowly spread outward, and *that*, Gray decided, was definitely sexual.

But, he argued to himself, as long as he didn't *do* anything then it should be fine. It wasn't like he hadn't thought about Lyall in this way before. Mateo had invited him into their bed after all. His mate was the reason that he knew what every bit of Lyall felt like, tasted like... He slammed down that train of thought. Lyall was still watching him and waiting for an answer.

"You don't have to stop," he said softly.

They stared at one another as Lyall returned his hand to Gray's hair. It was a struggle for the omega to not lean into the touch, to stop himself from nuzzling the scent gland at Lyall's wrist.

He pouted. There wasn't anything particularly sexual about that either so why did he feel so guilty?

Lyall cleared his throat and brought Gray back to reality. Embarrassed, the omega put his head down on the pillow a little firmer than necessary. Lyall let out an *oof*.

"Sorry," Gray mumbled. "I don't know why I'm such a disaster today."

"You're just a little high strung." Lyall chuckled.

The alpha resumed the soft touches that slowly drove Gray to distraction. He stopped listening to the movie and closed his eyes, revelling in the patterns Lyall traced on his scalp.

He shivered, looking up again. Lyall's mouth was slightly parted and his fingertips shook against Gray's hair just enough for the omega to take notice of it.

Balsam and honey flowed off the alpha in waves. and Gray buried his nose against the pillow to drown it out, but that only made him aware of the cock pressing against the underside of it. Gray shifted. Lyall shuddered beneath him, the alpha sucking in a sharp breath that had tingles shooting down Gray's spine.

Gray had been so preoccupied with his own reactions that he hadn't even stopped to consider he might be provoking the same in Lyall.

Lyall shot out from under him so quickly that Gray squawked and flailed, barely catching himself before he fell off the couch.

"Lyall, what the fuck?"

The alpha's eyes were wide with panic and the outline of his cock against his pants drew Gray's attention.

"I need to go," Lyall blurted out. "Downstairs, I mean."

Gray opened his mouth to speak, but Lyall was already running away, the basement door slamming behind him. The thoroughly confused omega stared after him. For a minute, he debated continuing on with the movie, but he wasn't that interested anyway and his body was demanding attention. Gray fished out his phone as he climbed the stairs to his room. It was easy enough to phone Mateo for another illicit session to curb his libido until his mate returned home to do it himself.

He sprawled back on the bed and had his cock in his hand before he could blink. His brain overloaded him with images—Mateo fucking into him, Lyall wrapping those beautiful lips about his cock, both of them bringing him to ruin while he begged for release—until he was overwhelmed and spilling over his hand in a few quick strokes.

Gray was riled as hell and unsatisfied with coming so fast. He wanted to be fucked. Rough and wild and desperate. Why did Mateo have to be away? Gray grabbed a pillow and shoved it to his face, letting himself scream into it until his lungs burned. He rolled around on the bed, rutting uselessly into the mattress while he whimpered.

It was *unfair*.

Someone needed to invent teleportation so his mate could return at night and give him the attention he needed. Growling, he climbed out of bed and swallowed down one of the sleeping pills he kept for restless nights. There was no way he was going to be able to sleep without one tonight.

Chapter Three

Morning dawned bright and utterly unwelcome. Gray was in a foul mood: unsettled and viciously hungry. His skin tingled, feeling too taut to accommodate his bones. He wriggled and sat up with a huff.

There was a missed call from Mateo on his phone screen. He thought briefly about ignoring it, but it wasn't his mate's fault that he was away or that Gray didn't feel well.

Gray:
Morning my love

Mateo:
Morning babe
I miss you

They went through the usual pleasantries. He hid his mood so Mateo wouldn't worry, and they planned for another video call that night.

The omega wondered if Lyall would let him get away with eating a chocolate bar for breakfast. He didn't bother to get dressed, instead wrapping himself in a robe, letting the fluffy softness soothe him. The scent of cinnamon, sugar, and yeast filled the air when he opened the bedroom door. He followed his nose downstairs and found Lyall reading on the couch. The alpha's gaze fastened onto him from over the top of the book.

"Rough night?" Lyall asked.

Gray only shrugged and yanked open the fridge to get himself a glass of milk.

"Would a cinnamon bun improve your mood?"

Gray looked back at the alpha. "It might."

Lyall hoisted his lanky form off the couch, and Gray watched him move with a graceful stealth to turn off the oven timer a second before it beeped. The alpha removed the tray of golden buns with their outdated Christmas oven mitts, and sat them, warm and steaming, on the stove.

"Did you make these for me?" Gray asked.

"There's a pretty good chance the answer is yes." Lyall smiled at him as he nudged the omega to the side so that he could get a bowl of glaze out of the fridge.

"I didn't know you bake."

"There are a lot of things you don't know about me," said Lyall. He grabbed a spatula out of a drawer, fished out a gorgeous bun for Gray, and set it on a plate, spooning glaze overtop of it so it melted and glistened, sliding over the dark swirls and golden bread.

"I don't know what I ever did to deserve you," Gray said. "You're like the perfect roommate."

"It's true." Lyall grinned and fetched himself his own cinnamon bun, urging Gray to sit at the table with his meal.

Gray shoveled in as much as his mouth would take, sitting in chipmunk-cheeked bliss while the flavors bathed his tongue and worked, molecule by delicious molecule, to undo the tension he'd woken up with.

"Slow down, sweetheart. You're going to choke, and Mateo would toss me onto the street if I let you smother yourself to death with baked goods."

Gray chugged some milk to speed up the chewing process and swallowed the lot of it down.

"But what a way to go. Almost as good as choking on..." he froze, suddenly remembering who he was talking to. "Nevermind."

Lyall laughed, and the sound made Gray's stomach clench. "Were you going to say something wildly inappropriate? Right in front of my cinnamon bun?"

"You're such a dork," Gray said, even as he shook his head and chuckled. "The sugar turned off my brain."

"Is that so? I know a few other things that do that, too."

Lyall's gaze glittered with mischief, and Gray's mouth turned dry. The omega stuffed another bite of cinnamon bun into his mouth, looking steadfastly away from the alpha that was now shaking with laughter.

"I'm sorry. You make it so easy."

"I do not." Gray pouted.

"Do, too." Lyall patted Gray's shoulder. "You're too cute when you're flustered. It's hard not to poke at you in that state."

The choice of words had Gray's cheeks burning. He stuffed his mouth again and kept his gaze down while he ate.

"Are you legit upset?" Lyall asked. "I'm sorry, if you are."

"I'm not. I'm in a weird ass mood and don't know what to do with myself." Gray sighed and slumped in his chair. "I wish I could turn emotions off like a light switch. Life would be a million times easier."

"Probably, but definitely less fun, I think."

"I guess." Gray inhaled the last bite of his bun. "Could I have another?"

"You can have as many as you can fit in that beautiful face." Lyall stood and prepared another cinnamon bun for Gray and set it in front of him. "I like watching you enjoy my food. It's really not the same when I make stuff for myself."

"I am a terrible cook and baker," said Gray, "so I much prefer having you make me stuff. I'll gush over it any day if it means you make more."

Lyall coughed awkwardly.

"Get your brain out of the gutter." Gray laughed.

"But then the extra home I keep there would go unused."

"Couldn't let that happen." Gray propped his chin on his hand and watched Lyall finish the last of his own food. There was a smudge of icing on the corner of his lip. Gray reached out without thinking and wiped it away with his thumb, sucking off the sweet remnants.

Balsam fir and honey flooded from the alpha. Gray froze, the scent rolling over him like a wave crashing against the shore. His thumb was still in his mouth, the lingering sweetness fading against his tongue.

Lyall shoved away from the table and stood there awkwardly. "I think I should go for a walk."

"It's raining," Gray pointed out. Light sprinkles danced against the windows. The sky outside the glass was pearlescent and overcast, pouring down its bounty on the grass.

"I have an umbrella." Lyall's gaze darted around, landing everywhere that wasn't Gray.

"Don't go." Gray found himself saying the words without realizing. That drew Lyall's attention, and their eyes locked.

"I really should."

"I want you to stay." Gray reached out and took hold of Lyall's wrist. His stomach clenched. It would be better to let him leave. Things were too weird for them to be alone together. If Mateo were home, Gray could have simply made the suggestion to his mate, and Lyall could have been invited into their bed. Whatever was floating around unsaid between them could be drowned out and broken down until there was no more need for words to make anyone understand what they wanted.

But Mateo wasn't home. There was only Gray's whisper-thin resolve and Lyall's instinct to flee standing in the way of some incredibly poor decisions.

Gray dropped his hand. "I'll go upstairs. You don't have to go out into the rain to avoid me."

"I'm not—that's not why—" Lyall let out a frustrated growl. "I'm trying to be respectful. You're stressed and haven't been feeling well.

You need to rest. *I* need to keep my distance."

Gray closed his eyes and curled into himself. More than anything he wanted to text Mateo to come home, to abandon his opportunities. They would find another way to get through everything. But he couldn't. He wrapped his arms around his knees, tucked his forehead down, and tried to stem the swell of emotion. He was being ridiculous. He knew that fact plain as day, but knowing did nothing to change how he felt.

His safe place was so far away.

A plate clinked against the table, and Gray looked up. Lyall had put a third cinnamon bun, absolutely drowning in icing, down in front of him.

"Will another help or make things worse?" Lyall asked.

Gray dipped a fingertip into the icing. "We'll find out."

Lyall nodded. "I think you should rest today. Pretend your to-do list doesn't exist and lounge as much as you can. We'll get you sorted out, so you'll be fit as a fiddle by the time Mateo is back."

"I can do that." Part of him wanted to ask if Lyall would rest with him so he could have the comfort of a warm body, of a heartbeat to lull him to sleep, but he couldn't bring himself to say the words.

"I'll be here if you need me."

Gray took his ill-advised cinnamon bun upstairs and deposited himself in bed. He sprawled out, curling around Mateo's pillow while he watched a movie on his phone and picked at his food.

He stayed prone as long as his body would allow. When his vision started to blur, he climbed out of bed and into the bathroom. Sweat prickled his temples, and nausea churned in his gut. He splashed cool water on his face, but it didn't help.

Gray turned on the shower and stepped under the lukewarm water. He shivered but stayed there trying to cool himself down and wash away the gross, sticky feeling that seemed to coat everywhere the water didn't touch.

The towel on his skin as he dried off was too coarse, and the heat it trapped was too uncomfortable. Gray was tempted to stretch out on the tile floor, but he needed to get his phone first.

A wave of heat rushed through him as he reached the doorway. He lurched forward and stumbled to his knees.

Gray staggered to the bed, sitting down before the wave of dizziness knocked him flat. The omega whimpered and rolled slowly over until he could fish through the bedside table drawer and pull out a small thermometer. He shoved it under his tongue and waited in silence until it beeped. The numbers on the read out stared at him. Apprehension twisted his gut.

"Fuck."

Maybe it was incorrect. He crawled to the bathroom and found the hormone test strips in the medicine cabinet. The finger prick made him jump. He set the strip to the droplet and waited. The indicator turned a dark green which meant, according to the chart, that he'd entered pre-heat.

Gray snatched up his phone and dialed his mate.

Mateo answered on the first ring. "What's wrong?"

"I'm starting early."

Mateo was silent for a few moments. "What do you mean early? What's going on?"

Gray relayed his various symptoms that had driven him to make the call. Lethargy pulled on him, and his vision wavered when he moved his head too quickly. Every sense was piqued, and his clothing chafed at him.

"I thought it was stress. It was too soon. I've just been trying to keep busy while you were gone. I'm sorry. I'm not ready. I don't have anything started. I haven't gone to the doctor."

"Shhh. You're going to be fine. Let me talk to my boss about leaving the conference early. In the meantime, try not to worry. Are you feeling alright?"

The omega whimpered. "I let it get too far."

"Take a deep breath for me."

Gray did so.

"We'll get everything handled, so try not to worry. You relax. I'll arrange what I can from here."

"Okay." Gray sighed. "I miss you."

"I miss you, too. I'll be home as soon as I can. Phone me if you need anything. I love you."

"Love you, too."

Gray indulged in a sulk and laid there pouting. At least it explained why he'd been feeling so strange. He'd been so diligent in his cleaning around the house that he'd removed so much of his mate's scent and never noticed the nesting impulses. He could hardly gather up what smelled like his mate when he'd scrubbed it all away.

Cursing himself, he gathered the bedding into a pile and flopped back into it. He wondered if he had enough time to slip out for some supplies before he got too deep, but when he sat up again, the lightheadedness hit him like a brick. He slumped back down.

Frustrated with himself for missing the signs, he curled up with his phone.

Gray:
I'm dizzy :(

Mateo:
Lyall's going to run out and get
what you need
Are you comfortable seeing
him in this state?

Lust flooded Gray's system as his brain pushed all the memories front and center from when all three of them had ended up in bed, with Mateo inside him and Lyall bringing him to completion with lips and hands made for sin. The last time they'd been together he'd come so many times between the two alphas' attention that he'd had to beg for a break. He swallowed hard, a small sound escaping his lips into the silence of his empty room.

Even knowing it was the pre-heat scrambling his brain, part of him still felt disloyal to Mateo for thinking of Lyall in such lewd

ways. There was no turning the thoughts off though. No way to
stem the needs and demands of his body and hormone-saturated
brain now that everything had started. It was a series of dominoes.
Unbeknownst to any of them, the first of them had tipped over before
Mateo had even left.

Gray:
Sure

Mateo:
Sit tight

Gray poked at one of his phone games while he waited, wiggling
around in the pile of bedding to get comfortable.

Mateo:
He's on his way out now

Gray:
Thank you <3

Gray took his time arranging the fabrics that still smelled like
Mateo and inched himself on hands and knees to the closet. He
pulled on one of his mate's oldest and softest sweaters then sank
back into the mass of blankets with his legs tucked into the sweater.
He nestled quietly, fussing on his phone and watching videos of
Mateo to soothe himself. Gray startled awake some time later when
the front door opened.

"Sweetheart?" Lyall called from the front door. "You okay?"

Gray let out an involuntary squeak into the sleeve of his sweater,
his blood sizzling from the sound of Lyall's voice. He listened from
upstairs, buried in blankets and pillows. His attention piqued
towards the sound, but he didn't answer back, focusing on his
breathing. A soft knock sounded at the bedroom door, and he let out
a low, involuntary growl now that the alpha was near his nest.

"It's just me," Lyall crooned.

Gray watched through a little crack between pillows. Lyall left the door open so Gray wouldn't feel cornered, but his hackles were still up, his mind struggling with the hormonal surges that whiplashed through territorial, horny, and desperate for comfort. He growled again when Lyall took a step closer. The alpha sat down on the ground, looking away purposefully. Gray kept watch, but the longer Lyall sat without moving, speaking, or looking at him, the more his attention waned. He snuggled back down into the nest, Mateo's scent a cocoon of comfort as much as the soft fabrics were.

Lyall's voice broke the silence after a while. "Sweetheart, do you need some water?"

Had he been standing, Gray's knees would have given out at the soothing tone, the use of *sweetheart*... It was so much softer than before. Lyall was the only one who called him that.

"Gray?" Lyall prompted again.

"Water, please."

"Do you want to come out? Or should I pass you some things in?"

Gray poked his head out of the nest. Lyall stood by the door, dressed in a pale blue T-shirt and jeans, his body language casual. His strawberry blond hair was tousled like he'd been running and his cheeks were flushed. Gray honed in on the rough stubble under those cheeks, his memory flashing back to when stubble had turned the inside of his thighs pink and raw. Everything about the alpha seemed too vivid, too sharp. Yet too soft and certainly far too inviting at the same time.

Lust rippled through Gray, and he pulled back into the nest.

"Okay, I'll be right back."

Lyall disappeared downstairs. Gray parted the pillows, catching the subtle mixing of the two alphas' scents—Mateo's ginger and juniper and Lyall's balsam fir and honey.

He shivered in his nest, waiting for the telltale sound of Lyall returning. Each footstep had goosebumps rising on his arms. He fought against the urge to pull back into the blankets. Mateo would want him to stay hydrated.

Lyall carried a tray and set it down inside the door, nudging it to the side.

"Hey, it's okay," Lyall crooned. "I guess this explains why we've been a little off lately. You don't have to get out. I'll bring everything to you." Instead of holding out anything he'd brought, Lyall held out both arms, palms up, and inched closer, eyes focused intently on Gray. The omega's breathing hitched. Lyall paused where he was, waiting for Gray's subtle nod. Every couple of feet that Lyall progressed, Gray's senses were flooded with balsam and honey. Gray let out a whimper as Lyall crossed the last bit of space between them, his palm resting on the omega's cheek. "You're doing so well. Mateo would be proud of you."

Gray turned his face, nuzzling at the scent glands in Lyall's wrist. The pheromones were like a hit of cocaine to his system. His fingers latched around Lyall's arm, and the alpha waited, soft and patient, for Gray to adapt to his nearness.

Lyall curled his fingers against the back of the omega's head, and Gray gasped, digging his nails into Lyall's arm, body shaking.

"Deep breaths, go slow. I'm here." Lyall cupped his other cheek. "Can I hold you?"

Gray's only answer was a barely perceptible nod as his hormones spiked, turning his brain to mush. The transitory phases of his heat always left him a mess, and, while having an alpha around *could* help with that, he was used to Mateo. Having Lyall instead was still confusing the fuck out of his body.

Gray climbed free of the nest and into Lyall's lap.

"Sweet *fuck*." Lyall groaned, digging his fingers into Gray's hips.

The omega pressed his face to the scent glands on Lyall's neck. It was so close to Mateo's but not the same. He zipped in and out of lucidity, only half aware of the escalation of Lyall's scent.

Lyall held him securely, nuzzling a soft cheek to Gray's hair, all the while shaking under the omega.

"Hold on to me," Lyall said.

Gray clung like a koala when Lyall stood up and squatted down next to the tray he'd brought in, hoisting it and both of them back up to the bed. Lyall passed over a glass of water and two pills.

"What are they?" Gray whispered.

"I got you an omega emergency kit from the twenty-four hour pharmacy. One is emergency contraception, and the other is to help with the heat fever."

Gray took them without complaint, still clinging to Lyall while he sipped the entirety of his glass of water. He ate his way through the sandwich and cookies that had been brought up as well, still nestled against Lyall's chest. The food helped immensely, and the medicine kicked in quickly, leaving him feeling almost normal.

When he pulled away, Lyall searched his face. "Better?"

"Much. Thank you." Gray's cheeks flared. He couldn't help his heats, but he hadn't been in that kind of vulnerable state around anyone but his mate for close to a decade and embarrassment had him cringing.

"I feel like I should have grabbed a respirator or something." Lyall laughed. "I thought I was going to lose my mind with you plastered to me like that and smelling as good as you do."

Gray pulled the neck of his sweater over his nose, hiding his blush. "I'm sorry."

"Not your fault." Lyall let out a shaky breath. "I should make you a proper meal."

"I just ate."

"Mateo told me that this is going to take a lot out of you and that I should get you to eat as much as I can before you hit the next stage. Even if you don't move, your body is running at maximum capacity and you need the calories. Do you want to come downstairs or wait here while I cook?"

Gray considered. He felt in control of himself for the moment so he opted to simply wrap a blanket arsound his shoulders and join Lyall downstairs.

The alpha opened the back door to get some of the sweet evening air in.

"What are you going to make?" Gray asked, tucking his knees up to his chest on one of the bar stools.

"Depends on what you like." Lyall pried open the fridge and surveyed the contents. "I picked up a decent supply earlier, so I should be able to accommodate pretty much anything."

"How have I never seen you cook before all of this?"

"That would be because your mate is a kitchen hog." Lyall laughed. "How about steak?"

"I like steak." Gray hid his smile behind the blanket.

Lyall glanced back at him, his face glowing with contentment. He pulled out a package of steaks, dug a couple handfuls of potatoes out of the pantry, and arranged the rest of his cooking implements across the counter. Although Gray wasn't much of a cook, he loved watching Mateo at work in their kitchen. Lyall didn't have the same familiarity with the space, but he knew what he was doing with the food. Gray was content listening to the sizzles, inhaling the heavenly aroma of everything Lyall had decided to make. There was way more food than either of them would be able to eat, but as soon as Lyall had plated them both up, he tucked everything else safely into containers and set them in the fridge for later.

"How come you don't have a mate?" Gray asked and immediately wanted to pull back the words.

"Hard to say." Lyall stared down at his plate. "I've never been very good at relationships."

"You've been friends with Mateo forever. That's a relationship."

"Cheeky." Lyall smiled softly. "That's not quite the same. I suppose I'm extremely picky. I've never found anyone that was able to hold my attention for long enough to consider bonding, and, when I did, they were already taken."

Gray swallowed hard, covering his reaction by shoving a bite of steak into his mouth. "Holy shit, this is good." His stomach turned suddenly ravenous, and he snared another bite.

Lyall watched him inhale his food with an amused expression. "You're cute when you eat."

Gray blushed. "I am not."

"I'm the one looking at you so I'm pretty sure I get to be the judge of that." Lyall quirked his head. "Are you embarrassed because it's me, or do you get like this when Mateo compliments you too?"

"That's different," Gray protested, his heart pounding. "Mateo is *allowed* to compliment me."

"But I'm not?" Lyall's blue eyes were watching him with an intensity that had him squirming.

"You're..." Gray trailed off, throat suddenly dry.

"I'm?" Lyall filled a glass with water and slid it across the counter.

The omega downed the liquid and dared to look him in the eye. "I don't know how to describe what you are."

"That's fair considering I don't know how to describe what you are either," Lyall said. "I know this is a weird time for you but I want you to be comfortable with me here."

"I'm not *uncomfortable*." Gray fidgeted. "It's just...my heat makes my brain go places it shouldn't."

"Where's it going?"

"I don't think that's very hard to guess." Gray bit the blanket, smothering the sound that climbed up his throat as his brain tipped straight into the memories. "I think about last time."

Lyall's lip twitched into a smirk, but it disappeared as fast as it had appeared. "And that's bad?"

"Mateo was here then. I don't know what to do with myself in this situation when he's not."

"Do you think he'd have asked me to take care of his mate in heat if he wasn't the teensiest bit comfortable with the possibility of what might happen? I'm not here to pressure you. I'm genuinely here to help with whatever you need, but I'm also open to sharing your heat if you want to."

Gray bit his lip and his cock twitched at the suggestion. Would Mateo really be okay if he and Lyall...

Lyall shot up from his seat and went to stand by the window. "Sorry," he mumbled apologetically, "you smell amazing. It's fucking with my head."

Gray's cheeks flushed with embarrassment. He'd never had to think about what his scent did during a heat when he got turned on because Mateo was right there. If Lyall was going to react like that every time Gray had a lustful thought, then they were in for a long night.

"If you don't want things to go that direction then you can tell me. Now's the time to be honest and I promise I can be good."

Maybe he didn't *want* Lyall to be good.

"Gray..." Lyall growled out his name and pressed against the screen door. "Fuck."

"Sorry." Gray chewed his lip. It was entirely unfair that Lyall was as attractive as he was. Not to mention attentive, kind, a beast in bed, as well as someone that his mate trusted deeply. Gray wasn't quite willing to admit out loud that he wanted to know what a heat would be like with Lyall and Mateo working together to keep him satisfied. Mateo always did a great job, but Gray was insatiable when the depths of his heat struck. Even the strongest alpha needed to sleep sometime.

"I've never shared a heat with anyone else since Mateo."

"Well, Mateo's coming back soon, so in all likelihood you won't have to."

Gray tucked his blanket under his chin.

"I did some reading while I was getting you supplies. It looks like it can be really rough in the early stages," Lyall said. "If you want me to help, you only have to ask."

Lyall's gaze burned right through Gray. The omega shuddered, tugging the blanket ever closer.

Gray's phone rang. He answered it when Mateo's name flashed on the screen.

"Hey, babe," Mateo's voice filled his senses, and he immediately relaxed.

"Hey."

"I finally got a hold of my boss. I'm leaving the conference now. I should be home in about four hours. How're you feeling?"

"I'm okay right now. Lyall fed me dinner, and I took medicine."

"Good. How far along are you?"

Gray squirmed, taking stock of his body. "I should be okay until you get home."

Part of him was too chicken to ask his mate for permission when he'd be home soon. It would be easier to avoid making that choice, to avoid breaking some new boundary between them, to avoid letting Lyall have him when Mateo wasn't there...

"Okay. I'll see you soon." Mateo's voice broke his mate's train of thought. The omega jolted. "Love you."

"Love you, too." Gray tucked the phone away and focused back on Lyall.

He *was* interested in another night like the three of them had shared, but he was also not the greatest at voicing what he wanted. He'd grown complacent being in a relationship with Mateo because his mate already knew him so well that he didn't often have to make a fool of himself asking for something new. Lyall didn't have that particular advantage, and Gray couldn't bring himself to say the words.

Lyall had returned to the kitchen during the call and was stirring something he'd tossed together.

"What are you making now?"

Lyall turned on the burner. "Chocolate pudding."

"You're going to spoil me."

"You deserve it." He whisked the mixture, eyes focused. "Your scent gets so soft when you talk to him."

"Soft?"

"Hmm, not less potent or anything, it's more...comforting, I guess would be the word."

The words warmed Gray through. He hummed in response. "What do I smell like?"

Lyall's eyebrow raised. "Mateo's never told you?"

"He has, but I'm curious if it's different to you."

"Oh. Um, I suppose the closest approximation would be apple blossoms. We had a tree in the backyard when I was growing up. I used to climb into it during the spring when the blooms were so thick you couldn't even see the branches. You smell like that, but with the tiniest hint of ginger, though that could be Mateo's influence."

Gray flushed. "It is."

He sat in silence watching the alpha at work until Lyall set a still-steaming bowl in front of him. Gray dug into the dessert and occupied himself with that until he was licking the last of it from his spoon.

"Why are you being so nice to me?"

"Why wouldn't I be nice?" Lyall rested his hands on his hips, and Gray couldn't help but notice how it stretched the fabric over his chest, lean muscles making themselves visible.

"I dunno," Gray murmured. "I've been *really* weird to you."

"A heat snuck up on you. That's not your fault. Are you asking because you think I'm buttering you up so you'll let me fuck you?"

Gray dropped his spoon, his face igniting. "Um."

"I'm going to be completely honest and say that I *do* want to fuck you, but I'm not going to push you on that. Mateo is my oldest friend, and he's never been shy about how much he loves you. If for no other reason, that would be enough for me to go out of my way to care for you. He asked me to be here for you and I'm more than happy to comply." Lyall's voice softened. "I like you. You're a beautiful man, and you're a good person who makes someone I love the happiest he's been in his life. Whatever you need and for any reason, I'm here."

"Thank you. I, um, I like you, too." Heat prickled up his spine, but Gray pushed the sensation away. "I'm going to go back to the nest for a bit."

"Okay. I'll clean up and join you in a bit if you want me there."

Gray nodded and slipped away in his blanket cloak, throwing himself into his nest when he made it to the bedroom. He whimpered into the fabric. Life was unfair. If Mateo were home, they would be naked and cuddled until the next phase. Gray debated stripping and chilling in his nest but couldn't bring himself to be quite that bold. He craved physical contact. The fever suppressant he'd taken earlier was already beginning to wear off.

"Lyall," Gray called out before his rational mind could stop him.

He clapped a hand over his mouth and burrowed into his nest. The omega shrank back when he heard Lyall's footsteps on the stairs.

"Do you need something?"

Even from the depths of his nest, Gray could hear the shift in Lyall's voice, sensed the tension in the air.

Say it.

Gray whimpered instead.

Lyall dropped to his knees next to the bed, bringing him to eye level. "Sweetheart, it's okay. I'm sorry if I got too intense downstairs."

Gray poked his head out of the nest. "Mateo would be holding me right now if he were home."

It took Lyall a few moments of staring before he grasped Gray's meaning. "Do you want to be held?"

Relieved he didn't have to speak, Gray nodded. He rearranged his pile and stretched out with his back to the alpha, holding his breath as Lyall's weight dipped the mattress and pressed against him. Lyall draped an arm around the omega's waist and tucked him close, allowing him to take hold of the alpha's wrist, moving it to cup his cheek so he had access to the scent gland. Gray let himself sink into the warmth. The balsam and honey scent managed to both soothe and provoke, but his body settled into rest, knowing what was to come.

"Can I ask a question while you're lucid?"

"Mmm sure." Gray forced himself back to full wakefulness.

"How did you get so far into your heat without noticing?"

"Mateo usually notices before I do. My scent changes beforehand, but he's been working late and it all gets kind of skewed and the stress scent can overwhelm the noticeable changes. It could have drowned it out, I guess. Plus, I'm earlier than I should be. It's easy to miss the signs if it's not time."

"I feel like I should know so much more of this."

"Have you ever been around an omega in heat before?" asked Gray.

"Nope."

"Then you'd have no reason to know. Besides, even if you did know, you wouldn't necessarily be able to tell without being able to compare different hormonal stages."

"That's fair." Lyall lapsed into silence for a while. "Would it be weird if I said that I wouldn't mind being around to learn?"

"You *are* around to learn," Gray pointed out.

"Yeah, but I meant...nevermind."

Gray spun in Lyall's embrace. "Tell me. Please?"

"I like living with you two. I mean, it's a little weird sometimes, but I don't really like living alone. My last roommate got married a year ago, and it wigs me out to be in a quiet home and for there to not be someone there when I get home. When Mateo asked if I was going to be okay after being laid off and offered your basement, I didn't even think twice."

"Do you mean that you want to move in permanently?" Gray toyed with the front of Lyall's shirt. "Or is my brain not interpreting right?"

"I'm just putting it out there. Obviously I'd have to talk to Mateo, too, but you're here, so I thought I'd float the idea."

In the midst of being cuddled and cared for, there was nothing Gray could think of to oppose the idea. "Okay. We should talk about it when this is all over."

Lyall tucked Gray closer and the omega let himself be lulled by the alpha's steady breathing.

Chapter Four

Gray woke covered in sweat, his body on fire, every nerve demanding attention. Each inhalation was infused with Lyall's balsam and honey. He whimpered into his pillow, hips rocking back against the alpha surrounding him. Gray nipped at Lyall's wrist, releasing a fresh burst of scent, sending his thoughts scattering as he pressed back, desperate for contact.

Lyall's arm tightened around him, and the alpha shifted. "Gray?"

His voice was rough, and the sound of his name melted over the omega.

He shivered, the cool air of the bedroom prickling his skin. His clothing stuck to him and a wetness between his thighs let him know he'd hit the next stage of his heat. Mateo still wasn't home.

"Please," Gray whined. "Where is he?"

Lyall's body shook behind him as he reached across and checked his phone, then cursed and grabbed Gray's, opening it up to his text messages. Gray clung to the last threads of clarity to read what his mate had sent.

Mateo:
My tire blew on the highway
I'm still waiting for a tow
I'll be there as soon as I can, but it

probably won't be tonight
If you want to be with Lyall for your
heat you have my full permission
I'm so sorry I'm not there
I don't want you to be alone
I love you

Permission.

The word rebounded in Gray's mind as the heat-haze dragged him under.

Too hot.

The fever was unbearable. Gray grabbed at his clothing, tugging off his shirt, which didn't work at all since he was still securely in Lyall's grasp. The alpha helped him with his fruitless endeavor. The omega followed the magnetism of his body and turned towards Lyall, climbing into his lap, face buried against the scent gland of Lyall's neck, hips grinding together.

"Please," Gray begged, the word dancing on his tongue like a mantra. Lyall shook beneath him, hands holding Gray's hips firm enough to bruise. "*Please.*"

Lyall slid his hand under the waistband of Gray's pajama pants. He paused to cup Gray's ass, his gaze unfocused and his breath sharp.

Another squirm and desperate entreaty from Gray prompted Lyall into action. He slid his fingers between the pert cheeks and pressed against the slick entrance. Gray groaned and rocked his hips, renewing his fevered mantra until the first finger was as far in as it could go. It slid away, joined by a second, then a third when he mewled in Lyall's ear, begging for more.

Gray clung desperately as Lyall finger-fucked him with a quick pace that Gray's hips met with frantic thrusts. Lyall's other hand slipped inside the front of Gray's pants and wrapped a firm hand around his cock.

The omega came undone with that touch, driving back and forth between Lyall's hands until the sensation spiked, overwhelming him as Lyall finished him off with a few well-timed strokes. The sensations didn't abate and Gray moved faster, growling as he drove Lyall's fingers inside.

"*More*," Gray pleaded.

Lyall nibbled the scent gland on Gray's throat. The omega's vision flashed white.

"I'll take my time with you later, but for now..." Lyall pushed Gray off and pressed him face first into the bed. Gray squirmed, bucking up as Lyall spread his cheeks and nudged a thick cock between them. "Can you hold still for half a second?"

The teasing cockhead was too much. Gray thrust back, burying Lyall to the hilt in one swift motion. Lyall released a guttural moan and snared the omega's hips as his knot swelled between them. Pleasure flared bright and hot, and Gray drowned in it, buffeted on wave after wave until he could no longer tell where he ended and Lyall began.

Gray surfaced when Lyall growled in his ear, the sound melting into a panting staccato that punctuated the tiny spasms of bliss where they were joined.

"Holy fuck." Lyall gasped. "I wasn't expecting you to come that fast. I wasn't ready."

Gray only half-listened, rutting his cock against the sheets and squeezing around Lyall. The alpha's words choked off.

Restless and needy, Gray whimpered. A chant of "more, more, more," poured from his lips. Pressure from the alpha's knot inside him had the omega shivering. Goosebumps painted his pale skin.

"You're not—" Lyall's voice broke as Gray writhed under him. "You're not making this easy."

"I *can't*," Gray whined. "Move more!"

"We're literally stuck together. I can't."

Gray broke into a sob and ground against the bed.

"Okay, calm down. Let me try." Lyall rolled over, bringing Gray with him.

The omega sprawled over the alpha's chest. He shivered from

the sudden cold and groaned when Lyall's hand wrapped around his waiting cock. Lyall pinned him with his legs, wrapping his calves over Gray's to keep him still.

He shuddered. The sensation of helplessness spiked his lust further. Lyall held his throat with one hand and stroked his cock with the other in a steady rhythm. He struggled as the orgasm overtook him, but Lyall didn't falter. The alpha panted in Gray's ear as the omega pulsated around him.

"That's a good boy," Lyall murmured. "Come for me."

The order stoked something deep inside him. Gray clutched the sheets, crying out. Lyall milked his cock, and Gray felt the hot spatter across his stomach.

"Again." Lyall kept up his pace, his own cock twitching inside Gray.

The omega sobbed out Lyall's name and writhed against the bodily restraints. Lyall sank his teeth into the scent gland in Gray's throat and his vision flared white as he came again so hard it choked off the air in his lungs.

Gray came back to reality slowly. His throat was raw, and it felt like he'd run a marathon. Lyall turned them sideways. The alpha slid his cock free, taking in deep lungfuls of Gray's scent.

"Fucking hell. You didn't give me warning it would feel like this."

Gray stayed quiet. He didn't have the energy to move quite yet. His neck pulsed and a thought niggled him. Lyall had bitten him. *Bonded.* The word flashed through Gray's mind and he gingerly turned to check Lyall's own throat. No bite marks. Gray collapsed back down, relieved he hadn't accidentally permanently bonded his lover during the heat-haze.

The omega blinked away tears as the temporary hormone drop turned him into a shaking mess. He craved his mate. Lyall held him tightly and murmured soothing words into his ear. The alpha's scent was overwhelming, and every breath pulled him deeper into Gray's being. When the quivering need became too much for him, he rocked against Lyall. The alpha pressed him back, hovering over him on all fours. The omega protested the distance and tugged at him. Lyall chuckled and lowered, pressing the length of their bodies together.

Lyall was gentle, as if he could tell the worst of the heat was over and the frantic force of before was no longer necessary to drive back the haze.

The weight was a welcome balm to Gray's anxiety, and he indulged in the quiet comfort of laying there, simply breathing in Lyall's scent.

"Hold on," Lyall murmured, and Gray complied as much as his limp-noodle limbs would allow. Lyall cradled him and took them both to the bathroom where he turned the shower on full blast. The alpha leaned against the wall with Gray plastered to him while they waited for the water to warm. He slid the shower door all the way open and deposited Gray onto the ledge seat inside.

Lyall sank to his knees in front of Gray, gently cupping his cheek, and the omega leaned into his touch, a purr reverberating in his chest. Then Lyall's mouth was on his, and Gray was lost again in the taste of him, the sweep of his tongue, the hot water, and the icy tiles pressed to his skin.

This was what he wanted. What he needed. Tenderness was as important as passion, and Lyall was willing to give both in excess.

Lyall soaped down his body, every glide igniting a new fervor that had him vibrating under the attention. Gray let out a sound of protest when Lyall moved away to rinse them both down, and the alpha gave him a self-satisfied smirk.

"I know it's the heat, but I am absolutely living for you being a needy mess for me." Lyall kissed him, soft and sweet, thumbs tracing the curve of his jaw.

"I'd think of a clever response, but my brain is basically mashed potatoes right now."

"Totally understandable." Lyall chuckled and hugged Gray closer. "How long do we have before you need to get fucked again?"

"It's already edging back in, but it's not as strong as the heat-haze," Gray replied as tingles skittered over his skin and slick dripped out of his ass. "I should be lucid for the rest of the heat if you keep up with me."

"Good to know. Let's get you back to bed." Lyall toweled him off and carried him out into the bedroom. He carelessly tossed a blanket over the absolute mess they'd made of the bed, and dropped Gray atop the fresh fabric.

"What way do you like to be fucked most during all of this?" Lyall asked.

Gray's cheeks flushed. He shrugged. "I don't know. I'm usually most concerned with the dick inside me. I'm not generally too fussed about the position I'm in when that happens."

"I don't want to hurt you by accident."

"You would have to try *very* hard to hurt me. Omegas are extremely resilient during heats. Plus, we heal faster and feel pain less."

"What about after?"

Gray climbed onto Lyall's lap, bringing them face to face. "Do *not* worry about hurting me. If you hold back, I'll be able to tell even in the heat-haze. It'll make it harder for me to come. Just be relaxed and let your body do what it does best."

"I can do that."

Gray kissed him, tongue delving to taste the recesses of Lyall's mouth, grinding their hips together with a slow precision. Lyall's cock rose to life under the attention.

"Hello there." Gray giggled against Lyall's mouth.

"I... don't usually recover quite that fast."

"It's the heat. Your body knows that I need you. Now, I want you to fuck me until I can't see straight."

The alpha let out a strangled sound and pushed Gray back down to the bed and shoved two pillows under him to hoist up his hips.

Gray stared at the ceiling in a daze, drunk with lust as Lyall's cock teased his entrance. Lyall's firm grip kept him pinned in place as the alpha slid inside with a groan, slow at first, moving in small experimental strokes, finding Gray dripping wet with slick and more than ready for him.

Lyall braced Gray's hips and thrust forward, burying himself to the hilt. The omega came instantly, the bone-deep pleasure rippling through him. Lyall dug his fingers into Gray's thighs. He panted and his eyes scrunched shut. Gray's body relaxed its vise grip on Lyall's cock, and the alpha's eyes slowly opened.

"*Fuck,*" Lyall gasped. "Thankfully I was ready for it this time."

Lyall laughed softly and traced soothing patterns on Gray's thighs. He pulled almost all the way out and slid back in with a fluid motion. Gray's eyes lost focus again as his senses fixated on everywhere he was being touched. He clung to the sheets and braced himself to take everything offered, riding the sharp crest of rapture, the slick friction pushing him over the edge again.

Before Lyall could pull away Gray locked his legs around him with a shuddering breath. "Don't stop." His voice was rough, ragged with a need that consumed him.

Lyall continued, a slow pistoning of his hips as he lowered himself, his teeth grazing the tender skin of Gray's throat, prompting a faint mewl from the omega. Gray threaded his hands into Lyall's hair. Each nip the alpha delivered sent little shockwaves of pleasure cascading through him, crashing against the rippling gratification of every thrust into his body. He arched as he came, grinding his cock against Lyall's stomach. Gray came twice more before Lyall joined him over that sharp edge.

The alpha sucked in long drags of air, face pressed to Gray's neck. He dropped a soft kiss there before slowly sitting up and sliding his cock free.

Lyall's gaze drifted over his prone form. "You're covered in cum."

Gray let out a laugh. "Yeah, that tends to happen when you get fucked into oblivion."

"You're in a chipper mood."

"That also tends to happen when you get fucked into oblivion."

"True enough." Lyall snickered. He tottered off to the bathroom and returned with a damp cloth, tenderly wiping down Gray's torso.

Lyall dropped down next to him like a lead weight. "I feel like I should have done some cardio training before all of this."

Gray chuckled. "It never hurts. I'm much easier to manage now than I was during my first few heats."

"Yeah?"

"Oh, definitely. I'm pretty sure Mateo lost weight every time because I was insatiable. My hazes took forever to break. He kept at it without food or sleep, trying to get me back to a lucid state. Now, if I'm lucky, it only lasts a few hours."

"You could have used me back then, you know." Lyall said the words casually, but they stirred something in Gray.

"I wasn't as confident then as I am now. I don't know what I would have done with the suggestion. It's not like I haven't thought about it before."

Lyall rolled onto his side to see Gray better. "You've thought about sharing a heat with me?"

He squirmed under the attention and dragged one of the pillows onto his chest so he could hide part of his face. "After we all had sex the first time, it might have crossed my mind. It would have been easier on Mateo in the early days if I'd been comfortable with him suggesting it."

"Whoa, whoa. Wait. Mateo never told me about this." Lyall poked the pillow over Gray. "Tell me about it."

"It's nothing really. You two had always been close. He told me about when you'd been together in college before we started dating. We both like men, and we both like you. I was just too shy. Heats are...intimate, I guess, in a way that regular sex isn't."

Lyall nodded thoughtfully. "Having been through part of one with you, I can totally agree with that statement."

The alpha tucked his fingertips under Gray's chin and brought the omega closer. Gray whimpered into Lyall's mouth. The soft caress of warm lips made him shiver, his body slowly reawakening.

"I know that you weren't expecting to do this with me," said Lyall, "but I'm glad you felt comfortable enough with me to let it happen all the same."

Gray pulled him back in and indulged in a tender kiss. "Thank you for doing this for me. I know I was weird about everything, but

I'm glad we could share this experience. Especially since it's not very comfortable or safe for me to go through it alone."

"Not safe?" Lyall's arm tightened around him.

"If an omega in heat is alone, especially after having had a partner for as long as I have, their bodies don't react well. It's almost impossible for us to satisfy ourselves, and we tend to get hurt."

"But I thought you said omegas didn't get hurt during them."

Gray shook his head. "I said it was very difficult to do. That doesn't mean it doesn't happen. Sometimes we end up in hospital. It's even worse if you're caught unaware and don't even have safe supplies on hand. You can't think straight. Your whole body is on fire. Sometimes it feels like you'll burn to ash and relief never comes. It's not something I would wish on anyone."

"You sound like you have personal experience with this."

"Once." Gray went quiet, his thoughts churning. "I'm sorry, this isn't really the time to be talking about this."

"If you want to talk, I'm here to listen." Lyall nuzzled Gray's head.

"It was my first. It came out of nowhere, almost a year earlier than expected. I was home alone at the time, and my parents were out of town. I was totally out of my mind. Nothing helped, or at least nothing that my heat-brain could think of at the time. When my parents finally came home I was a mess—dehydrated and malnourished and miserable—at least the bleeding had stopped from when I'd tried to abate the heat myself. Even with the resiliency, I fucked up my hips and shoulders and had to get physiotherapy for a few months. It was not an enjoyable time."

"I am so sorry you went through that." Lyall squeezed Gray to him. "What did you do between then and Mateo? There's a two year gap."

"Oh. My parents hired me heat helpers."

"Those are the sex workers who specialize in omega care, right?"

Gray nodded. "My experiences with them were infinitely superior to my first. I was very well taken care of on all accounts."

"Good. I know you're forced to have heats, but I'm glad that you're able to get some positive experiences out of them."

"Me, too." Gray sighed, melting comfortably into the bed. "I'm having a pretty positive experience right now."

Lyall snuggled in, breathing deeply against the omega's throat. "Thank you for telling me. Know that I don't take this all lightly. I'm happy I get to share at least part of your heat with you, that I could help."

Gray rotated and pressed them back together, hooking a thigh over Lyall's waist. "You've been a fabulous heat partner."

"Another skill to add to my resume." Lyall traced twirling patterns over Gray's hip. "Did you know that you're magnificent during all of this?"

"Magnificent? You turn into a total cheeseball when you get laid." Gray laughed and nuzzled in to inhale more of the balsam and honey scent.

"I'm serious. You smell fucking incredible. You get absolutely lost in the sensations; you're entirely uninhibited, and that's not something people always get to see in a lover. Everything about you in heat is perfect."

Gray snickered and smacked Lyall on the ass. "You're going to give me an ego, and it's not going to last past my heat."

"All the more reason to let me say every ridiculous compliment that comes to mind."

Lyall's fingers shifted along the curve of Gray's ass and the omega's eyes lost focus.

"Again?" Lyall asked.

Gray nodded, trembling as the heat rose up in him again.

Lyall rolled him over, hoisting his hips back into the air and gripping his shoulders for leverage as their bodies slid together. Held up this way, every moan he made was exposed rather than muffled into the sheets. Each sound seemed to trigger Lyall to move faster, thrust deeper, and squeeze tighter to meet the omega's unspoken demand.

As Gray neared coming once more, his senses flooded with juniper and ginger. He turned his head sharply to see where his mate filled the doorway. Mateo's eyes were wide and wild, chest heaving like he'd run the entire distance home. Gray's heart rate jumped. Lyall went motionless behind him, nails digging into his shoulders.

Mateo moved like a tempest, filling Gray's vision as he was shoved up, sandwiched between the two alphas. Sensation cascaded over him as the warmth of their bodies surrounded him. Lyall resumed his pace, his hands locked on Gray's hip after adjusting for Mateo's sudden appearance. He whimpered into his mate's mouth, his blood simmering as the familiar scent enveloped him, kicking his desire into overdrive. Mateo took Gray's cock into his hand and matched Lyall's pace with his strokes, his teeth sinking into the remaining untouched scent gland on his mate's throat.

Gray's vision whited out, his whole body seizing, breath stalling in his throat, the thrill of pleasure sizzling up his spine. Lyall cursed as Gray's muscles contracted around him, and Mateo growled, his teeth still holding firm.

Chapter Five

"Babe, wake up." Mateo trailed soft fingertips over his cheek and the omega slowly rose back to full consciousness. His muscles twitched as the rebounding sensitivity slowly abated.

"You're back," Gray croaked.

"I am."

"What time is it?"

"Almost seven in the morning." Mateo continued the soothing motions, cradling the omega in his arms, and Gray looked to Lyall for the first time since Mateo's arrival.

He looked almost abashed now that Mateo was here. Gray reached out a hand and tugged Lyall closer when he took it. The omega closed his eyes, blissfully relaxed between the two alphas.

"I'm sorry I bit you without permission," Mateo murmured.

"It's okay. I'm too tasty to resist," Gray said, laughing softly. "Lyall bit me too."

Mateo traced the matching bite marks on Gray's throat. "I see that."

"I didn't mean to," Lyall blurted out. "It was instinct. I wasn't ready."

"Don't worry about it." Gray squeezed Lyall's hand. "I like how it feels. I'd have it done all the time if I could."

"Does it do anything strange for an omega to be claimed by two alphas at once?" Lyall asked, his thumb moving in soft circles over the back of Gray's hand.

"Your guess is as good as mine," said Mateo. "I don't know if it's happened often enough for them to study it."

"No science. Only love." He tugged both alphas to lay next to him and curled into Mateo's embrace. "I missed you."

Gray drowned in the kiss Mateo dropped onto his mouth. The sweep of tongue and scrape of teeth stoked the embers in Gray's belly, and the omega groaned. His cock climbed to attention.

"Mateo." The name melted into a moan. Gray pressed his mate's hand between his thighs where the slick had pooled, ready and waiting.

"Should I...leave?" Lyall asked.

"No!" Gray's eyes snapped open. "Stay."

"I don't want to intrude."

Gray pawed at Mateo. "Tell him. Do you want him to stay?"

Mateo chuckled and pressed two fingers into his mate, pumping them slowly while the omega squirmed around him. "I knew I made the right choice giving you permission."

"You're not secretly mad?" Gray asked, leaning in to nuzzle at Mateo's scent gland.

"Mad that my best friend took care of my mate when I couldn't be here? If I thought it was a bad idea I'd have run from that conference without telling anyone no matter the sacrifice to my career. I'm glad that Lyall was here to help you and that you trusted us both enough for that to happen." Mateo buried his nose against Gray. "You smell different now."

Gray squirmed. "In a good way? Or an 'I regret everything' way?"

Mateo's tongue slid over Lyall's bite, and Gray gasped.

"In an 'I want to devour you' way."

"Oh." A quiver slipped down his spine. "I am entirely unopposed to being devoured."

Mateo laughed against his skin and nibbled his way down his mate's chest, tonguing each nipple in turn on his way to the juncture of Gray's thighs. He took the entirety of Gray's cock into his mouth, and the omega arched off the bed. Gray fisted his free hand in

Mateo's hair, every hot lick sending him spiralling. Lyall slid down next to him and nibbled at the bite mark he'd left, flinging Gray over the edge of orgasm, his hips thrusting up into Mateo's mouth.

Mateo pinned him down sharply and dragged him closer until Gray's naked body was pressed against Mateo's still clothed hips. Gray gasped as his mate ground against him and the omega sat up, grabbing onto Mateo's shirt collar for purchase.

"Let me. You came all this way for me. You deserve a reward."

"Collars first." Mateo reached into the drawer of the bedside table and fastened a collar of black mesh around his throat, passing a second one to Lyall.

"What exactly are they for?"

"He's already got a bonding bite from each of us," said Mateo, "and this gives access to the scent, but prevents him from accidentally doing a permanent bond on one of us if he gets too nippy."

"Does this mean you two *aren't* already bonded?" Lyall asked. "I thought you'd have done that ages ago."

"It was the plan for our tenth wedding anniversary," said Mateo.

"Why not at the actual wedding?"

"We wanted to be practical. There's no way to ever undo a full bond, and it can really fuck up a person if you had to separate for some reason. I didn't want to be in a job where I had to travel all the time and leave him with the weight of a bond."

"Huh. I guess I've never thought about it before." Lyall fastened the collar around his own throat.

It gave Gray a deep sense of satisfaction to see them both with the collars. For some, it was a sign of ownership, and, while he gave little credence to that concept, he had to admit that he liked the look of both alphas collared and ready to appease his every desire.

Impatience burned through him. He whined, hands reaching for the hem of Mateo's shirt. At Mateo's nod, Gray set to work stripping the alpha down, covering every newly exposed inch of skin with hands and mouth, breathing in the scent of his mate until Mateo was bare and waiting.

Mateo slid his hands into the omega's hair, squeezing gently on the back of Gray's neck. Shivers slid through him as he lowered down to take Mateo's cock into his mouth. The alpha growled, hand fisting in Gray's hair as the omega relaxed, gliding forward until his nose was pressed to Mateo's stomach. He slid back, sucked in a breath, repeated the motion, spurring a litany of curses from Mateo. Much as he adored coaxing those sounds from his mate, Gray's body was demanding attention as well. He pulled back with a whimper and turned pleading eyes to Lyall.

"Please?"

Lyall looked to Mateo for permission.

"You heard him."

Gray returned his attention to Mateo's lap as Lyall got behind him, firm hands gripping his hips. Lyall pulled him back, sinking into him with a groan and then pushed him forward until his nose hit Mateo's stomach again. He followed the motion with ease, allowing Lyall to control the rocking movement. The low growl in Mateo's throat had Gray's blood sizzling every time his tongue swept over his mate. He curled needy hands against Mateo's thighs and stroked the tender skin there, soothing, even as his mate's grip on his hair grew sharper the closer he got to coming. Every time Lyall dragged him backwards, Gray let out a soft mewl as the sensation crackled through him.

When the taste of Mateo finally spilled over his tongue he was pulled up and away, his mouth devoured by his mate. The fingers in his hair still tugged on him and he relaxed into the possessiveness as Mateo scraped his teeth over the bond bite he'd left earlier. It took only Mateo wrapping his fingers around Gray's cock to make him come, decorating them both with the results. Lyall cursed as Gray squeezed around him, and emptied himself into the omega.

Mateo spun Gray in his arms and beckoned Lyall to join them. The security of his new position, surrounded by both alphas, had him melting, a soft purr reverberating in his chest.

Lyall chuckled and pressed a kiss to his forehead. "Is someone happy?"

"I challenge anyone to not be if they were me." Gray trailed gentle, wet kisses over Lyall's chest and tucked his nose against the scent gland. Instinct told him to bite, to bond, but the mesh prevented it and he huffed, disappointed, until he felt Mateo stir against him, prompting the opposite emotion.

The omega gasped against Lyall as Mateo slipped in with a slick glide that had Gray shuddering in Lyall's arms. Mateo inched impossibly closer and snared Lyall's mouth. The other alpha let out a sound of surprise that lasted only a moment before the two were squeezing Gray between them. Mateo pulled out, leaving both Gray and Lyall panting. Mateo slid confident fingers over his mate's entrance and coated them, wrapping his slick-coated hand around Gray and Lyall before plunging back into the omega. Gray lost focus, his world narrowing down to heat and friction, and the slap of skin on skin.

He came sharply, coating Mateo's hand, but the alpha set a relentless, driving pace, not slowing for even a moment. Lyall dipped between Gray's mouth and Mateo's, a greedy man devouring the previously forbidden.

Both alphas began to waver sometime after Gray lost count of his orgasms. Lyall shuddered and buried his face against Mateo's throat as hot stripes of cum hit Gray's stomach. Mateo gave a few final thrusts, fingers digging bruisingly into his mate's hips as he buried himself to the hilt, his knot catching the omega off guard. It sent a cascade of pleasure through his body and pushed him over the edge a final time.

Lyall dropped flat onto his back breathing harshly. Mateo lowered Gray and himself with more grace since they were attached and curled around his mate. Lyall's face glowed. All three were luminous with sweat and contentment.

Gray fought to keep his eyes open.

"There are so many things that happened today I would have never expected." Lyall laughed and curled towards them, threading his fingers into his Mateo's hair.

"Good things?" Gray hummed softly as sleep teased him.

"Very good things." Lyall kissed his forehead and draped an arm across the joined alpha and omega.

Mateo's deep purr vibrated against the omega's back as he finally surrendered to the siren call of rest.

Tomato and garlic filled the air when Gray woke again. His stomach rumbled obnoxiously, and Mateo laughed softly behind him. They were no longer attached, but Mateo was still curled around him.

"Good morning." The alpha nipped Gray's earlobe. "Lyall's making breakfast. We should shower and join him."

"Carry me."

Mateo gathered his mate into his arms and continued that level of care and tenderness as he scrubbed them both clean, toweling his mate dry again after, and wrapping him in a plush robe.

"I'm glad you're home," said Gray. The flood of emotion made his throat feel thick. "I missed you."

"I hated every minute I was gone," Mateo confessed. "Honestly, if I don't get that promotion, I think I'm going to apply elsewhere for something that stays more local. I hate having to be away so much."

"I am entirely for that idea. Lyall mentioned moving in more permanently."

The alpha's eyebrow climbed his forehead. "Did he now? What do you think about that?"

"I think we should keep him." Gray grinned sleepily. "If you want to. I like him."

"I like him, too." Mateo swept an arm around Gray's waist and ushered him downstairs where Lyall was plating up their meal.

Lyall's face brightened as they entered the kitchen, and he set a tiny sprig of basil atop each plate of spaghetti and meatballs. "I know it's morning, but I figure this would be good to refuel."

"I will never say no to spaghetti." Gray parked himself at the bar.

Mateo crooked a finger at Lyall, waiting quietly for the other alpha to set down his tools and come closer. Gray watched Lyall's languid movements and the casual ease with which he carried himself.

Mateo dragged Lyall into a fierce kiss that had lust pooling in Gray's gut. Far from the jealousy he had expected at seeing his mate kiss someone else, he only wanted to be part of it. Contentment warred with desire, but he pushed away the latter so that he might have a chance to eat. The alphas were locked around one another as Mateo had Lyall pressed up against the counter.

Gray's deep purr had the alphas breaking their kiss to look at him.

"You're too fucking cute." Lyall winked at him.

"Ahem," Gray coughed, "*we* are too fucking cute."

Lyall stepped away from Mateo and grabbed a plate and fork for Gray before he sat down with his own plate. "As much as I am very into kitchen make outs, I need to restock my energy supplies a little."

Mateo snort laughed. "Yeah. Gray is a bit of a work out."

"Oh, hush," said Gray. "You can thank me for your incredible body."

"That's true." Mateo shoveled a meatball into his mouth. "God, this is good. I should let you cook more often."

"If you promise to quit hogging the kitchen, then I will absolutely make more meals."

They ate in companionable silence.

Gray patted his stomach when his plate was empty. "That was so good. I'm so full."

Lyall pressed his nose to Gray's throat. "You smell so good. Like both of us."

The thought warmed him through. He liked the idea of smelling like his mate and his lover. *Their* lover. His heat wasn't over yet, but his head felt clear, and the thought of belonging to both of them set off his purr again.

Mateo set a firm hand on the back of Gray's neck, his thumb massaging circles on the scent gland until he was half-asleep and blissed out in his grasp.

"This is fascinating to watch. I've never seen it in action," said

Lyall. "I know some stuff from school, but I've forgotten most of it. Can I?"

Gray bobbed his head, and Lyall's hand replaced Mateo's. It wasn't as finessed, but he wasn't bothered in the least. Mateo attended to one of Gray's wrists, tongue sliding over the scent gland until Gray was vibrating between them. Lyall took his other wrist, replicating what Mateo was doing, and Gray squirmed in place.

"Does this work outside of a heat?" Lyall asked, delivering another lick to the omega's wrist.

"To an extent," said Mateo. "It's not nearly this intense, but if you get him good and riled up, he'll react the same."

Gray didn't have the wherewithal to be embarrassed about Lyall having that information. He *wanted* Lyall to touch him like that again, whenever he wanted. Gray whined, and Mateo gathered him into his lap.

He was lulled by the soft hand on his hair and the sweet scent in his nose. "Best heat," he mumbled.

Mateo chuckled. "Is it because you're being doubly spoiled?"

"Maaaybe." Gray hummed and buried his face into Mateo's neck.

"Man, how do you ever go anywhere when you have this at home?" Lyall chuckled, shaking his head.

"It's literally hell sometimes." Mateo fell silent until Gray pawed at him. "You could have it at home, too."

Lyall's gaze snapped between the two. "What?"

"Gray said you were asking about moving in permanently."

"I don't want to push or be awkward." Lyall looked steadfastly away.

"You're hardly pushing," Mateo insisted. "We've lived together before."

"That was you and I. This feels...different."

"It *is* different." Mateo smoothed a hand over Gray's hair. "But I think it's better. We both like having you around."

"What would we be?" Lyall asked.

"Whatever you'd like us to be," Mateo answered. "I'm rather a fan of the advancements in our relationship."

"Me too!" Gray piped up.

Lyall laughed. "Me three."

Gray held out a hand, waving it at random until Lyall finally took it and let himself be pulled towards the cuddling pair. "All mine."

A cloud of balsam and honey flowed from Lyall. "I'd say I'm surprised that I like the sound of that, but I've let myself think about it before."

Gray snickered against Mateo. "Lyall's been holding out on us."

"Not on purpose." Lyall pouted. "It's a big deal to suggest joining a relationship. You're mates. I'm just...me."

"You're ours," Gray said.

Mateo purred, the sound infinitely louder in Gray's ear pressed against him. "We don't have to make decisions right now. We should wait until the heat is over at least, but if you want to stay with us, know that you're welcome to."

Gray squeezed Lyall's hand. "Stay."

Lyall set a hand atop their joined ones. "Okay."

Chapter Six

Gray stretched out, luxurious and content, between the two alphas.

In the lull between heat waves, he indulged in a cuddlefuck with Mateo, his mate's cock nestled inside him while they lay unmoving. Lyall kissed him, slow and sweet.

The two alphas traced patterns over his skin, the caresses lulling him into a blissful near-sleep state. A long sweeping motion brought Lyall's hand down the side of the omega's body, hooking his knee to tug him even closer.

Lyall wrapped a gentle hand around Gray's cock and stroked, barely touching, the lightest tease that prodded the embers of his desire.

The edge of his vision wavered.

"More," Gray whispered.

He inhaled sharply when Lyall gripped a little firmer and Mateo nudged closer. The alphas dove in, each suckling a scent gland as Gray craned his neck to give them access. Electricity raced over his skin and sank into his bones.

Mateo's fingers dug into his mate's hip, hard and possessive. The heat rose through Gray like a torrent. He writhed between them, craving the friction and force that he needed to appease the deep primal parts of himself.

"Present," Mateo growled in Gray's ear.

The omega pulled away from them, whining and moving on

shaking limbs to press his face to the bed and lift his ass into the air. Mateo pressed a hand to the back of Gray's neck and squeezed the scent glands until the omega was pliant and whimpering beneath him. He gasped as Mateo fucked into him, relishing the slap of skin on skin.

Mateo lifted him up, his hand sliding around, pinning his mate to his chest by the omega's exposed throat. Gray reached out, searching for stability and found Lyall moving into place to support him. They sandwiched him. One alpha devoured his mouth while the other buried themselves to the hilt with each thrust until he was a begging, mindless mess only held up by the bodies around him.

He was so close.

"You can take us both, can't you, babe?" Mateo's voice was a ragged whisper in Gray's ear.

The desperate *yes* was gasped out.

Lyall sprawled out on the bed and Mateo slid out of Gray, letting the omega sink down into the other alpha before taking hold of his neck again to force him down against Lyall's chest. The alpha's heart was a pounding drum beneath Gray's ear.The warmth of Mateo's body inched up behind him and the omega held his breath, waiting for the pressure and stretch as Mateo pushed in slowly alongside Lyall's cock.

Every muscle in his body shook. Lyall locked his arms around Gray's waist and held him still. He whined, wet and desperate, held on the knife's edge of pleasure. Mateo muttered curses behind him, sinking inch by gratifying inch.

"Sweet *fuck*." Lyall muttered beneath him.

Gray tried to wriggle, the irrational heat-haze part of his brain demanding to be dominated and dragged even further into submission.

Mateo squeezed Gray's hips, the grip biting, and the rooted knowledge that he would bruise from it was satisfying in a way Gray couldn't quite describe. He struggled a little more.

"*Gray*." Mateo grunted his name, holding tighter.

It wasn't enough. He rolled his hips and both alphas cursed. Lyall slid one hand along Gray's back and wrapped it over the omega's throat.

"Be still." The tone was almost begging. Gray loved it.

He tensed his muscles, and Mateo paused in his invasion.

"Have you not gone deep enough, babe?" Mateo asked.

"More." It was the only word Gray could think.

His mate grabbed both of his arms and pinned them behind his back, bracing them there with a firm hand that the omega wasn't strong enough to overcome.

"Move slow, Lyall." Mateo rocked his hips, and Lyall matched the pace.

Gray cried out, cum painting his stomach. He twitched and whined, shivering and seizing as the two alphas overwhelmed him.

"Bite him," Mateo ordered.

It was the only warning he had before Lyall's mouth fastened over the scent gland in the omega's throat, teeth baring down. Gray screamed as his body convulsed, and he sank under.

He woke slowly. Soft fingertips traced over his skin. His eyelids were too heavy to open, and his body had no strength to move. He was limp and sated, listening to the heartbeat beneath him. Nothing mattered except for this.

"He's coming back." Mateo's voice was soft and rough off to his side.

Gray pulled in a breath that seemed to inflate the entirety of him. When he released it, the weight of his own corporeal form was too much to manage.

"Wake up, my love." Mateo kissed his shoulder. "Wake up."

The soft lips and prickly stubble moved in a pattern, kisses marching up Gray's back, down his arm, and against the back of his neck. He shivered.

"He's still dead weight," said Lyall. "How long does he stay like this?"

"If you drag him deep enough, it can last a couple of hours."

Gray listened to them talk, but he was perfectly content to not move a muscle. He was warm and comfortable, albeit rather sticky from the sweat and cum that clung to him.

"Do you want me to take him for a while?"

"I'm good," said Lyall, "but if you want him, you can."

Gray let them pry him off his resting place against Lyall and resettle him in Mateo's lap. His mate's arms held him securely, and his face rested against the scent gland of Mateo's throat so he could breathe in the juniper and ginger.

Warmth pressed against Gray's back and the mattress shifted as Lyall joined them. Delicate fingertips drew patterns on his skin, and he delighted silently in the attention.

Little by little the strength returned to him. He sighed happily and finally opened his eyes. The room was dark, a blessing.

Mateo's thumb and forefinger captured Gray's chin and lifted his mouth. He let Mateo take as much as he wanted, accommodated his delving tongue and questing lips, until he pulled back and pressed a final tender kiss to his mate's mouth.

"Welcome back."

Words didn't work quite yet, so Gray tucked back against his mate, mumbling what he hoped conveyed his thanks.

"God, he's cute," Lyall chuckled.

"Blissed out Gray is one of my favorite versions of him," said Mateo. "This doesn't happen every heat. It's always special when he can completely surrender and let the omega part of himself take over outside of the haze."

Gray tipped his head back to look at Lyall. He let out a squeak and dropped his gaze to Lyall's mouth. The alpha leaned in and indulged Gray's silent request.

Peace settled into his bones.

The claiming bites on his throat thrummed. Instinct pulled at him, urging him to return the claim. The metallic mesh at Mateo's throat thwarted him. His mate slid his hand into Gray's hair and tugged him away.

"Are you trying to keep us?"

"Yes," he finally said.

"We're not going anywhere," Mateo murmured, soothing his mate.

"I want it," Gray whined.

"I know." Mateo pressed a kiss to Gray's forehead. "But you know I can't let you without you agreeing to it before the heat starts. You're stuck with me whether or not you stake your claim."

Lyall took Gray's hand and kissed the palm before sliding down to nip at the scent gland on his wrist. "You might be stuck with me, too"

Gray smiled. "Good."

Heat Play Love Bonus Story

A prequel story about Lyall and Mateo back in
their college days.

Content notes: This story is m/m and contains shower sex,
mutual masturbation, butt stuff, and alcohol consumption.

Bonus

Mateo stumbled into his dorm, drunk as a skunk and probably smelling equally delightful after a freshman had tripped into him with a full beer at the party. The only light in his dorm was a desk lamp, partially obscured by his roommate's broad shoulders, which were hunched over a textbook. The light teased out the strawberry tones in his blond hair and reflected off the scruffy stubble that had grown in during exam season. It took all of Mateo's fleeting willpower to stop himself from walking over to rub his own darkly stubbled cheeks against Lyall's.

Lyall turned toward him, brow furrowed, as Mateo swung their door shut.

"You're still studying?" Mateo squinted into the light and draped himself around Lyall's shoulders.

"I really wish I weren't." Lyall sighed and rested his hand on Mateo's wrist. "This class is going to be the death of me."

"Oh, probably." Mateo grinned and gave Lyall a squeeze. "But after tomorrow you'll be a free man."

"If I pass."

"You're going to pass," Mateo assured him. "You're way too smart to fail."

"God, I hope so. I need a shot of your confidence straight into my veins to get me through this stupid final." Lyall slumped hopelessly.

"I can't even let you distract me because I'm pretty confident I'm going to fail if I stop studying right now."

Mateo made a psh sound and dragged Lyall's desk chair backward until there was enough room for him to sit on his roommate's lap. "Yesterday-Mateo would have understood. But Today-Mateo has only two brain cells left after exams and those two are very intoxicated."

Lyall shifted beneath him. His balsam and honey scent bloomed out and Mateo breathed deeply, inhaling it until his head was swimming.

They'd been teasing each other for weeks, never quite stepping over the edge to indulge in a forbidden love affair. Well, perhaps forbidden was the wrong word. Taboo, then. They were two male alphas housed together to keep them away from the women and the omegas. While Mateo had initially been annoyed by the outdated concept and puritanical ideals of the university, he hadn't minded so much when Lyall had become his roommate.

"You're drunk." Lyall's words were soft as he leaned toward Mateo. "You should go to sleep, but drink some water first."

Mateo deflated. "You're no fun."

"I wish I could be fun tonight."

Mateo gave Lyall a long look, absorbing the intensity in his bright blue eyes, mulling over the tone as well as his tipsy brain would allow. He followed his first instinct, leaning in to brush his lips against Lyall's, instantly electrified by the pulse of longing that fizzed through him like champagne popping free of its cork.

Lyall shuddered, and for a moment he lingered, lips pressed to Mateo's, before pushing him away. "You have the worst timing. Holy shit." Lyall chuckled and let his forehead rest against Mateo's.

A magnetic force pulled Mateo in again. He wanted more kisses and Lyall's warmth was a beacon, a siren's song that Mateo was helpless against. But Lyall held firm, a hand braced on Mateo's chest.

"Mateo, you're drunk and I have to be awake in about four hours. I can't do this with you in this state. Please. Go to sleep. Tomorrow..."

His words trailed off and Mateo reluctantly climbed off Lyall's lap. "If I have to sleep, so do you." Mateo flopped onto his bed and wiggled uncomfortably, his cock straining against his jeans. He undid the button, unzipped, and freed himself.

Lyall squawked. "That's not sleeping."

"Shhh."

"Mateo..."

Mateo wasn't even listening as he let his hand fall to his cock and gave it a stroke, swirling his thumb over the tip before sliding to the base.

The desk lamp clicked off and Lyall fell onto his own bed. "You're unfair."

"Stop that. You need it. You're so tense."

Lyall laughed. Mateo heard the zipper and then a hiss of breath. Mateo grabbed the lotion from the bedside table, and pumped out a generous amount into his hand before focusing on the matter at hand. He turned to the silhouette of Lyall in the dark, barely illuminated by the threads of light sneaking through the curtains. The distance between them seemed unbearable, insurmountable, despite the fact that if they both reached out they would be able to brush fingertips.

Mateo's hand moved, slow and smooth, every motion making him gasp with the deliberate friction. His drunk brain spurred him to move and he rolled off the bed, crossing the room.

"Mateo, what the—"

He slumped down onto the floor, his back leaning against the side of the bed. "I'm still being good."

"That really depends on your point of view," Lyall said with a laugh.

"Shhh. Let me be close. I want to hear you better."

The bed shifted behind him and Lyall resumed stroking his own cock. Mateo listened to every infinitesimal stutter of breath, the slick sounds of their hands stroking their cocks. He could turn his head so easily, take Lyall into his mouth, and stroke himself off while he helped his roommate de-stress.

No.

He was being good.

Good meant waiting.

Maybe touching just a little would be okay. Mateo reached out and set his hand on Lyall's arm, feeling the flex and movement of the muscles beneath his fingertips. It was so much easier to imagine that Lyall was the one touching him now. Easier to fill his thoughts with images of the blond's gaze losing focus, his lips stretching to take Mateo in, of the bite marks that could be left on that pale skin.

Mateo's soft whimpers filled the small space, lacing with Lyall's answering moans and sharp breaths. Mateo groaned, pleasure flowing sharp and sweet as he spilled over his hand with a shudder. Lyall's arm jerked, moving quickly before faltering, carrying him over the edge until he and Mateo were both panting quietly in the dark.

"I like the sound of you," said Lyall.

"I could have been so much louder." Mateo chuckled, letting his head rest on the bed.

Lyall sat up and nudged Mateo with his toes. "Like I said, tomorrow. Wash up for bed."

They crowded into their minuscule en suite bathroom and cleaned up their bodies. Mateo couldn't help but stare. He'd seen Lyall naked too many times to count since neither were particularly shy, but that had been as roommates and not on the vibrant precipice of becoming lovers. He wanted to sink to his knees and—

"Quit looking at me like that." Lyall tipped Mateo's chin up. "You're being too tempting and I have boundaries to maintain."

Mateo huffed a sigh. "Okay, fiiiine." He shuffled back into their room and collapsed face first onto his bed. Sounds faded away as the exhaustion and alcohol took him under.

Mateo woke to their door closing. He opened one eye to see Lyall standing there, kicking off his shoes.

"Am I dead?" Mateo asked.

"Nope." Lyall chuckled. "Just extremely hungover."

Lyall flopped down on top of Mateo, who let out a yelp.

"Shouldn't you be nice to me when I'm hungover?" Mateo asked, barely able to lift his aching head from the pillow.

"Also nope." Lyall rolled over and stretched out next to him.

Mateo wrapped an arm around Lyall's shoulders and closed his eyes. Lyall's scent was muted, exhaustion and stress souring the notes of it. Mateo's head pulsed angrily. Mateo rolled into Lyall, burying his nose in the curve of his roommate's neck, taking long, deep breaths. The longer he snuggled, the more Lyall relaxed into him, sweetness sneaking back into his scent, muscles losing their tension.

"How was the exam?" Mateo kept his voice low and soft for the sake of his head.

Lyall sighed and answered just as quietly, "Not as bad as expected. Unless it was all trick questions, I think I did okay."

"Nap with me?"

"I'm already here," said Lyall. He slid his fingers into Mateo's hair and stroked lightly.

"Good. Don't go anywhere. Once I can exist without wanting to remove my head from my shoulders, I'm going to take you up on your promise from this morning."

Lyall laughed and wriggled himself under the blankets. "I look forward to it."

When Mateo woke again, he felt much more human. Lyall was fast asleep, his arms wrapped around Mateo. There wasn't enough room for both of them on the single bed and one wrong move would have Mateo on the floor, but none of that mattered when he was infinitely more comfortable than he'd been in ages. Minus the fact that his cock was definitely awake and pressed against Lyall. Subtle hip movements sent sparks of pleasure through Mateo, soft moans and hot breath whispering against Lyall's throat.

The other alpha woke slowly. "Are you dry humping me?"

"Only a little." Mateo inched closer, rocking with intention. "My hips have a mind of their own."

"Every bit of you has a mind of its own." Lyall chuckled and rolled slightly to face Mateo. "You know, I had plans for our first kiss. It was supposed to be when we'd be able to fall straight into bed afterward, pawing at each other until we couldn't stand it any longer."

Mateo hummed and pressed a kiss to Lyall's lips. "What about our second one?"

"You know I adore you and you're the hottest thing on two legs, but your morning breath is strong enough to knock a person out. Why don't you go wash up and we'll get some food before I let you rail me senseless."

"*Fuck.*" Mateo's cock twitched, lust zinging up his spine, and he reached between them to rub his palm over the length. "I'm never going to get this to go down if you have me thinking about that."

Lyall's hand nudged Mateo's out of the way. "Conveniently, this part of you doesn't have morning breath. You want some help with it?"

"It's not possible for me to say no to that offer. I've wanted your mouth on me for as long as I've known you." Mateo's gaze unfocused as Lyall slid down the bed.

Tentative fingers curled around Mateo's length and Lyall dipped his head, tongue swirling around the tip. Mateo cursed and lifted his hips off the bed, thrusting himself through Lyall's fist and deeper into his mouth. This moment had run through Mateo's mind probably a lot more often than it should have. It wasn't his fault that Lyall had a pouty mouth shaped for sin, or that the other alpha's sky-blue eyes turned dark and stormy when their gazes lingered too long on one another. How was he supposed to *not* think about climbing him like a tree?

Mateo knew he was no slouch in the looks department, with dark hair and eyes, a trim body, and a smile that drew people in, but he always got *unreasonably* distracted by how goddamn beautiful his roommate was. Mateo's purr came to life, rumbling as Lyall slid a wicked tongue up his cock and swallowed him back down again.

"Pass me the lube." Lyall held out his hand and waited.

Mateo fished around under his bed and pulled out a small bottle. He usually stuck to lotion for rubbing one out, but he kept fancier stuff on hand for when he had sexy guests. Mateo passed the bottle to Lyall and held his breath as the other alpha squirted a dollop onto his hand and wrapped it around the base of Mateo's cock. Firm, slippery strokes had Mateo arching off the bed.

Thoughts melted into a rippling puddle of lust and friction.

"Fuck, that feels so good." Mateo let out a whine that slid into a growl when Lyall paused to adjust. "Don't fucking stop."

"Yes, sir." Lyall nipped Mateo's thigh and resumed his stroking, swirling his tongue over the tip of Mateo's cock again.

Those words were a spark that fell onto a dry forest inside Mateo. The inferno exploded and he came with a buck and a shout, Lyall taking him deep into his throat.

The blond kept up his efforts, head bobbing until Mateo hissed and wriggled away from the onslaught of sensation.

"Holy shit." Mateo sucked in a deep breath.

"How's that hangover doing?" Lyall wiped his mouth and sat up on his knees.

"Made me forget I had one." Mateo sat up slowly. "Want to shower together and lock everyone out?"

Lyall grinned. "I can get behind that."

Mateo pulled on some discarded lounge pants to avoid getting an indecency complaint. They gathered their supplies and trotted off to the shared showers. No one else was there when they arrived so Lyall flipped the lock closed behind them.

Mateo hurriedly brushed his teeth while Lyall hung up their towels and shower caddies, turning the water on hot to steam up the room. Refreshed and minty, Mateo slipped out of his lounge pants and watched Lyall peel off his clothing. A low growl filled his chest as the expanse of skin and cock at full attention were revealed.

Loping forward in his shower sandals, Mateo pinned Lyall to the tiled wall and pulled him down so he could reach his mouth. Sweet honey coated his tongue as Lyall's scent flared, hot and sweet with the rising steam.

Lyall went pliant under Mateo's touch. Seeking hands traced over Lyall's lean muscles, tweaking peaked nipples, making patterns in the water droplets. They'd held off so long and now that all of Lyall was available to him, Mateo took his time touching all he could reach as he drank his fill from Lyall's lips.

"You taste too delicious," Mateo murmured and licked into Lyall's mouth. Mateo reached blindly for the soap and filled his hands with suds, working them in circular motions over Lyall's chest, around his shoulders and down his stomach before Mateo grabbed a bold handful of Lyall's cock. The taste of one part of Lyall only made Mateo more curious about the rest of him.

Spinning Lyall under the spray, Mateo rinsed away the suds and followed the cascade of water with his mouth. It was hard to get the actual flavour of Lyall with the water stealing it away, but that didn't stop Mateo from trying. He fastened his lips around Lyall's nipple and revelled in the sensation of Lyall weaving his fingers through Mateo's wet hair, kneading softly as a moan escaped. Honey and balsam perfumed off Lyall's body and Mateo breathed it in. His teeth scraped Lyall's nipple, earning a hiss from the other alpha.

Mateo wrapped his hand around Lyall's cock and Lyall's head thunked back against the tiles with a whispered *fuck*.

Their scents mingled, Mateo's juniper and ginger flaring out to twine through Lyall's balsam and honey. Who needed a spa when you could toss two randy alphas into a shower? Mateo inhaled their combined scent until he was dizzy from it, lazily stroking Lyall's cock and sliding down to rest his head against Lyall's hip. He wasn't quite sure if he wanted to satisfy Lyall here or leave him needy and aching so he could be teased further while he was getting fucked.

Decisions, decisions.

Mateo nipped at Lyall's hip and let his purr rise up as he nuzzled the same spot. He inched closer and took his first taste of Lyall's cock with a slow, hot lick up the length of it. Lyall whined, his fingers twitching in Mateo's hair.

"You're such a fucking tease." Lyall gave a shaky laugh and pulled in a sharp breath as Mateo slid his other hand up to cup Lyall's balls, stroking them softly with his thumb.

"If you want to pretend you don't love it, I'll just shower and go." Mateo looked up from his spot on his knees, tongue darting out to tease Lyall's cock.

"Selfish lover, too." Lyall stroked his hand through Mateo's hair.

Mateo narrowed his eyes and moved before Lyall could react. He took Lyall in until he couldn't breathe, pulling back *just* enough to let his purr rumble through and vibrate his mouth around Lyall's cock. It was especially gratifying when Lyall cursed and bucked against Mateo's mouth. Mateo wasn't usually the one in this position so he didn't have as much practice as he'd have preferred for this encounter, but he was finding he didn't mind the experience of being on his knees, unravelling his lover lick by lick. The power rush might even be stronger than seeing his partner on their knees for him. He'd have to experiment to see what he liked best.

"I'll let you have a vote," Mateo said after he pulled away again. "Do you want me to finish you here or while I'm buried in your ass?"

"I'm pretty partial to coming while being fucked." Lyall sucked in a breath, his fingers curling at the back of Mateo's neck. "But you've got a wicked tongue and I'm enjoying it on me. I've had too many thoughts about it all to choose."

Mateo slid up Lyall's body and tugged his head down for a kiss. Their bodies pressed together, hot and slippery and perfect. Mateo grabbed the soap again, coated his hand, and wrapped it around both of their cocks in a slick glide.

"I'll play with you here. Get you all clean before I turn you into a mess." Mateo purred and stroked their cocks until Lyall was squirming again in his grip. He soaped up his other hand and reached around, slipping sudsy fingers between Lyall's ass cheeks to gently tease the puckered hole.

"*Fuck.*" Lyall whined, his hips rocking back and forth between Mateo's hands.

Mateo stood on his toes and nipped at the scent gland on Lyall's throat, teasing the honey flavour onto his tongue while Lyall shook and panted. It was probably for the best that they hadn't played together before this. If he'd had an accessible lover in his room, they'd have both failed out of so many classes, getting distracted by fucking instead of studying.

"I'm impatient for you," murmured Mateo against Lyall's skin. "Wash fast so I can take you back to the room."

They separated enough to wash their hair and rinse off the remaining soap before slinging towels around their hips and dashing back to the dorm with their things in tow, shower sandals slapping down the hallway. Everything they carried tumbled to the ground as they spilled into their dorm. Mateo flipped the lock closed before stealing away Lyall's towel and dropping his own.

Mateo's growl vibrated his chest as he backed Lyall up to his bed, pushed him backward, and climbed on top of him. "You look perfect like this."

Lyall's cheeks flushed pink.

Mateo snared Lyall's wrists and pinned them above his head. Lyall's scent bloomed again and Mateo dipped down to inhale it. "You like that, hmm?"

"A lot, yeah." Lyall wiggled his wrists and Mateo pressed down tighter until he stilled. "Nice to give up a bit of control. To you, anyway. Not sure I trust anyone else with that right now."

"I'll take good care of you." Mateo picked up the lube bottle. "I kind of want to see your face during all this, but if it's more comfortable for you we can do doggy."

"On my back is fine. I'll let you know if we need to switch." Lyall's blush had extended down to his chest, his skin a gorgeous rosy tone that Mateo couldn't help but kiss.

"How flexible are you?"

"I guess we'll find out." Lyall laughed. "I used to do gymnastics but we'll see how much of it stuck."

Mateo picked up one of the discarded towels and folded it into a thick pad and tucked it under Lyall's ass before grabbing both of his ankles and hoisting them up and forward slowly until they were over Lyall's head.

The other alpha gasped and wriggled in the new position.

"Hold those for me," Mateo ordered. Lyall was spread open like a fucking buffet—ass exposed, cock and balls waiting for attention, a glorious expanse of thigh begging to be touched. Mateo purred as he slid his hands over the backs of Lyall's thighs and trailed down to brush the lightest touch over his asshole. "Ready?"

"Mhmm." Lyall nodded.

Mateo squeezed the bottle of lube. There was something so satisfying about watching the fluid glide over Lyall's most intimate areas. Mateo rolled one finger through the lube and pressed gently, working bits of the liquid inside in the tiniest movements while he listened to Lyall's mewling whines.

"Barely even inside you yet and you sound like I've ruined you already."

Lyall let out a shaky breath. "We could switch and see how composed you are in this position."

Mateo laughed. "I'm content where I am." He tucked his finger inside to the first knuckle, enjoying the reflexive squeeze of the muscle around him. "You're going to feel so fucking good when I get my cock in there."

Mateo closed his eyes and focused on the feel. He added more lube, pressing deeper and pumping the single digit until Lyall was quivering.

"Ready for one more?"

"*Please.*"

Another finger pressed inside and Mateo savoured the low moan from Lyall. Both of their purrs buzzed in Mateo's ears, getting louder with each thrust.

Mateo pulled his fingers free and wiped the excess lube onto his cock before adding extra to coat himself. He leaned over Lyall for a quick kiss. Sitting back up, he lined himself up and pressed in with slow ease, rocking his hips and steadying himself on Lyall's thighs as the ecstasy of gliding into the alpha's body had his muscles shaking.

"Sweet fucking hell." Their hips met and Mateo paused to catch his breath. "Fuck. Okay, it's definitely for the best that I didn't know what you felt like before this because neither of us would have gotten any sleep this semester."

Lyall laughed and squeezed around Mateo. "There are worse things than no sleep. Besides, I'm intending for neither of us to get a lot of rest before we go home for break."

Mateo wrapped his hand around Lyall's cock and the blond alpha threw his head back into the pillows. Soft strokes matched the gentle thrusts Mateo made to get them both used to each other. Lyall held him in a vise grip that pulsed, utterly obliterating any thought in Mateo's head. He arranged Lyall's legs over his shoulders, wishing he'd been more diligent at the gym before this.

"You look so perfect like this, taking me so—" He grunted as Lyall squeezed around him again. "—so well."

Mateo pulled out slowly, already panting from the exquisitely tight glide, and pressed back in, earning a heady moan from Lyall. It was Mateo's favourite sound. Unravelling his lover was a power trip that left his blood simmering. Not everyone could—or wanted to—give their partner the level of pleasure that Mateo sought to. He'd always been of the mind that if his partner wasn't having even more fun than he was, then he was doing something wrong.

He stroked Lyall's cock with smooth motions, matching them to the slow thrust of his hips while he fell into a rhythm. Lyall dropped one hand over Mateo's, fingers clenching as he guided Mateo's movements. Their laboured breathing melded together as easily as their scents, filling the tiny dorm room with gasping echoes.

Each thrust into the snug, slick heat pulled Mateo closer to the edge. Lyall's calves tensed and relaxed against his shoulders. The peak of pleasure raced toward him and Mateo tipped over, bucking hard into Lyall, doing his best to keep up his strokes as his vision blacked out and his head swam. Blessedly Lyall was already at the tipping point and tumbled over the edge with him. The sound of them both coming—sharp, sweet, and desperate—branded itself into Mateo's brain. He was definitely going to need a repeat performance.

As reality descended again, Mateo smiled down at Lyall, resting his cheek on the other alpha's calf. Streaks of white decorated Lyall's chest and his blue eyes were closed, a brilliant smile on his lips.

"You look fucking gorgeous like this, you know that?" Mateo patted a sticky hand on Lyall's ankle.

"Mmm," Lyall hummed. "Looking forward to staring down at you like this at some point, too."

"You will." Mateo slid his cock free as they both hissed at the sensation. He leaned over Lyall, stretching out atop him so he could bury his face against the blond's throat, breathing in the honey scent. "But before that, I'm going to take my time exploring all the ways to ruin you until I have to go back home for the season."

"I can think of worse ways to spend my time." Lyall chuckled and slid a hand into Mateo's hair. "I'm going to need another shower."

Mateo laughed and pulled Lyall into a languid kiss. "Later."

Thank you for Reading!

If you enjoyed this collection of stories, please consider
leaving a review on Amazon and/or Goodreads
and telling your friends about it.
Thank you so much for supporting an indie author.

Happy reading!

Also by Sierra Cassidy

Omegaverse
First Heat
First Heat: Second Chances
Heat Play Love
Conference Confidential
First Heat: Tying the Knot
Nicky and the Night Owls

Paranormal
Into The Depths

Contemporary
Salacious Salvation
Playtime with Professor
Instant Kicks Anthology

Follow Sierra on social media to get updates on even more
omegaverse stories coming your way soon.

Twitter: @SierraCassidyXO
Instagram: sierracassidyauthor

Get more information at sierracassidyauthor.com

About the Author

Sierra is an erotica and romance author with a passion for writing cinnamon roll heroes, loads of consent, and spicy stories dipped in sweetness. She lives in Western Canada with her husband and cats.

www.ingramcontent.com/pod-product-compliance
Lightning Source LLC
Chambersburg PA
CBHW030807210726
48290CB00002B/470